LEFT DEFENSELESS

His right hand could never recover. He had been told so by a doctor who never missed in his judgments any more than Peter Blue, in the old days, had missed with a gun. Nothing but the left remained to him, and with that left he knew that he could never attain the old heights of skill.

He mastered himself with a great effort, but, as he walked out through the hills, he wondered what he could do. In a wave of weakness, he wished to let the world know of his stricken condition. Very shame might then hold back his enemies. No, the hundred faces looked suddenly in upon his mind—dark eyes, sneering lips, keen, cruel faces, as merciless as the faces of wolves. They would never forget and they would never forgive, and they would pity him no more than the wolves pitied a failing moose, caught in the snow.

—From "Peter Blue, One-Gun Man"

MAX BRAND®

PETER BLUE

LEISURE BOOKS   NEW YORK CITY

A LEISURE BOOK®

May 2006

Published by special arrangement with Golden West Literary Agency.

Dorchester Publishing Co., Inc.
200 Madison Avenue
New York, NY 10016

ISBN 0-8439-5698-4

Visit us on the web at www.dorchesterpub.com.

PETER BLUE

TABLE OF CONTENTS

Speedy's Mare

Frederick Faust's saga of the youthful hero Speedy began with "Tramp Magic," a six-part serial in Street & Smith's *Western Story Magazine* (11/21/31–12/26/31). As other of Faust's continuing characters, Speedy is a loner, little more than a youngster, and is able to outwit and out-maneuver even the deadliest of men without the use of a gun. Stories of his adventures, in addition to the serial, eventually numbered nine. The serial has been reprinted by Leisure Books under the title *Speedy*. The first story, "Speedy—Deputy," published in *Western Story Magazine* (2/13/32), can be found in *Jokers Extra Wild* (Leisure Books, 2005), and was followed by "Seven-Day Lawman" in *Flaming Fortune* (Leisure Books, 2006). "Speedy's Mare" was first published in Street & Smith's *Western Story Magazine* in the issue dated March 12, 1932.

I

"Gloomy Gun"

High on a hill above Sunday Slough, in the dusk of the day, three horsemen sat side-by-side, two very large, and one a slenderer figure. The sun had set, twilight had descended on the long gorge of the mining ravine, and the last dynamite shots of that day had exploded, sending a roar and a hollow boom whizzing upward through the air. From the highest of the surrounding mountains, the rose of the day's end had finally vanished, leaving only a pale radiance, and now the smallest of the three silhouetted horsemen spoke:

"*Señor* Levine, as you know, I've come a long distance, because it is the pleasure of a gentleman to defy miles when one of his brothers calls for him. But it is already late, and I must inform you that, instead of going to bed, I intend to change horses and return, before the morning, to my own house."

He spoke his English with the formality and the accent of a foreigner.

The largest silhouette of the three, a gross shape that overflowed the saddle, answered: "Now, look a-here, *Don* Hernando. I ain't the kind that hoists up a white flag before I gotta need to."

"That's the one thing that he ain't," said the third member of the party. "You take Levine, before he hollers, he's got his back ag'in' the wall."

"Aw, shut up, Mike, will you?" demanded the big man, without the slightest passion. "What I wanna say, if you'll let me, is that I ain't called for you, *Don* Hernando, except that I needed help. And everybody knows that *Don* Hernando is *Don* Hernando. It would be a fool that would yell for him, unless there was really a wolf among the sheep, eh?"

"Thank you," said the Mexican. He raised his hand and twisted his short mustaches, forgetting that the dimness of the light robbed this gesture of half its grace and finish. Then he said: "We all love to see reason according to our lights. What reason do you think you can show me, *Señor* Levine? This a wolf . . . those sheep . . . which may they be?"

"This sheep," said Levine, "we're the sheep. Me and my friends down there in Sunday Slough. There was a time, not far back, when we owned the town. What we said went. But then along comes the wolf, which his name is Speedy, what I mean to say. You don't need to doubt that. Because he's the wolf, all right."

"I have even heard his name," said the Mexican politely.

"You have even heard his name, have you?" said One-Eyed Mike Doloroso. "Yeah, and you'll hear more'n his name, if ever you got anything to do with him. You'll hear yourself cussing the unlucky day that you ever bumped into him. That's what you'll hear."

"One never knows," said *Don* Hernando. "He is not a very large man, I am told."

"Oh, he ain't so big," said Sid Levine, "but he's big enough. There was me and Cliff Derrick. Maybe you heard of him?"

"He was a very great man," said *Don* Hernando. "Yes, yes, some of my friends knew him very well, and one of them was honored by having the *Señor* Derrick steal all that he owned in this world."

"Cliff would do that, all right," said One-Eyed Mike. "I tell you what I mean. Derrick, he'd steal the gold fillings out of your teeth, while you was saying good morning and glad you'd met him. Derrick, he was a man, what I mean."

"Yes," said *Don* Hernando, "I have heard that he was such a man. And he was your friend, *Señor* Levine?"

"Yeah," said Levine. "I had Sunday Slough all spread out, and along comes Derrick, and him and me get ready to take the scalp of Sunday Slough so slick and careful that the town won't hardly miss its hair. Then along comes this no-good, guitar-playin' hound of a tramp, name of Speedy, that looks like a worthless kid, and that turns the edge of a knife, and

11

bites himself a lunch out of tool-proof steel . . . what I mean."

"That I hardly understand," said *Don* Hernando.

Mike Doloroso explained: "What the chief means is this Speedy looks soft, but he's hard-boiled. He's more'n an eight-minute egg, is what he is. You take and slam him the works, and they just bounce off his bean, is what the chief means. He lunches on boiler plate, and dynamite sticks is toothpicks for him, is what the chief means."

"Aw, shut up, Mike. Lemme talk for myself," said the chief, "will you? *Don* Hernando, he understands English like a gentleman, all right."

"I think I understand what you mean about *Don* Speedy," said the great *Don* Hernando. "It is to get a surprise, to meet him."

"Yeah, you said it then, Hernando," said Levine. "A surprise is all that he is. I was saying that me and Derrick, we had things planned, and we had this here county all lined up, and tied, and ready for branding. And then we find out that Speedy is in the way, and first Derrick stumbles over him and pretty near breaks his neck, and then along comes my best bet, which it was my old friend, Buck Masters, that I had got made the sheriff of the county.

"Why, Buck Masters was worth ten times his weight in gold to me. He was set with diamonds, was all he was to me, and along comes that sneak of a wolf of a Speedy, and he picks off Buck Masters, too, and all that Buck gets is fifteen years minus hope, for pushing the queer, which was a rotten break for any gent, I say. And there's Derrick in for life, and a matter of fact, I mean to say, that there ain't any fun around here, like there used to be in the old days, when we had Sunday Slough all spread out and waiting to be scalped."

"I seem to understand you," said *Don* Hernando. "I also, in a small way, have a little town at my service. It is not much.

We in Mexico have not learned the big ways of you *americanos*. It is very small that we work, in a modest way. Still, it is a comfortable town. Everybody pays me a little bit, not much, partly because I love my people, and partly because they have not much to pay. But we understand one another. If my friends make five *pesos,* one of them they pay to me, and all is well.

"They are poor, simple people. Some of their *pesos* they pay to me in oil, others in wine, others in chickens, or in goat's flesh. Fine flour and cornmeal they send to me. Their donkeys toil every day up and down the steep road that goes from my castle to their city. So we understand one another. I am not one who rides down suddenly and robs a man's house. No, not I . . . unless the scoundrel has refused my rightful tribute to me. But I leave all of my people in peace. Like a great family, we live all together, *Señor* Levine, and that, I dare say, is how you lived here in Sunday Slough before this accursed Speedy, who I already despise, came to spoil your happiness."

"Yeah," said Levine with a sigh. "You can say that we lived like a happy family, all right. I won't say no to that. The boys didn't know where they stood, except that it was better a lot to stand on the sunny side of me. I can talk out to a fellow like you, *Don* Hernando, I guess?"

"Frankness is as frankness does," said Hernando, wasting a smile on the darkness—only the gleam of his teeth showed through.

"Now, then," said Levine, "in the old days, I ran the biggest gambling house in the town, and I got everything my own way. There's only one side to be on in Sunday Slough, and that's my side, what I mean. All the boys in the know are on the right side of the water, believe me. But along comes this runt of a singing fool, this here Speedy, and slams everything,

13

and busts up the picture, and why, I ask you?"

"That I cannot tell," said the great *Don* Hernando.

"Because," said Levine, his voice warm with indignation, "because, if you'll believe it, I wouldn't let the low-down son of a sea hound get away with nothing. And there was a half-witted sap of a crooked prospector that was a friend of his, by name of Pier Morgan, that claimed to own a mine, and my friend, the sheriff, he turned that mine over to a friend of mine and got Pier Morgan jailed for vagrancy, which is being a tramp, to say it in good English. And Pier Morgan starts shooting his way out of jail, and only shoots himself onto the junk pile, and along comes this here Speedy that nobody had ever heard of, and he takes and picks Pier Morgan off the tin cans.

"Then he takes him off into the hills, and goes and gets him well, what I mean. And while he's getting well, Speedy, he comes down and gets himself a job as a seven-day man, I mean, as a deputy sheriff. You know how it goes. The deputy sheriffs, they didn't last more'n about seven days apiece, in those times, that's what kind of a wide-awake town we had around here, *Don* Hernando. But Speedy, he starts throwing monkey wrenches into the machine. He goes after my scalp, unbeknownst to me, and he picks off Cliff Derrick, and then my pal, Buck Masters, that was sheriff.

"And now comes along the election for sheriff . . . and whatcha think? If they don't go and put up Speedy for sheriff! Why, he ain't got no name, even, and he calls himself John James Jones, and they laugh their fool heads off, but they get all ready to vote for J.J.J. just the same. Now, I ask you."

"That would be hard on you, *señor,* to have him for the sheriff of the county?"

"It was heart failure and rheumatism to me to have him only for the deputy sheriff," sighed Levine, "so what would it be to have him for sheriff? There was a time, when my house down there, the Grand Palace, it took in nine tenths of the coin that was pushed over the felt or over the bar in Sunday Slough. And now what kind of a trade have I got? Nothing but the crooks that hate Speedy so bad that they won't patronize the joints that he lets run. So they come to me, and drink my booze, and run up bills and don't pay them, and the roulette wheel, it don't clear five hundred a week."

He hung his head for an instant with a groan, and then he went on: "Now, I'm gonna tell you what, *Don* Hernando. I know how to clean out this here Speedy. There's a friend of mine called Dick Cleveland, Crazy Dick, that was smeared around by Speedy once, and he's spotted the place where this Pier Morgan is finishing up, getting well and sharpening his knife for my throat at the same time. Now, *Don* Hernando, if I can snatch this here fellow, Pier Morgan, away, and put him in a safe place, this here Speedy will line out after him, and that'll take him out of my path, and, while he's gone, I clean up on Sunday Slough. Is that clear . . . I mean, is it clear if you're the place where Pier Morgan is taken to?"

"I see your reason, *señor,* but not mine," said *Don* Hernando rather crisply.

"I got five thousand reasons for you," said Levine.

"Reasons, or dollars?" asked *Don* Hernando.

"Both," said Levine.

II

"The Mexican Hand"

In Sunday Slough, later on that day, Speedy, public choice
for sheriff, sat in his office, which had formerly been office and
home of the late sheriff, Buck Masters, now in the peniten-
tiary where Speedy had put him. He sat at his window, much
at ease. In dockets upon his desk were various documents
that had to do with his workmen wanted by neighboring
states, by neighboring counties. But Speedy allowed such
business to roll off his back. He was interested in only one
thing, and that was cleaning up the town of Sunday Slough.

The job would have been more than half finished, at that
moment, except that Sid Levine was still decidedly at large.
The great Levine was the major force with which, as Speedy
knew, he had to contend. Although he had cut away, as it
were, the right and the left hand of the gambler, there still
remained the man himself, with his brain so resourceful in
evil, and upon the subject of the great Levine the thoughts of
Speedy were continually turning.

He heard a light, stealthy step crossing the porch in front
of the little wooden building that housed him and his office.
Then came a light knock at the door.

"Come in, Joe!" he called.

The door opened. Joe Dale, short, thick-shouldered,
strong as a bull and quick as a cat, came into the room. He
waved his hand in the dusk.

"Why not a light, Speedy?" he said.

"I like it this way. I think better by this light," said Speedy.

He began to strum, very lightly, the strings of the guitar that lay across his knees.

"If you don't stop playing that blooming thing," said Joe Dale, "I'm gonna go on out."

"All right. I'll stop," said Speedy gently. And stretching himself, he settled more deeply in his chair and watched the other man.

"What's up, Joe?" he asked.

"I meet up with Stew Webber," said Joe Dale, "and the fool don't know that you've gone and got a pardon for me out of the governor. When he recognizes me, he pulls a gun. I kicked the gun out of his hand. I slammed that bird on the beak so hard that he nearly busted the sidewalk when he sat down on it. Then I told him what was what. He was gonna collect some blood money out of that, Speedy."

"He's a fool," said Speedy. "He's a fool, though I don't know him. How are things in town, Joe?"

"Everything's so good that it'd make you laugh," Joe Dale said. "I'll tell you what. There was a bird come into the Best Chance Saloon, and he starts telling the boys that he won't vote any ex-tramp for sheriff of this here county. And the boys listen to him a while, and then they take him out and tie him backward on his hoss, and give him a ride out of town. That's what they think of you, Speedy."

"I hope the poor fellow doesn't get a broken neck," said Speedy.

"No, he didn't get no broken neck," the deputy replied. "All he got was a fall, and a dislocated shoulder. One of the camps took him in off the road. He wasn't hurt bad."

"Dog-gone it," said Speedy, "I'll have to go and see him, tomorrow."

"Say, what are you?" asked Joe Dale. "A visiting sister of mercy or what?"

"Oh, lay off that, Joe," Speedy said. "What's the other news?"

"There was a riot started down in the Thompson Saloon. I got there as the furniture begun to break. A big buck hauled off and was about to slam me, but somebody yelled . . . 'That's Speedy's man!' Well, the big bozo, he just backed up into a corner and hollered for help, pretty near. He started explaining how everything was wrong that he'd been thinking. I lined him up and made him pay for the breakages, which he done plumb peaceable. Afterward, he bought drinks for the crowd. Thompson, he says that any bird that don't vote for you, and announces it loud and high, he don't get no liquor in his saloon. And election day, he's gonna run wide open, with free drinks for everybody. I told him that was a fine idea, but the Best Chance Saloon already had the same idea. He said that he'd go in one better than the Best Chance, because he'd loosen up and give a free barbeque, along with the drinks. It's gonna be a great day when you're elected, Speedy."

"Humph!" said Speedy.

"Like you didn't care, is what you mean to act like, eh?" Joe Dale commented. He sat down on the window sill, his big shoulders silhouetted against the street light.

"I care, all right," said Speedy. "But what I'm after is Levine, not the job of sheriff of the county. I don't want that job, Joe, unless I have to have it before I can get Levine."

"I know you want Levine," Joe Dale said, "but you're human, Speedy. You want the sheriff job, too."

"I don't," said Speedy. "I'm human, all right, but not that human. Hunting men isn't the kind of excitement that I want. Only I have to get Levine, because he's got so many others."

"I've gotta believe you, if you say so," answered Joe Dale. "But, if I was you and circulated around the town and heard the boys singing songs about Speedy and J.J.J., it'd give me a thrill, all right."

"What's the rest of the news?" Speedy asked.

"There ain't any other news except you. It's all that anybody is talking about. All the big mine owners are gonna close up shop, that day, because they want to make sure that their men get a chance to vote for you on election day."

"That's kind of them," said Speedy. He yawned. "Anything about Levine?" he asked.

"Levine is cooked. His place don't draw no business, no more," said Joe Dale. "The tables are mostly empty, day and night. Levine is cooked in this town. It's a funny thing that the fool keeps hanging on."

"He'll hang on till he gets me, or I get him. He's no hero, but his blood's up."

"He's beat," declared Joe Dale. "He's only a joke, now. He's got no hangers-on."

"He'll have them five minutes after I'm dead," answered Speedy. "Oh, I know how it is with the boys. They like the top dog. You say Levine is beat, but I tell you that I'm more afraid of him right now than when he was on top of the bunch here. Bad times sharpen good brains, and Levine has a brain in his head, don't doubt that!"

"He has a lot of fat in his head, is what he's got," said the other. "You're all wrong, Speedy. Levine is finished in Sunday Slough. Gents have had a taste of law and order, and they like it better than Levine's rough-house. Only, Speedy, we oughta do more about the outside jobs. We get letters every day about thugs and crooks that've come over into our county. We're expected to clean up some of those boys. We oughta do it."

Speedy yawned once more, very sleepily. Then he said: "They behave, over here. They don't even lift cattle. They pay their way. I know a dozen of 'em around town, right now. But as long as they stay quiet, this can be their port of missing men. I don't mind having them about. I don't care how many other states and counties want them . . . all I want is peace in Sunday Slough. It was a rough nest when we came here, Joe, and now it's settling down, I think."

Joe Dale grunted, but, before he could answer, a rapid drumming of hoofs was heard, the rider stopping before the shack. Then, he threw himself from the horse and ran forward.

"Speedy! Speedy!" he called, in a guarded voice.

"It's Juan. It's the half-breed," said Speedy. Instantly he was through the window, going like magic past the form of Joe Dale.

The panting runner paused before him.

"Juan, you idiot," said Speedy, "what are you doing showing your face in town with a price on your head?"

Juan shook the head that had a price on it, as though disclaiming its importance, then he said: "Pier Morgan, the *Señor* Morgan, he is gone, Speedy!"

Speedy got him by the shoulders and backed him around until the street light, made of the dull shafts of distant lights, fell upon his face.

"Say that again!" he demanded.

"The *Señor* Morgan, he is gone. I, *señor,* have a bullet hole through the side of my neck. That is why the bandage is there. I still bleed, my friend. It is not for lack of fighting, but the evil one himself came and took Pier Morgan from me."

"D'you know the name and address of this evil one, Juan?" asked Speedy.

"It is *Don* Hernando of Segovia, *señor.* I saw his face only in part. But I knew the scar on his forehead. I was once one of his people. It was *Don* Hernando, and you will never see Pier

Morgan again. He is gone to Segovia. He is gone forever."

"Where's Segovia?" snapped Speedy.

"A little on the other side of the Río Grande. It is more than a day's ride from this place, *señor*. But it might as well be the journey of a life, for those who go into it never come back. They are held in the teeth of *Don* Hernando forever! Ah, *señor*, it was not carelessness on my part, but. . . ."

"Be still, Juan," said Speedy. "You know the way to Segovia?"

"I know the way, *señor*."

"Will you take me there?"

"I take you within sight of it," Juan said. "I do not dare to go closer. I have been in the dungeons of Segovia. I shall never go there again."

"I'll go all the way, Speedy," offered Joe Dale.

"You'll stay here and run Sunday Slough," Speedy answered. "I'll find out about Segovia on the way down, but I imagine that this is a one-man job. You know, Joe, that an army often can't take a place by open assault, but one crook can pick the lock of the gate."

III

"Intrepid Youth"

Segovia stood among rocky hills, bare as the palm of the hand. The town itself was an irregular huddle of whitewashed adobe, without a tree in the streets, without a bush to cast shadow. In fact, vegetable life could not exist beside the famous goats of Segovia which, men swore, could digest not only the labels of tin cans, but the tin as well.

How these people lived was a mystery which it was hard to solve. The naked eye could see almost nothing except, now and then, a dun-colored patch of cattle, scattered here and there in the distance. But distances mean little in Mexico, and a cow will run two days to drink of water on the third. A cow will walk thirty miles a day, grazing on a few blades of grass or tearing at a frightful cactus now and then. Still the cow will live and grow, becoming fat enough for marketing in the early spring.

So it was that the outlying herds fed the town of Segovia. In addition, it was said that some of the hardy inhabitants worked along the river, not as boatmen or agriculturists, to be sure, but in other sorts of traffic, generally done at night, work that pays well per hour, but whose pay and pleasure is well salted with death, now and then, death that spits out of the guns of federal patrols and Texas Rangers on the northern side of the stream.

Some of the sons of Segovia, also, went at times to the mines, or to very distant ranches, returning to their homes with money to blow in. They helped to support the two *cantinas* of the town and the little stores, where the women bought each day enough food to keep starvation off for twenty-four hours. There was even a store, in Segovia, where one could buy clothes, and it was notorious that the second-hand department of that store was filled with wonderful bargains, usually in styles and materials from north of the great river.

These people of Segovia were a race apart, a race all to themselves. Almost to a man, they were slender, agile, and strong. They were like their own goats, which seemed to eat the sand and the sunshine, for there was little else on the ground where they grazed. They and their ancestors had inhabited this place since the days of the *conquistadores*. The old Spanish blood mixed with the Indian in their veins. They were paler than other *peónes*. They bore themselves like *caballeros*. They were fierce, cruel, revengeful, patient, enduring. They loved their friends with a passion; they hated their enemies with still more fervor. They were people to be noted, and to be feared.

All of these terrible clansmen, for like a clan they clung together, looked down on the rest of the world, and looked up to the castle of *Don* Hernando Garcías.

It was not really a castle. Once, to be sure, the walls had been of stone, cut and laid together with the priceless skill of the Mexican stonecutters. But the centuries had cracked, molded, and eaten the big stones until they had fallen from their places, and a ragged mass of adobe finished in part the outline of the earlier walls.

Still, it remained a castle to the proud, stern *peónes* of Segovia, the new. When they raised their eyes, a saying had it, they never found heaven or aught higher than the walls of the castle. For in that building, for three centuries and more, there had always been a Garcías called Hernando.

They were as like one another as peas in a pod, all those lords of Segovia. They all looked like the villagers themselves, that is, they were lean, hardy, tough-sinewed, erect, quick-moving, passionate of eye. They all wore the same sort of bristling, short mustaches. They all bore themselves like conquerors.

Sometimes when the people of the town were called the children of their overlord, there seemed to be more than words in the phrase, such a family resemblance existed among them. Their devotion to their lords of the castle, therefore, was all the more passionate and profound because they looked upon them, in true medieval style, as children upon parents. They rejoiced in the pride, cruelty, and wealthy grandeur of their masters and paid the heavy exactions of the Garcías family with perfect calm of mind. Most Mexicans are resolved democrats, but the men of Segovia preferred to be under the thumb of an autocrat.

For one thing, he preserved them from paying taxes to the state, for when tax collectors came to Segovia, they strangely disappeared, and finally they had fallen out of the habit of going to the mysterious little white town above the river. For another thing, according as he was a great and lordly freebooter, they themselves picked up plenty of profit from his expeditions. The present Hernando Garcías filled all the requirements.

He was rapacious, stern, and ruled them with a rod of iron. On the other hand, in settling their village disputes, he was as just as he was cruel. Furthermore, he had always had some large employment on hand. It might be the organization of a long march into the interior, where he harried wide lands and brought back running herds of the little Mexican cattle, to be rustled across the Río Grande and sold "wet" into the northern land. It might be simple highway robbery, organized on a smaller scale, but paying even better. It might be a midnight attack upon an isolated house or a mountain village. It might be a stealthy smuggling of liquor or drugs.

But he was always occupied and always providing employment for his "children", as the men of Segovia loved to call themselves. Since he had come into power, they rode better horses, wore brighter sashes, ate more meat. The *cantinas* offered them beer, wine, and distilled fire; they had money to buy it. What other elements could they have desired in a terrestrial paradise?

The sun of the day had set, and in the twilight the white town had been filmed across with purple, and the lights had begun to shine out of the doorways, flashing upon groups of children who played and tumbled in the deep, white dust of the streets. Then night gathered about the town, and it seemed to huddle, as though under a cloak, at the knees of the castle, and about the home of Garcías the stars drew down out of the clear sky—or so it seemed to the villagers.

It was at this time that a rider on an old gray mule came into the town, and stopped in front of one of the *cantinas* to play on a guitar and sing. His voice was good, his choice of songs was rich and racy on the one hand, profoundly sentimental on the other. His hair was dark, so were his eyes; his skin was the rich walnut color of Mexico; his handsome face seemed to fit exactly into his songs of love.

So a crowd gathered at once.

He was invited into the *cantina*. He was offered drinks. Then they brought him some cold, roasted flesh of a young kid, cold tortillas, hot tomato and pepper sauces. He ate with avidity, leaning well over his food, scooping it up with the paper-thin tortillas.

A jolly, ragged beggar was this minstrel, with a ragged straw hat on his head of the right Mexican style, its crown a long and tapered cornucopia. In the brim of it were a few twists of tobacco leaf and the corn husks for making cigarettes. Furthermore, somewhere along the road, he had found a sweetheart, who had rolled up a number of cigarettes and tied them in pretty little bundles, with bits of bright-colored ribbon. These, also, were attached to the brim of the hat.

He had on a gaudy jacket, the braid of which had tarnished here and ripped away there. His shirt was of silk, very soiled and tattered, and open at the throat. However, a splendid crimson sash was bound about his waist and narrow hips. The flash of his eyes and his white teeth as he ate, or as he sang, or as he danced, made the tawdry costume disappear, particularly in the eyes of the women who crowded about the door of the *cantina* to look on at the diversions of their lords and masters.

Particularly was he a master of the dance, and it was really a wonderful thing to see him accompany his flying feet with strumming of the guitar, while he retained breath enough in his throat to sing the choruses, at least. Furthermore, and above all, his spinning was so swift that he could unwind the sash that girded him and keep it standing out stiff as a flag in the track of his dancing, and so remain while, without the use of hands, he wound himself into it again.

The old men sat in the corners of the room and beat time with their feet and hands. Their red-stained eyes flashed with fire. The younger men stirred uneasily, nearer at hand. Sometimes one of them would fling his voice and his soul into a chorus. Sometimes one of them would dart out, with a bound, and match the steps of the visiting master. Whenever a village dancer came out to rival the minstrel, the ragged fellow welcomed him with such a grace, such a bright smile, and nodded in such approval of the flying feet, that each man felt Segovia had been honored and flattered.

It was almost midnight before this entertainment ended. By that time the minstrel had collected, it was true, not very many coins, but he had been surrounded by good wishes and ten men offered to give him a bed for the night. However, it appeared that the little glasses of stinging brandy had done more than their work on the minstrel. Like a drunkard, he declared that he would not bother any of them to put him up for the night. Instead, he would gain admission to the castle, where there were sure to be many empty beds!

They listened with amazement. Some of the good-hearted warned him that García's household could not be wakened with impunity in the middle of the night, but the fume of the liquor, it appeared, had made him rash and, therefore, the whole lot of them flocked along to see the performance.

They even pointed out the deep casement of the room of Hernando Garcías, and then they crept away, into hiding in nooks and corners and shadows among the nearer horses to watch the fortune of the rash young entertainer, as he strove to sing and dance his way into the house of the great man.

IV

"Music on the Air"

Don Hernando was about to sink into a profound slumber with the peaceful mind of one who has done his duty and done it very well.

For a little earlier, that evening, he had arrived with his prisoner, the *gringo*, Pier Morgan, and had ridden up to his house, not through the village streets, but up the narrow and steep incline that climbed the face of the bluff and so came directly to the outer gate of the building. By this route he came home, partly because he did not wish to be observed, partly because he would thus have his prisoner closer to the dungeon cell in which he was to be confined, and partly, also, because he loved to impress and mystify his townsmen.

He knew that some of the household servants would soon spread everywhere in Segovia the news that a prisoner had come, a *gringo*. Even the little children would soon be buzzing and whispering. But just as surely as the story was bound to fill every house in Segovia, so sure was it that not a syllable would pass beyond. The secrets of *Don* Hernando were family secrets, as it were, and the whole town shared in them

27

and rigorously preserved them.

The good *Don* Hernando, having lodged his captive in one of the lowest and wettest of the cellar rooms of the old house, posted a house servant with a machete and a rifle to watch the locked door. He had then gone on to his repast for the evening, content.

He had been told by Sid Levine that he would have to use every precaution to keep his prisoner from falling into the hands of Speedy again, and this subject constituted part of his conversation with his lady, as they sat together at table. She was a dusky beauty, and now that the years were crowding upon her and she was at least twenty-two, she began to be rounder than before, deep of bosom and heavy of arm. Her wrist was dimpled and fat, and so were the knuckles of her fingers. But her eyes were bright, and she carried her head like a queen, as befitted the wife of *Don* Hernando Garcías.

When she had seen and distantly admired the new thickness of the wallet of her spouse, he explained the simplicity of the work which he had done. It was merely to receive from one man the custody of another, and to ride the man down across the river and hold him in the house.

"This Levine, who pays me the money for the work, is a simpleton," he said. "He seems to feel that his enemy, Speedy, is a snake to crawl through holes in the ground, or a hawk to fly through the air and dart in at a casement. But I told the *señor* that my house is guarded with more than bolts and locks and keys, for every man within the walls of it has killed at least once. This vagabond, this Speedy, of whom they talk with such fear, had he not better step into a den of tigers than into the house of Garcías?"

The same fierce satisfaction was still warm in his breast when he retired to sleep, and he was on the point of closing his eyes when he heard the strumming of a guitar just under his window. For a moment he could not and would not believe his ears. Then rage awoke in him, and his heart leaped into his throat. It was true that the townsmen took many liberties. It was true that they acted very much as they pleased within their own limits, but those limits did not extend to the very walls of the castle. No, the space between the last of their houses and his own outer wall was sacred ground, and no trespassing upon it was permitted!

"A drunkard and a fool," said Garcías to himself, as he sat up in his bed.

He listened, and from the outer air the voice of the singer rose and rang and entered pleasantly upon his ear. It was an ancient song in praise of great lords who are generous to wandering minstrels. On the one hand, it flattered the rich; on the other hand, it poured golden phrases upon the singers who walk the world.

The purpose of the song seemed so apparent that Garcías ground his teeth. No man could be sufficiently drunk to be excused. He, Garcías, was not in a mood to allow excuses, anyway.

He bounded from his bed and strode to the window, catching up as he went a great crockery wash basin from its stand. With this balanced on the sill, he looked over the ledge, and below him, smudged into the blackness of the ground, he made out clearly enough the silhouette of the singer, from whom the music rose like a fountain with a lilting head. Garcías set his teeth so that they gleamed between his grinning lips. Then he hurled the great basin down with all his might.

It passed, it seemed to him, straight through the shadowy form beneath. Even the stern heart of Garcías stood still.

It was true that his forebears, from time to time, had slain one or more of the townsmen, but they had always paid through the nose for it. The men of Segovia were fellows who could be struck with hand or whip, by their master, but, when it came to the actual taking of a life, they were absurdly touchy about it. They insisted upon compensation, much compensation, floods of money, apologies, declarations of regret in public, promises that such things should never happen again. On certain occasions, they had even threatened to pull the old castle to bits and root out the tyrants.

So Hernando Garcías stood at his window, sweating and trembling a little, and cursing his hasty temper. For the song had ceased, or had it merely come to the end of a stanza?

Yes, by heaven, and now the sweet tide of the music recommenced and poured upward, flowing in upon his ear. At the same time, *Don* Hernando unmistakably heard the tittering of many voices.

"By heavens," he said, "the louts have gathered to watch this. It is a performance. It is a jest, and I am the one who is joked at."

He said other things, grinding them small between his teeth. It was excellent cursing. It was a sort of blasphemy in which the English language is made to appear a poor, mean, starved thing. For the Spaniard swears with an instinctive art and grace. There are appropriate saints for every turn of the thought and the emotions. And *Don* Hernando called forth half of the calendar as he cursed the minstrel.

He turned. The washstand was nearby, and on it remained the massive water jug, half filled with a ponderous weight of water. It was not so large a missile as the wash bowl, but it was at least twice as heavy, and it was the sort of thing with which a man could take aim.

The fear that he might have committed murder, the moment before, now died away in him. He wanted nothing so much as to shatter the head of the singer into bits. He wanted to grind him into the ground. So he rose on tiptoes, holding the jug in both hands, and he took careful aim, held his breath, set his teeth, and hurled that engine of destruction downward with the velocity of a cannon ball.

It smote—not the form of the minstrel. It must have shaved past his head with only inches to spare, but the undaunted voice of the song arose and hovered like a bird at the ear of *Don* Hernando. The jug was too small. He needed a large thing to cast. And presently his hand fell on the back of a chair. It was an old chair, the work of a master. It had been shipped across the sea. Even its gilding represented a small fortune, and on the back of it was portrayed the first great man of the Garcías line.

That was why it stood in the room of the master of the house. For every morning, when he sat up in bed and looked at the picture on the back of the chair, he was assured of his high birth and of the long descent of his line, for the picture might have stood for a portrait of himself. There were the same sunken eyes, the same hollow cheeks, the same narrow, high forehead, and even the same short mustache, twisted to sharp points. He thought not of the portrait, alas, as he stood there by the window, teetering up and down from heel to toe, in the grand excess of his wrath. But, catching up the chair, he hurled it out of the window, and leaned across the sill, this time confident that he could not fail of striking the mark.

It did not seem to him that the minstrel dodged. But certain he was that he had missed the target entirely, for the song still arose and rang on his ears! Then, lying flat on his stomach across the window sill, he remembered what it was that he had done. The chair must be smashed. Undoubtedly the portrait was ruined. Woe coursed through his veins. For it was plain that he had cast away with his own hand what was as good, to him, as a patent of nobility? He groaned. He staggered back into the room, gasping, and buried his fingers in his long hair.

Then he flung himself on the bell cord that dangled near the head of his bed, and pulled upon it frantically, not once, not twice, but many times, and, when he heard the bell jangling loudly in the distance, he hurled a dressing gown over his shoulders.

Hurrying feet came to the door of his room. There was a timid knock; the door opened.

"Manuel, fool of a sleepy, thick-headed, half-witted muleteer, do you hear the noise that is driving me mad?"

"I hear only the noise of the singer, *señor*," said poor Manuel.

"Music! It's the braying of a mule!" shouted Garcías. "Go down. Take Pedro with you. Seize the drunken idiot by the ears and drag him here. Do you hear me? Go at once! Go at once!" He seized the edge of the door and slammed it literally upon the face of Manuel.

It eased his temper a little to hear the grunt of the stricken man, and to hear the muttered names of saints that accompanied him down the hallway.

V

"The Angry *Don*"

Don Hernando lighted a lamp and paced hurriedly up and down the room. From the windows, he heard again the tittering of many voices. Yes, it was as on a stage, and the crowd was enjoying him as one of the actors. Rage seized upon his heart. He thought of the ruined portrait on the chair and a sort of madness blackened his eyes.

At one end of the room hung various knives. He fingered a few of them as he came to that side of the room but, remembering the revolver, pistols, rifles, and shotguns that were assembled in a set piece against the opposite wall, he would hastily go back and seize on one of these, only to change his mind again. Nothing could satisfy him, he felt, except to feel the hot blood pouring forth over his hands.

Then came rough voices in the outer court and stifled exclamations from the near distance. That soothed him a trifle. He shouted from the window, leaning well out: "Bring up the wreck of the chair and, if you pull off the ears of the singer, I, for one, shall forgive you!" He retired and sat in another chair, deep and high, wide as a throne and with a tall back. Seated so, nursing his wrath, his fingers moved convulsively, now and again, as though he were grasping a throat.

Presently up the hall came the voices and the footfalls of Manuel and Pedro. The door opened. They flung into the room the body of a slender man, who staggered, almost fell to the floor, and then, righting himself and seeing the glowering face of *Don* Hernando in the chair in the corner of the room, bowed very deeply, taking off a tattered straw hat and fairly sweeping the goatskin rug with it.

"*Señor* Garcías," said the minstrel, "I have come many miles to sing for you. One of my ancestors sang for yours, generations ago. And so I have come."

The master of the house glared.

Pedro, in the meantime, was presenting him with the wreckage of the chair. The old, worm-eaten wood had smashed to a sort of powder. Of the back panel, in which the face was painted, there remained no more than scattered splinters. He picked up a handful of that treasured panel. Only a twist of a mustache, only one angry eye glared forth at him from the ruin. Garcías dropped the wreckage, rattling upon the floor, feeling sure that he would kill this man.

He surveyed him, the dark head and eyes, the large, over-soft eyes, like the eyes of a lovely woman. He regarded the smile, the sort of childish delicacy with which the features were formed.

Then he said: "*Señor* minstrel!"

The stranger bowed, brushing the floor once more with the brim of his hat.

The fool seemed totally unconscious that he was about to receive a thunderbolt of wrath that would annihilate him.

Suddenly *Don* Hernando smiled. It was a smile famous in the history of his family. Every Garcías had worn it. Every Garcías had made that same cold smile terrible to his adherents. All of Segovia knew it. Manuel and Pedro shuddered where they stood. But the idiot of a minstrel stood there with high head.

One thing was clear. To act on the spur of the moment would be folly. Together with the rich, red Castilian blood, there flowed in the veins of Garcías a liberal admixture of the Indian. That blood mastered him now and, still smiling, he told himself that time must be taken with this affair. The painting on the chair had been a work of art. The revenge he took would be a work of art of equal merit, a thing to talk about. Why not? The fellow was not of Segovia. He was not of the chosen people. He came from a distance.

So Garcías cleared his throat, and, when he spoke, it was softly, pleasantly.

Another shudder passed through the bodies of the two servants. Like all the others in the house, each of these had killed his man, but the smile and the voice of *Don* Hernando, in such a mood, seemed to both of them more terrible, by far, than murder.

"The Garcías family keeps an open house for strangers," he said. "We have rooms for all who come. But chiefly for such good singers. I wish to hear you sing again. Manuel, Pedro, take him down to the most secure room in the house. You understand?"

His fury mastered him. He thrust himself up, half out of the chair, with glaring eyes, but the half-witted minstrel was already bowing his gratitude and sweeping the floor with his hat, so that he entirely missed both the gesture and the terrible expression of the eyes.

Don Hernando managed to master himself. Then he said: "My friend, you will be well looked after. You will be put in a safe place. All the enemies you have in the world could not disturb your sleep, where I shall put you. You, Pedro, will sleep outside of his door, armed. You understand?"

"*Señor*, I understand," said Pedro. He had heard the songs of this man. In his heart he pitied him, for he saw that the naked wrath of the master was about to be poured out upon his head. But it never occurred to him to disobey. Besides, he was really a savage brute. So were all of that household, hand-picked brigands. He soon mastered any feelings of pity or of remorse.

"I understand," he repeated. "The deepest room of the house, *señor*, if you wish."

"Yes, the deepest . . . the deepest! The one with the strongest door," repeated the great Garcías through his teeth, "the smallest window, and the heaviest lock . . . the one where sleeping clothes are always ready, bolted to the wall. You understand? You understand?" His voice rose to a high, whining snarl, like that of a great cat. Then he added: "And in case he should want to sing, let him have his guitar. Yes, let him sing, by all means, if he wishes. I am only afraid that I shall not be able to hear the songs."

35

Manuel and Pedro grinned brutally. Their master laughed, but the fool of a minstrel was again bowing to the floor and seemed to fail to see or to understand his dreadful predicament. That was all the better. He would learn, soon enough, what was to befall him. The guards took him to the door of the room.

"Strip him!" shouted the great Garcías, and slammed the door behind the trio.

He went back, then, to the wreckage of his precious chair and picked up, again, the splintered wood upon which the remnants of the portrait appeared. Holding them tightly grasped in his hand, he groaned aloud, with such pain that he closed his eyes.

He went to the window. His rage was overcoming him, and he was feeling a trifle in need of air. From the open window, he could hear long, withdrawing whispers and murmuring down all the alleys that approached the face of the castle.

"Well," he said through his teeth. "Very well, indeed. They shall learn that the old spirit has not died in the blood of Garcías. They shall learn *that*, if nothing else." His spirit was eased as he thought of this. There is nothing that impresses a Mexican more than the signs of absolute, even cruel power. He was right in feeling that the men of Segovia would be impressed by the object lesson that he would give them in the person of the young minstrel, the unlucky stranger.

Still, when he lay upon his bed, about to fall asleep, he roused to complete wakefulness. For it occurred to him that the many bows of the singer, as he stood in the presence of danger, might have been useful in concealing a certain smug expression of self-contented pleasure which, as Garcías remembered, had seemed to be lingering about the corners of the eyes and mouth, every time he straightened. At all events, one thing was clear, the man was an idiot.

Then he soothed himself by devising torments. It was clear, above all else, that for the destruction of the famous Garcías portrait he deserved to die. With the placid emotions of a cat about to torment a mouse, the great *Don* Hernando finally fell asleep.

VI

"Guest Room"

The two house servants were conducting the young dancer and singer down winding stairs that sank toward the bowels of the earth, as it seemed. They grew narrower and narrower. The feet slipped in the moisture that covered the stones. The stones themselves were worn by the centuries of footfalls that had passed over them. Their steps echoed hollowly up and down the descending corridors. The head of the tall Pedro bowed, as he avoided the roof of the passage, rounded closely in. Finally they passed the mouth of a black corridor.

"Down there," said Manuel, "is the last dear guest that the *Señor* Gracías brought home with him. He, also, has a secure room. He, also, is guarded against intrusion. Oh, this is a safe house, friend. Danger never breaks in from the outside." He laughed, and his brutal laughter raised roaring echoes that retreated on either hand.

The minstrel merely said: "This should be cool. But also rather dark. However, darkness and coolness make for perfect sleep in summer."

They went on, the two servants muttering one to the

other, and so they came to the last hall of all, in which there was the door of a single room. In the hallway lay slime and water half an inch thick, and the horrible green mold climbed far up the walls on either hand. There was a low settle in the hall.

"You'll sleep there, Pedro," said Manuel with a chuckle.

"A plague on my luck," said Pedro. "If I don't catch rheumatism from this, I'm not a man. It needs a water snake to live in a hole like this."

Manuel was unlocking the door. It groaned terribly on its hinges and gave upon a chamber perhaps eight feet by eight, and not more than five in height. It was like a grisly coffin. A breath of foul air rolled out to meet them.

"Is this . . . is this the room?" gasped the poor minstrel.

"Yes, you fool," said Manuel. "Strip him, Pedro."

They put the lantern on the floor. Between them they tore the clothes from the body of the poor singer and flung them to the floor. But when he was stripped, they paused, and looked him over in bewilderment.

For he presented not at all the picture which they expected to see, of a starved and fragile body. He seemed slender, in his clothes, to be sure. But he was as round as a pillar. He was as deep in the chest as he was wide, and over arms and back and legs spread a cunning network of muscles, slipping one into the other, strand upon strand. An anatomist, with a pointer, could have indicated his muscles without effort.

"Hey!" said Manuel. "He could be a bullfighter." He thumbed the shoulders of the captive. It was like driving the thumb into India rubber.

"But what does it mean, my friends," said the minstrel. "Why am I stripped? Alas, I am a poor man. I have done no wrong."

"Be quiet," said Pedro. "You were told about a secure

room and this is it. And you were told about bedding and this is it, perfect to fit you, like a suit of clothes ordered from the tailor." As he spoke, he dragged a mass of chains from the wall, and then locked them around the wrists and the ankles of the trembling minstrel.

"Ah, my friends," said the youth, "this is cruel and unjust. Trouble will come upon your master for this act. Trouble, for sure, will follow him."

They left the room, slammed the door upon him, and turned the key in the lock.

"There's a guitar against the wall beside you. You can play and sing in the dark, *amigo*," were their last words.

They were hardly gone, when the minstrel raised his manacled hands to his head, and, from the base of a curl, he drew forth a little piece of flattened steel, like a part of a watch spring. With this, he began to work, cramped though his fingers were for space, upon the lock of the manacle that held his left wrist. He did not work long before the manacle loosened. It slipped away, and presently its companion upon the other wrist likewise fell to the floor. The singer stooped over his anklets. They presented a little more difficulty. But they, also, presently fell away, and he was free in the room. After that, he felt his way along the wall to the heap in which his clothes had been flung. There was a bitter chill in the air of the dungeon, and he hastily pulled on his garments, one by one, the shoes last of all. They had soles of thin whipcord, silent as the furred paw of a cat for walking over stone, and light as a feather.

When he was dressed, he went to the door and felt of the lock. To his dismay, he found that the whole inside of the lock was simply one large sheet of steel. The key did not come through the massive portal! He stood for a time, taking small breaths, because the badness of the air inclined to make him dizzy. But eventually he had a thought. Outside, in the corridor, Pedro the guard was already asleep, for the sounds of his snoring came like drowsy purring into the dungeon cell. So the prisoner found his guitar and lifted his voice in song. He took care in the selection of his music. The ditties that found his favor, now, were the loudest, and he sang them close to the door.

It was not long before there was a heavy breathing against the door, and then the loud voice of Pedro, exclaiming: "Half-wit, I, Pedro, wish to sleep! If you disturb me again, I shall come in there and make you wish that it were Garcías instead of me. He shall have only half of you. I'll eat the other half."

"Ah, *amigo*," said the minstrel, "I am as cold as a poor half-drowned rat. May I not have covering? The floor of the room is covered with wet slime and. . . ."

"Shiver, then," said the Mexican angrily. "I have told you before, what I shall do if you sing once more."

The singer waited until he heard the snoring begin again, and then, for a second time, his voice arose like a fountain of light.

The answer came almost at once. The key groaned in the lock, the door was thrust wide, and in rushed big Pedro, cursing.

From the shadow beside the door, the minstrel struck with a fist as heavy as lead, hitting home beneath the ear. Pedro slumped forward on his face in the slime.

He was quickly secured, ankle and wrist, in the manacles, which had just held the singer. The wet filth in which he lay brought back his senses after a moment or so. He opened his eyes, groaning, in time to feel the revolver being drawn from its holster on his hip and, by the light of the lantern, he saw the minstrel smiling down upon him. Exquisite horror overcame big Pedro. Agape, he looked not so much at the slender youth before him as at a terrible vision of the wrath of Garcías when the lord of the house should hear of this escape. He could not speak. Ruin lay before his eyes.

"Good bye, Pedro," said the minstrel. "Remember me all the days of your life and never forget that I shall remember your hospitality. As for your master, who you are fearing now, don't worry about his anger. He shall have other things to think of before many minutes."

He left the room before the stupefied Pedro could answer and closed the door gently behind him. He picked up the lantern and quickly climbed to the black mouth of the corridor down which, as he had been told, the last guest of Garcías was housed. He could guess the name and the face of that poor stranger.

Down that corridor he went, and presently around a sharp elbow turn the light of another lantern mingled with that of the one that he was carrying. He went on at the same pace, dropping the revolver that he carried into a coat pocket. He could take it for granted that, if a guard waited outside the door of this prison, the face of the singer would not be known to the man.

So he went on fearlessly and now saw the man in question seated on a stool that he had canted back against the wall. With his arms folded on his breast, he was sleeping profoundly. The minstrel laid the cold muzzle of the revolver against his throat and picked up the sawed-off shotgun from his lap. Then, as the rascal wakened with a start, he said: "Be quiet and steady, my friend. There is no harm to come to you except what you bring with your own noise. Stand up, turn the key of that locked door, and walk into the cell ahead of me, carrying the lantern."

"In the name of the saints," said the guard, "do you know

that it is an enemy of Garcías who lies there?"

"I know everything about it," said the singer. "Do as I tell you. I am a man in haste, with a loaded gun in my hand. Pedro loaned it to me," he added with a smile.

The guard, one of those Oriental-looking fellows one sometimes finds south of the Río Grande, with ten bristles in his mustache and slant eyes, studied the smile of the stranger as he looked up and suddenly he felt that he recognized in this man a soul of cold iron. He rose with a faint gasp and, striding to the locked door, turned the key and stepped into the gloom within.

There, stretched on a thin pallet of straw, was the prisoner. He had not been stripped; there were no irons upon him. Plainly he had not excited the wrath of the great Garcías to the same degree as the singer, who now stooped over and fastened the manacles that were chained to the wall upon the wrists and the ankles of the guard.

The latter was moaning and muttering faintly: "The saints keep me from the rage of *Don* Hernando! Oh, that ever I was born in Segovia!"

The prisoner, sitting up, yawning away, settled his gaze beneath a frown at the other two and suddenly bounded to his feet.

"Speedy!" he cried. "I didn't know you, with the color of your skin and. . . ."

"We have to go on," said Speedy calmly. "There's something more for us to do before we leave the house of the great Garcías. He's fitted the two of us with such good quarters that we ought to leave some pay behind for him, Pier. Come along with me. This chap will be safe enough here. Rest well, *amigo*. When the others find you in the morning, or even a little before, they will give you the last news of us."

42

So he passed out from the cell and locked the door behind him.

Pier Morgan, in the meantime, was gaping helplessly at him.

"Speedy," he said, "I'm tryin' to believe that's your voice that I'm hearing. I'm trying to believe that. I've never seen anything finer than your face, man, and never heard anything sweeter than your voice. But how did you come here? Did you put on a pair of wings and hop in through a window?"

"*Don* Hernando asked me in," Speedy said, smiling faintly. "He even sent out his men and insisted on my coming in. He's a hospitable fellow, that man Garcías, and I can't wait till I've called on him again. How do you feel, Pier? Are you fit to ride a bit, and do some climbing, perhaps, before we start the riding?"

"I'm fit to ride . . . I rode all the way down here," said Pier. "And I can ride ten times as far in order to get away. This here place is a chunk of misery, Speedy. I've had something like death inside of me ever since I smelled this dungeon. Let's get out quickly and let your call on Hernando go!"

VII

"The Hanging Hernando"

The door of the bedroom of Garcías was locked from the inside. He had gone to bed, with the flame turned down in the throat of the lamp. Now he awoke, not that he had heard any suspicious sound, but because there was a sighing rush of wind through the room, as though a storm had entered.

The nerves of Garcías were not entirely at ease. His

43

dreams had been pleasant, but very violent. In his sleep, he had killed the insolent *gringo* singer by scourgings that had flayed his cursed body to the bone. Again, he had toasted his feet at a low fire, he had tormented him with the water cure, and he had hung up the American by the hair of the head. Also, he had dreamed of various combinations of these torments, and, although it was true that Garcías was to be the torturer, and not the tortured, it was also true that his nerves were jumping. All the tiger in him had been fed in his sleep. And the tiger in him now demanded living flesh, so to speak.

At the noise of the murmuring in his room, like the rising whistle of a storm wind, he raised himself impatiently on one elbow and turned his head toward the door. To his amazement, that door was open! He rubbed his eyes and shook his head to clear away the foolish vision, for he knew that no one in the house would ever dare to attempt his locked door. Even if there were someone foolish enough to make such an attempt, the lock of the door would itself give simple warning, for the key in the bolt could not be stirred without making a groaning sound, audible all up and down the corridor outside.

He opened his eyes again and scowled at the offending door, but now the vision was more complicated. A man stood in the doorway and was gliding with a soundless step straight toward his bed. The light of the lamp was very slight but, as he stared, the bewildered Garcías saw that it was the face of the *gringo* minstrel who was all the time drawing nearer to him.

He grunted. In the distance, the door was being closed by a second shadowy figure. But there was always a weapon at the hand of Garcías, and now he snatched his favorite protection from beneath his pillow. It was a rather old-fashioned double-barreled pistol, short in length, but large in caliber. It was equipped with two hair triggers, and it fired a ball big enough and with sufficient force to knock a strong man flat at fifteen yards. He always had it with him, in a pocket during the day and under his pillow by night. It had served him more than once. He had killed men many a time in his life, but all other weapons had been less deadly than this old-fashioned toy.

So, snatching it out, he tried to level it at the *gringo*. But he found his hand struck down, a cleaver stroke, as it were, falling across the cords of his wrist and benumbing the entire hand.

The pistol slipped into the sheets of the bed. A second stroke, delivered with the flat edge of the man's palm, fell upon the neck of Garcías, where the nerves and the stiff tendons run up to the skull. He floundered a little, but with only vague movements. He was stunned as though with a club.

Before he was entirely recovered from the effects, he found that the minstrel was sitting comfortably on the edge of his bed, toying with that double-barreled pistol with his left hand, but in his right was a short-bladed knife, the point of which he kept affectionately close to the hollow of *Don* Hernando's throat.

The second shadowy form had drawn closer and stood on the farther side of the bed. With disgust, *Don* Hernando recognized the face of Pier Morgan. He had received twenty-five hundred dollars for taking Morgan into the southern land across the river. He would receive twenty-five hundred more for keeping him there, or for making away with him. This was a bad business, all around. He wished for wild hawks to tear the flesh of the minstrel.

"I see," said Garcías, "how it is. You tricked the guards and got away from them, but you know that you can't get out of the house. Well, then, I am to let you go . . . through me you wish to manage it, but I tell you, my friends, that you never can persuade me. I know that you will not kill me, because you fear what will happen to you before you manage to get clear of the house. You think that you still have a chance to talk to me and to give me orders, but every door and every entrance to the house is guarded night and day!" He laughed a little as he ended. His fury made his laughter a tremulous sound.

"Speedy?" said Pier Morgan, "we can't waste time. We must hurry."

He said it in English naturally. But *Don* Hernando understood the language perfectly. Also, the name itself struck his ear like the blow of a club. He stiffened from head to foot.

"You are not Speedy," he exclaimed through his teeth. "Your skin is as brown as. . . ."

"As walnut juice, *amigo?*" suggested Speedy.

The lips of the Mexican remained parted, but no word issued from them.

Then Speedy said: "You see how it is, *Don* Hernando? I knew that your house was so guarded that only a bird could fly in safely through a window. And I had no wings. So I came and sang at night, to disturb you. Do you understand?"

The teeth of the Mexican ground together. He said nothing.

"Then, when you were sufficiently annoyed," Speedy said, "you sent for me to get me into your house and throw me into your hole of a prison. But I expected that, Garcías. I was prepared for all of that trouble, and it was worthwhile, because I had to reach my friend, Pier Morgan. I knew that it would be hard to hold me in a cell, because I know the language of locks."

Garcías rolled his eyes toward the door of his own room.

"The others were no harder," said Speedy. "Besides, your men are all fools. Like dogs that are kept half starved. They have plenty of teeth, but no brains whatever. They pointed out the room where Pier Morgan was kept on the way down to your slimy pigpen in the cellar. One of your servants sleeps in one of those cells, and another sleeps in the second. They are not happy, *Don* Hernando, because they are afraid of what you will do to them when they are set free."

"I will have them cut to pieces," said Garcías, "before my eyes. I will have them fed to dogs, and let you watch the feeding, before you are cut to bits in your turn!"

"You are full of promises, *Don* Hernando," Speedy observed, "but that's because you don't understand how simply we can get out of your house through that window with a rope of bedclothes."

"Idiots!" said *Don* Fernando. "Segovia lies beyond, and will have to be passed through. And there are always armed men there!"

"True," said the minstrel, "and I shall let them know that I am passing. I shall sing to my guitar."

"Are you such a half-wit?" Garcías said with a snarl.

"They know that I was dragged into your house," said the other, "but they don't know that I was treated like a whipped dog."

"Ha?" said Hernando.

"Besides," Speedy said, "I shall have something to show them, which will prove that Garcías forgave me for disturbing him in the middle of the night."

"What?" demanded the man of the castle.

"A ring from your finger," said Speedy.

Don Hernando gripped both hands to make fists. His fury was so great that his brain turned to fire and threatened to burst. For he could see that the inspired insolence of this *gringo* might very well enable him to do the thing that he threatened.

"I shall believe when I see," said *Don* Hernando.

"You will believe and see and hear, all three," Speedy said, "for I shall put you on a high chair to look things over. I shall put you where you'll be found in the morning. Tie his feet, Pier. I'll attend to his hands."

Hand and foot, the lord of the town of Segovia found himself trussed and made utterly helpless. That was not all, for then a gag was fixed between his teeth. The language of Speedy was more terrible than the insulting treatment he was giving to his host. He apologized, every moment, for the necessity of being so rough with so great a gentleman in his own house. For his own part, he regretted such a necessity. He would do much to avoid the occasion for it. It was only, after all, that murder and cruelty and dungeon tortures were not popular on the northern bank of the river, and even here, to the south of it, the people must be shown an example. They must be shown that tyrants are also cowards and that cruel beasts are really fools. For that reason he, Speedy, intended to give the people of Segovia an object lesson in the person of their master.

As he spoke, he drew from the struggling hand of *Don* Hernando almost his dearest possession, his signet ring. It was merely a flattened emerald of no great value, but it was carved with the arms of the house of Garcías. That ring and the portrait which had been ruined that night were his two clear claims and proofs of gentility.

He saw the second one departing in the possession of the same scoundrel; he turned blind with fury. When he recovered from the fit, he was hanging from the sill of a window of his room by the hands, his back turned to the wall. Strong hands held him at the wrists. Presently his arm muscles

48

would weaken. The strain would come straight upon bones and tendons. And then the real torment would commence. But what would that matter compared with the exquisite agony of being found in this humiliating position in the morning by the loyal populace of Segovia?

VIII

"In Segovia"

In all the house of Garcías, among all of his people, was there not one careful soul to look out a window, at this time, and see the two villains who now clambered down their comfortably made rope of bedding to the ground?

No, well filled with food and drink, they were snoring securely in their beds. As for the guards, they would be awake. He always took pains to be sure that they would sooner risk their necks than fall asleep either at the main door or at the one that opened over the bluff. But now he wanted a guard outside the place, and not within the massive old walls.

His anguish grew. He turned his head and saw the wretches standing upon the paving stones at the base of his wall. He bowed his head to stare down at them, while rage choked him, and there he saw Speedy remove from his head the hat with the tattered straw brim and sweep the ground with it, making a final bow.

Anguish, shame, fury, helplessness, fairly throttled the great Garcías. He became alarmed. He was unable to breathe well. He had to give all his attention, for a time, to drawing in his breath deeply. Fear of strangling at once made his heart flutter desperately. He compared it to the beating wings of a trapped bird, a bird dying of fear. Aye, he was like a bird, he thought, like a chicken hanging by the feet in the market, plucked, ready for the purchasers to thumb before making sure that it was fat enough to buy and take home. If only he could cry out!

He had only his bare feet to kick against the wall, and he soon bruised the flesh of his feet to the bone. But no one answered. No one looked out of the adjoining windows to discover the master, so crucified in shame and pain. Then he heard a sound that fairly stopped the beating of his heart again. It was rising from the lower streets of the town, and it was the strumming of a guitar, and the sound of a fine tenor voice that rose and rang sweetly through the air.

It was true, then, that the rascal had determined to do all as he had said? Was he to outbrave the fierce men of Segovia and increase the shame of Garcías? A demon, not a man, was walking down the street and playing on that guitar, singing the words of those old songs.

But Speedy and Pier Morgan did not get unhindered from the town.

It was said that the men of Segovia slept as lightly as wild wolves, which they were like in other respects, also, and, when they heard the voice of the minstrel, one, then another and another, jumped up in the night and went out to see what the disturbance might be. For they had seen the fellow dragged within the walls of the house, and what had happened to him in there was much pleasanter to guess than to see.

So they came running out, a score of those ragged, wild men, and found the minstrel, as before, mounted on the ancient gray mare, with a white man walking at his stirrup. This was too strange a sight to let pass.

There was one elderly robber, long distinguished in

forays, known as by a light, by the great white scar that blazed upon his forehead. He was gray with years and villainy, and music did not particularly tickle his fancy.

He took the mule by the bridle and halted it. "What is the meaning of this?" he demanded. "I saw you snatched into the door of the castle like a stupid child. High time, too, what with your caterwauling. Now you are here. Who set you free?"

"An angel, father," said Speedy, "walked into my room, wrapped me in an invisible cloak, and took me away, with this man."

"So?" said the desperado, darkening. "I'll have another kind of language out of you, before I'm through." He pulled out a knife as long as a sword, and glared at the boy in the saddle.

"If you're in any doubt," Speedy continued, "take us back to the house. If Garcías is wakened again, tonight, he will be interesting to the people who disturb him. You, however, are a wise man and know best what is to be done."

The veteran scowled. Some of his companions had begun to chuckle. They enjoyed this predicament.

"I ask questions when I can't understand," he said. "Now let me ask these questions again. *Señor* the singer, you will sing a new tune, if you try to make a fool out of me. You are here after midnight. So is this man. People do not start a trip at this time of the night."

"Look at his hands," said Speedy.

"Aye," said the other, "I see that they are tied together behind his back. And what do I understand by that?"

"You will understand," Speedy said, "when Garcías knows that you have stopped me in the streets and made me explain before the people. I am taking this man to a friend of Garcías."

51

"Ha!" said the man with the scar, coming a little closer, glowing his disbelief. "Taking him where? How will you prove that?" He snatched a lantern from the hand of another, and held it up to examine the face of Speedy.

The latter used the light, thrusting forward his left hand with the emerald ring on the largest finger. "Do you know the signet of Garcías?" he demanded harshly. "Would he give it to me for pleasure, or because of an important errand in his name?"

The other was stunned. He squinted at the ring. The face of it was well known. His companions were already falling back from the scene. They did not wish to interfere where the will of the master of Segovia was expressed in such unconditional terms as this.

The man of the scar no longer hesitated. He released the head of the mule and stepped back. "Well, *amigo*," he said, "there is a time for talk and a time for silence. This is a time for silence. Go along."

"Perhaps you wish to know to what place I am taking the prisoner?" asked Speedy. "You are many and I am one. You can force me to tell you even that."

The man of the scar muttered: "You can take him to Satan, for all I care."

Speedy rode on, slowly, through the last street of Segovia and into the plain beyond.

Once down the slope, he cut the cord that confined the hands of Pier Morgan and the latter gasped: "Speedy, I thought that we were finished when we came to the gang of 'em. I thought they'd certainly drag us back to the big house. And if they had . . . eh, what then?"

"Garcías would have burned us alive," Speedy answered. "That's what would have happened. But it didn't happen, old man, and the more luck for us. I thought that the ring would turn the trick, and it turned out that way."

"I've got other things to ask," said Pier Morgan. "But I'll ask 'em after we get on the other side of the river."

It was Pier Morgan who rode the mule across the shallows of the ford. It was Speedy who waded or swam behind until they struggled up the farther bank. There they turned and looked back over the dim pattern of stars that appeared, scattered over the face of the famous river.

Then Pier Morgan said: "Yesterday, I thought that I was ridin' my last trail, Speedy. And today it don't seem likely that I'm really here, on safe ground, and you beside me. You've got through stone walls, and locked doors, and raised the mischief to get me out of trouble. I ain't thanking you, Speedy. Thanks are pretty foolish things, after all, considering what you've done for me. I've used up nine lives, like any cat, and you've kept me on the face of the earth. That's what you've done. But still I'd like to ask you a coupla questions."

"Fire away," said Speedy, beginning to thrum very softly on the strings of his guitar.

"I dunno that I understand very well," said the other, "why you wanted to make this here Garcías so crazy mad at you. You done that on purpose, but I dunno what the purpose is."

"You could guess."

"Yeah, I could guess," Pier said. "I could guess that life was kind of dull for you up there in Sunday Slough. I could guess that you didn't have your hands full, and that you wanted to crowd in a little more action. So you got Garcías practically crazy. You wanted to make sure that he'd get together every man that can ride and shoot and come up to the Slough looking for your scalp."

Speedy chuckled a little. "Garcías can be a pretty dangerous fellow, I imagine," he said. "He has that reputation. But I wanted to have him so blind crazy with rage that he would hardly know what he's about. He'll never rest till he gets at me again, do you think?"

"No, he'll never rest," agreed Pier Morgan. "He'll certainly never sleep until he gets a whack at you in revenge."

"When he comes, he'll come like a storm," Speedy said, "and the first thing that he does will be to get in touch with friend Levine. Isn't that fairly clear?"

"Yeah. That's pretty likely."

"When that happens, I have a chance to scoop him up along with Levine. And then the charge is kidnapping, with you and me both for proofs of what's happened. Kidnapping of a man and taking him across a frontier is pretty bad and black for everybody concerned. I think, if my scheme works, I'll have Levine in for fifteen years, at least. That's my hope. Then I've done what I wanted to do . . . I've cleaned up Sunday Slough and given it a rest."

"All right," murmured Pier Morgan. "I'm behind you every step, but you must carry a pretty steep life insurance, old man."

IX

"The Return"

Levine was at the breakfast table. His coat was off. He had not put on the stiff white collar that made him respectable for the day. He had rolled his sleeves. By way of a bib, a large cotton hand towel was stuffed in at his throat. This kept him from the necessity of leaning far forward every time he raised a dripping forkful from his plate. Fried eggs will drip. A ragged half of a loaf of bread remained at his left hand; a tall coffee pot and a can of condensed milk were at his right. The eggs were well flavored by numerous strips of bacon. The precious juices that might slip through the fork were salvaged by using the bread as a sort of sponge. In this way he made excellent progress.

He had a newspaper propped up in front of him, but he paid less attention to its headlines than to the cheerful conversation of One-Eyed Mike Doloroso, who was lolling in a corner of the room. Mike had just come in and made himself at home.

"Have something?"

"Nope," said Mike.

"Slug o' coffee, maybe?"

"I fed my face a coupla hours ago," said Mike. "I ain't a lazy hound like you, what I mean."

"You got nothin' on your brain to worry you, like me," said Levine. "You got nothin' but hair."

"Ain't I got Speedy to worry me, too?" asked Mike.

"Him? Aw, he don't pay much attention to you. It's me that he wants. What's that yowling out there?"

Mike went to the window. "Aw," he said, "there's a coupla dozen poor fools walkin' down the street carryin' a big banner that says J.J.J. for sheriff."

"Close the window and shut the yapping out, will you?" asked Levine testily. "That tramp, I'm kind of tired of thinking about him."

"Yeah," said One-Eyed Mike, "you shouldn't go and get yourself into a stew about him now. You're gonna have plenty of time later on, when he throws you into the pen for life."

"He's gonna throw me into the pen, is he?" asked Levine.

"Sure, so you'll be sure to have plenty of time to think

about how he's trimmed you."

Levine paused with a large slice of egg dripping from his raised fork. Twice he tried to put it into his mouth. Finally he gave up the effort and lowered the fork to the plate. "Whatcha drivin' at, Mike?" he asked. "Stow that chatter, will you? You wanna spoil my breakfast?"

"You've had enough for three men for three days, already," said Mike. "I was just thinking how you and Derrick and Buck Masters had the town all laid out and ready for a trimming. And here comes Speedy, and he gets Derrick first, and then Buck Masters that was sheriff, and now he's gonna get you."

Levine pointed at Mike with his fork. "You think I'm asleep on the job, do you? Well, right now, Mister Deputy Sheriff Speedy has disappeared from Sunday Slough, and the town's gonna wake up to the fact, pretty *pronto*."

Mike rose stiff-legged from his chair. "You think that he followed Pier Morgan?" he said.

"I don't think. I know. He started right out. I've sent off another rider, riding fast, to let Garcías know that Speedy has a gray mule that he's riding on. The kid may try to disguise himself or something. Another day or two, Garcías will make fish bait out of him."

"Speedy ain't so easy," One-Eyed Mike advised.

"You're telling that to somebody that don't know?" suggested Levine, resuming his eating. "But Mexico ain't home soil for him. He's out of the water, down there. And this here boy Garcías has done a couple things in his life, lemme tell you!"

"All right," said Mike. "You're an optimist, is all I say. But one of these days you may be rotting like Buck Masters. I got a letter from Buck just the other day."

"Why didn't you tell me about it?"

"Because you didn't want to see it."

"Why not?"

"Because Buck is pretty sore. He says that he trusted you to fix things for him. He says that he's the goat and went to jail to save your scalp."

"Did the fool say that?" asked Levine, losing a splotch of color out of either cheek.

"Yeah, he said that."

"Prison letters are opened and read!" gasped Levine.

"Aw, they've all heard more than that about you a long while before this," declared One-Eyed Mike. "Talk ain't gonna kill you, or you'd've been a sick fish a long while ago, I guess. But Buck is sore, is what I mean."

"I spent a lotta money on that case," Levine said sadly. "You know what I mean."

"I know what you say you spent," said Mike.

"Look," protested Levine, "are you gonna lie down and croak on me, too? Are you fallin' away, Mike? Gonna do a State's evidence, or something like that on me?"

"Aw, shut up," said Mike Doloroso. "You know that I ain't that kind. But I ain't a fool. And I'm worried. County courts, they're one thing. You can get to a jury and fix a coupla jurors, or maybe you can buy up a judge. But I tell you what . . . a federal judge is a lot different. Look at Buck and Derrick, both. There was plenty of money working for both of them two, but it didn't do no good. Not a damned bit."

The window that looked onto the street was thrust up with a screech. The face of young Joe Dale appeared in the square. "Hello, boys," he said.

"Hello, beautiful," said Mike. "Whatcha want here, kid?"

"I just wanted to clap eyes on you bozos, was all," said Joe Dale. "I just wanted to ask you where you seen Speedy last."

"We ain't seeing Speedy these days," said Levine. "He

don't seem fond of me, no more. We was good friends once, but he's gone and got proud, since those days."

"Has he?" asked Joe. "That's all right, too. But how far south would your partner, Garcías, trail him?"

"What Garcías?" asked Levine. But he glanced at One-Eyed Mike.

"No, you never seen Garcías, did you?" Joe Dale said. "Lemme tell you, brother. I'm inside the law, just now. But I was outside of it for a long time and got along pretty good. If Speedy don't come back, I'm gonna be outside the law ag'in. I'm gonna be outlawed for shooting the brains out of a pair of fatheads that I'm looking at right now."

"Breeze along, Joe," said Levine. "You're all right, but you're young. You ain't got any sense."

"I'm just telling you, that's all," said Joe Dale.

"Look," broke in One-Eyed Mike. "Speedy licked you so good that you love him now, don't you?"

"He licked me," agreed Joe Dale. "But I can lick you, you slab-faced Irish bum. That's all I gotta say to you."

"Get out of the window," said Levine. "You're standing on my ground."

Another voice struck in cheerfully from the distance, down the street.

"Hello, Joe! Hello!"

Levine started up from his chair. "It's Speedy!" he gasped.

One-Eyed Mike grunted. There was a sawed-off shotgun standing in the corner against the wall, and this he picked up and held at the ready. Revolvers were the favored weapons of Mike but, where Speedy was concerned, experience taught him that a gun with a wide spread of shot was more likely to touch the elusive mark. He stood firm, but his face was very pale.

Sid Levine had slumped down into his chair again. A

frightful weakness in his knees had attacked him.

The cheerful face of Speedy now appeared outside the window, at the shoulder of Joe Dale, and behind Speedy loomed Pier Morgan.

Sid Levine became smaller in his chair, a watery pulp. That window seemed to him to open upon the inferno itself, three such enemies were gathered there before his face.

Speedy said: "I took your regards down to your friend, the great Garcías, Levine. He'll be up, before very long, to see you. Just dropped in to say hello to you, Levine. And Morgan wanted to tell you that he'd enjoyed his trip with *Don Hernando*."

"I don't know what you mean," said Levine. He shook his head; his fat cheeks wobbled and bulged from side to side.

"You may understand later on," said Pier Morgan. "We're gonna do our best to clear up the idea in your mind, anyway. Hello, Mike! I ain't seen you for quite a spell."

But Mike Doloroso answered nothing at all. He was rather sick at heart.

So the three outside the window passed out of view, laughing.

They left a silence behind them in the room which had been such a cheerful breakfast scene the moment before. Levine was resting his fat forehead in a fatter hand. Mike remained still, as one stunned by bad news. But at last he began to pace up and down along the floor.

Then he said: "Chief, it looks like we got our backs against the wall."

Levine slowly roused himself and leaned forward. "There's one thing that we can still try," he said. "And there's one thing that will work."

"What's that?" asked Mike.

Levine beckoned, and the big Irishman came closer to him and leaned over.

Levine whispered one word, and Mike Doloroso, although a man of exceptionally steady nerves, jumped away as though a knife had been thrust into him.

X

"The New Danger"

Speedy and Joe Dale sat in the sheriff's office. Pier Morgan, exhausted by his long journeying, was asleep in the side room. The deputy sheriff who, as nine tenths of Sunday Slough declared, was to be the sheriff in full at the next day's election now sat slumping in a chair, yawning a little from time to time, and making short answers to the questions of Joe Dale.

"You ought to let the people know what you did down there, Speedy," said Joe Dale. "That'll poll all the votes for you. You'll be unanimously elected, I tell you!"

Speedy yawned. "Ask Betsy about it," he said. "Ask her what I ought to do."

Betsy was grazing in the lot behind the shack which housed the sheriff's office. It was a good, deep lot, and the grass grew tall in it. Betsy, now that the heat of the day was over, moved slowly, step by step, spreading her forelegs a little and scratching her long neck as she moved about for choice tufts. Now and then she snorted, shook her head, and lifted it to look about her.

Joe Dale went to the window and looked upon her with a loving eye.

"She's always a little wild in the eye," commented Speedy.

"She's been in some wild places with me," said Joe Dale. "She's a cross between a horse, a friend to talk to, and a watchdog. I'm as safe sleeping out, with her to keep an eye around, as I'd be with two men on guard. Safer, even, because she can use her eyes and her scent, as well."

"Ask her about me," said Speedy.

"What about this fellow?" Joe Dale asked, pleased by the suggestion. "Come here, Betsy, and tell me about him."

Speedy went to the window as Betsy came up to it.

"Tell about him, Betsy," repeated her owner. "Is he a good fellow?"

She stretched her head through the window and sniffed Speedy's hand, then she drew back a little and shook her head.

"I'm gonna look out for you, Speedy," said Joe Dale. "I thought you were all right, but trust Betsy. She knows the right sort of a man." He began to laugh, immensely pleased. Then he added: "Come here and tell me about him again, Betsy. I want to see you vote twice on him. Tell me what sort of a bad egg he is, will you?"

Betsy came and again sniffed the hand of Speedy, but this time she pricked her ears mischievously and began to nibble at it.

"She knows you're no good and she's trying to bite you," declared Joe Dale. "I'm going to keep an eye on you, Speedy. Here's Betsy saying that you're no good at all. Betsy, you're a wise old girl. You know more than I do."

"I've never ridden her," said Speedy.

"You'd better not try," answered Joe Dale.

"Why? I thought that she was as gentle as a lamb."

"She's gentle with me. She's gentle with others, too, but she knows some little tricks."

"Such as what?"

"She hates spurs. One touch of 'em and she'll buck like a fiend. She's an educated little pitching witch, I can tell you. She learned young."

"How did she learn?"

"Got into the hands of a half-breed son of trouble and learned how to pitch him off every time she jumped, even if he was a pretty slick rider. She's had other chances, too. I've had people try to steal her a dozen times, and she generally gets them out of the saddle before they've gone a mile. A touch of the spurs will always start her."

"Anything else that she doesn't like?"

"She's a balky brute, at heart. She even tries it on me, now and then," confessed Joe Dale. "Sometimes she doesn't like to pass a stump or tree with a funny shape. And sometimes she'll stop dead at a bridge, and start turning in circles like a crazy thing. I can bring her out of those wrong notions with a touch. But nobody else can."

"What's to do, then?" asked Speedy.

"Get off and lead her. That's the only way. She's always as quiet as a lamb when she's on the lead. She seems to be sure that a man walking on the ground really knows the way better'n she does." He added: "You planning to steal her, Speedy, asking all these questions?"

"I'd rather have my gray mule." Speedy grinned. "He's slow but he's sure. But someday I might want to make a fast move and need Betsy."

"You don't wear spurs, so you'd be all right on her," said the other. "And I've told you about the bucking."

"How fast is she?" asked Speedy.

"She's no racer," Joe Dale admitted. "She looks a lot faster than she is. Somehow, she doesn't seem able to stretch out in a real, long gallop. But her point is that she can last all day and all night, and she'll live on thistles and drink the wind for a week, and still be able to lope along like a wolf."

"That's the horse for this country," declared Speedy. "Next to the iron horse, that's the way to travel in this country."

"You're still a tramp." Joe Dale grinned now. "You'd like to be back on the bum, riding blind baggage, and going nowheres."

"Going nowhere is the best place to go," Speedy said.

"How come?" asked Joe Dale.

"Well, you ought to know how it is. You straighten out for you don't know what, and the fun is all in the getting there. There's no place I've ever seen where I'd like to drop anchor. But to drift from one spot to another . . . that's a good deal better."

The other stared curiously at him. "Look a-here, Speedy," he said. "Look at Sunday Slough. Take a place like this, and you could live here the rest of your days. The people are all proud to have you around. You could be sheriff here till kingdom come. They'd give you a fat salary. You wouldn't have to keep smiling, up here. The boys know what you can do."

"I've had a good time here, but it's lasted long enough," said Speedy.

"You want to be on the road again?"

"Yes, I want to be going nowhere. I'm tired of having a fixed home address."

A horse beat down the street, came to a grinding halt before the sheriff's office, and a big man in shirt sleeves rolled to the elbows, with salty sweat stains on his breast and shoulders, came clumping into the room.

He had been riding against the western glare of the sun, and now he paused, scowling and blinking, growing accustomed to the dim light inside the house.

"Hullo, Speedy," he said.

"Something wrong?" asked Speedy.

"You bet there's something wrong," he replied. "You know me?"

"I've seen you. I don't know your name."

"I'm Sam Jedbury. I got a claim up there at the head of the ravine. I went about a mile beyond everything else, and I struck it pretty good. I struck it too good for my health. I'm working along, and getting out my share and a little more of the bonanza, and today along comes a low-down hound of a Swede and pokes a rifle into my stomach and tells me that he staked that claim a year ago. Why, there wasn't even a jack rabbit in Sunday Slough a year ago. But that's what he says. And what am I to do? Argue? You can't argue with a rifle, unless you got a gun in your hand. And I didn't have no gun. So I come in here to let you know."

Speedy sighed. "What sort of a looking fellow?" he asked.

"Big and hairy is all I can say," said Sam Jedbury. "Got a mean-looking eye, too. It was like poison to me."

"What sort of a rifle?"

"Winchester."

"I'll go and call on him," said Speedy.

"I'll go along," said the other.

"No, you stay here. You, too, Joe."

Dale had picked a gun belt from a nail on the wall and was strapping it around his hips.

"Hold on, Speedy," Joe Dale said. "You let me tell you something. You've handled a lot of the wild men around here, but you've never handled a claim-jumper before. Those fellows know that trouble is ahead of 'em, and they plan on doing a little shooting. Besides, everybody in Sunday Slough, by this time, knows that you don't carry no gun."

"That's right." Sam Jedbury nodded. "You let us both go along."

"I don't carry a gun . . . everybody knows it . . . so guns aren't likely to be used on me," Speedy stated.

"Don't be so sure of that," said Jedbury. "Every gunman in the Slough would be pretty proud if he could slam a slug of lead into you, no matter whether you carry a gun yourself or not. Neither does a wildcat or a grizzly pack a gun, but gents will go shooting for them."

Speedy shrugged his shoulders.

"I'll go alone," he said. "Don't be surprised if I don't come back for a while. The fact is that I may have to do a little scouting around." He turned to Dale. "Suppose that I borrow Betsy?" he asked.

"You can have Betsy," said Joe Dale, "but I'd a lot rather you'd let me go along with you. You're taking too many chances, Speedy. Someday you'll lose your bet. Do you realize that?"

"I told you before that I wanted to be on the road," said Speedy. "Here's a trip on a sideline, anyway. It may not be much, but I'm going to take it."

So, straightway, he took the mare and rode off. The other two remained staring after him.

"He loves trouble, I reckon." Jedbury sighed.

"It's the only fun he gets," said Joe Dale, and he sighed in turn.

XI

"The Trap"

Twice the beautiful mare balked on the way up the valley, and twice Speedy dismounted and led her forward until her step became free and willing and her ears were pricking. But he had been so delayed by these halts that it was after sunset when he got to the claim of Jedbury, at the head of the ravine.

The claim-jumper was in full view, sitting on a broad-topped stone at the mouth of the shaft, which lay on top of a dump. It was apparent that he had been working inside the shaft or, at least, making a thorough survey. But now he was merely intent on keeping his fort. He smoked a pipe with a quiet concentration, and he had across his knees a shining new Winchester that would hold fifteen shots—fifteen lives, perhaps.

He was what Sam Jedbury had described—a hairy fellow, with a very considerable jaw to be guessed at behind the tangle of his beard. His great eyebrows bushed out and downward, and the eyes themselves were as bright as bits of flame.

He paid no heed to the approach of Speedy and the mare, but continued to smoke his pipe. It was only when the deputy sheriff was a few yards away that he picked up his rifle and held it like a revolver in one hand, his forefinger on the trigger and the long barrel pointing at Speedy.

The latter spoke to Betsy, and she halted. "How's things?" asked Speedy.

"Things are fair to middling," replied the other in a noncommittal way.

"Been here quite a time?" Speedy asked.

"On this stone? No. Whatcha want?"

"Just to spend some time with you," said Speedy, and he dismounted.

"I can't offer you no hospitality," said the man at the mouth of the mine's shaft. "I ain't got no chuck to offer you, stranger. Sorry."

"That's all right," said Speedy. "I just wanted to have a chat with you." He sat down on a rock near the claim-jumper, facing him. The muzzle of the rifle followed his movements like the magnetic needle pointing toward the pole.

"You go on and chat," said the miner. "Whatcha gonna chat about?"

"A fellow came into town," said Speedy, "and told me a wild yarn about his mine up here. He said another fellow, who answers your description, had arrived and jumped it. It sounded like a cock-and-bull yarn, but I had to come up here and investigate. I'm the deputy sheriff, you see."

"Wait," said the other, frowning. "You call yourself Speedy?"

"Yes," said the man of the law.

"The Speedy that runs Sunday Slough?"

"I don't claim to run it."

"Hold on, now. You say that you're Speedy, and I say that you lie. Whatcha think about that?" He thrust his head forward and uttered the last words with a sneer.

"Are you sure that I'm a liar?" Speedy asked, smiling.

"Sure? Of course, I'm sure."

"Have you ever seen Speedy?"

"I don't need to see him," answered the claim-jumper. "I heard him described enough times. Back in the mountains they don't talk about much else of a winter evening, except to swap lies about Speedy . . . what he's done and what he ain't done. I been damn' sick of hearing the name, just to speak personal."

"Too bad," said Speedy. "Maybe I'm not big enough to be the right man?"

"Well, he ain't so very big," said the other. "I'd say maybe he was about six feet, not weighing more'n a hundred and eighty or ninety. But that's big enough. And you're only a runt. You ain't more'n five nine or ten. You wouldn't weigh a hundred and fifty pounds hardly. Why, kid, you're a plain fool if you think that you'll kid me into believin' that you're Speedy!"

The latter opened the breast of his coat and showed the steel badge that was pinned inside of it. "That's all I can say," he said. "You can believe me or not, but I'll have to take you into Sunday Slough."

"You?" cried the miner.

"I'm afraid that I shall," Speedy said. "Unless you can prove that the mine belongs to you. You drove out Jedbury. He was the first to work it."

"That's a lie," said the ruffian. "I'll tell you what. I staked out this claim pretty near a year ago. I broke the ground. I started things going. Jedbury, he never would've found nothing here, except that he saw where I'd been working and. . . ." He paused, scowling. "I done enough talking," he said. "Talking ain't my style."

"Fighting is more your line, I suppose," suggested Speedy.

"I've done my share of that," declared the miner. He glared at the smaller man as he spoke.

"I think Jedbury was telling the truth," said Speedy. "You'll have to come to town with me, partner."

"Where's your warrant?" asked the man of the beard.

"Warrant?" Speedy echoed. He lifted his brows and stared in turn. "We don't bother about those little formalities in Sunday Slough. Not when we have fellows like claim-jumpers to handle."

"I'm a claim-jumper, am I?" asked the other. His teeth glinted through his beard as he spoke. Then he added: "You're gonna take me back, are you? Would you mind telling me what you're gonna take me with?"

"Yes, with my hands," said Speedy. He stood up. "It's getting toward dusk," he observed. "We'd better be starting along."

When the miner spoke, it was as if a dog were snarling.

"You don't dare do it," he challenged. "If you're Speedy, I'll tell you what else you are. You're a fake. That's what you are! Now, if you're the wild man that I've heard so much talk about, start something, kid." He rose in turn and held the rifle stiffly toward the breast of the man of the law.

"Resisting arrest may be hard on your eyes and bad for your health," declared Speedy. "Have you thought about that, partner?"

"You talk like I needed advice or asked for it," said the stranger. "Now, shove up your hands. I'm gonna make an example out of you. You may run Sunday Slough, but you can't run me!"

Speedy obediently raised his hands, and the other came closer, slowly. "You have a gun," said Speedy, "and you know that I don't carry one."

"I could lick you without a gun," said the miner, "except as how they say that you're a whole pack of tricks. I reckon that I don't really need a gun, but why should I throw away a bet on a sure thing? I'm gonna skin you alive, Mister Deputy Sheriff, that's what I'm gonna do. I'm gonna teach you what it means to mix up with Bill Parry, and. . . ." With savage satisfaction he drew nearer to the boy, so near that the muzzle of his gun, although still out of reaching distance, was not, however, out of range of a kick.

And that was what Speedy tried. It was a difficult target, the narrow, gleaming barrel of that rifle, and, if he missed, a bullet would take his life the next instant. Murder was no new thing, he could guess, to this ruffian. But he took the chance.

It was a partial miss. Only with the side of his shoe did he touch the rifle a glancing blow. It exploded almost on the instant, but the force of the kick had been sufficient to make it swerve to the side, and the bullet ripped the shirt under Speedy's armpit. Half an inch closer in, it would have broken

69

his ribs and knocked him down.

Bill Parry, as he fired, leaped backward to avoid danger, but he was far too slow of foot. All the tangled padding of his beard was not sufficient to dull the force of a blow that clipped him close to the point of the chin and staggered him, bent his knees. His head was flicked back by the blow and, although he managed to fire again, it was blindly, at an unseen target.

What happened to him after that, he was never quite sure. He simply knew, all in an instant of time, that he was tripped up, disarmed, half stunned by a blow on the temple and, in general, felt as though he had been tackled by a combination of wildcat and grizzly bear. Then he was lying flat on his back, looking up toward the darkening sky and toward the face of Speedy, who stood erect, panting.

"You'd better get up, Bill Parry," Speedy advised. "As I said before, you'll have to come into Sunday Slough with me. You've resisted arrest, attempted murder, and in general played a bad hand. I'm going to see that you get the limit. I'll be lucky if I keep the men of the Slough from taking you out on a necktie party."

Parry did not move. He merely said: "There'll be a necktie party, all right enough."

"I'm not threatening you," Speedy assured him.

"Ain't you? But I'm threatening you! You fool, we got everything set ready for you. We got you trimmed and trapped, you swine. If you don't believe me, look around you."

Although he did not turn his head, Speedy was suddenly certain that figures had moved up behind him during the fight, and that now they were in readiness. The chill of an unknown dread flowed suddenly like liquid ice through his blood.

Then from behind him, he heard the last voice in all the world that he wished to hear, the voice of Garcías, saying with a tremor of joy: "Now, Pedro, now Manuel, take him on each side. If he moves a finger, fill his skin with lead!"

For the first time in his wild young life, Speedy made certain of death!

XII

"A Digression"

Chains, irons, and locks they knew better than to try upon the magic hands of Speedy by this time. They used ropes, instead, not big ones that may be slipped, but thin, powerful cords that will fit into the very knuckles of joints and that hold on as if with conscious force, steadily applied. They took no chances. They tied his hands together. They tied him across the elbows. They tied his feet and ankles together; they bound his knees. They put a stout pole down his back, and wrapped him to it with lashings.

Then he heard a voice saying: "There ain't anything he can move, now, but his brain and his tongue."

It was the voice of Levine, and the voice of One-Eyed Mike broke in to add: "Yeah, he can think and he can talk. We're gonna see how he can talk himself out of this here pickle." He came and stood over Speedy, and kicked him brutally in the ribs with his heavy boot.

"You go on and tell me, Speedy. You tell me how you're gonna cut these here cords with your tongue. You got a bright brain in your head, and you got a tongue with a fine sharp edge to it. But now, you tell me how you're gonna talk your way clean out of this, will you?"

"Oh, I'll tell you," said Speedy. "I don't at all mind telling you that I'll get out of the tangle."

"You hear that, *Don* Hernando?" said the great Levine, laughing softly. "He says that he'll talk his way out of this here trouble. He ain't the kind to boast, neither."

The Mexican came nearer, glaring down at the victim. "Pedro, give me a whip," he commanded.

Pedro handed him a double-lashed quirt, and *Don* Hernando struck the bound man across the face.

"There is your answer, dog," Garcías said.

The knotted tip of one of the lashes cut through the skin of Speedy's cheek, cut deeply, and brought a stream of blood. But he hardly felt any pain. The imminence of death made all lesser things of no moment whatever.

"You are here again, *Señor* Garcías. This time I did not have to wake you up by singing," he said.

Garcías smiled. Suddenly he squatted like an Indian on his heels, to bring his face closer to that of the helpless prisoner. "You had a moment in my own house," he said, "when you could have run a knife through my throat. You could have killed me as the mountaineers kill pigs in the autumn, when the frosts begin. But you did not, *Señor* Speedy. Tell me why, like a blind fool, you let me go."

"Because," Speedy answered, "I wanted you up here."

"And so you have me, eh?" said the Mexican.

"So I have you," agreed Speedy. "And Levine with you, and your two man-killers, there, and One-Eyed Mike, also. I am only baiting a trap that will catch you and swallow you all."

Hernando sprang up and looked about him in alarm. Then he raised the quirt as though to strike again. "You lie," he said, "and your lies are the lies of a fool. There is no danger near us. I have other men posted. They can see everything that comes near. We are alone here with you, and we intend to see you die slowly." He turned toward Levine, saying: "I told you that this would be the better way." Then he added, to the prisoner: "Poison was the last thought of Levine, my dear friend Levine. He has a good, quick mind, but I am not a fool, either."

"Find a death for me," said Speedy, "that takes plenty of time, because there won't be any shame in it. There'll be no shame like hanging out a window of my own house, like a suit of old clothes taking the air. How much do the people of Segovia laugh when they think of you, *amigo* Hernando?"

The Mexican, in frantic anger, fairly howled out an oath, and whirled the lash of the whip above his head.

It was caught from behind and the voice of Bill Parry exclaimed: "No more of that, Garcías!"

Pedro, on one side of Parry, drew a knife. Manuel, on the other, had a revolver ready. They waited the signal from their chief before laying the rash *gringo* dead.

But Levine called out: "Stop 'em, Garcías! We don't want anything to happen to Parry. He's all right. He's played the game straight and square with us. We wouldn't've had Speedy now, except for him."

"He . . . he," exclaimed Garcías, stammering with rage, "he dared to hold my . . . ! What shall I do to . . . ?"

He could not find words, and Bill Parry said calmly enough: "It's all right, Garcías. I know that the kid has to die. He's done too damn' much. He's spoiled too many good times. It's the day for him to be bumped off. But don't slam him like that when he can't slam back. You'd never have the nerve to try it, if you and him was alone, and his hands was free."

"Shut up, Parry!" called Levine.

Don Hernando had drawn himself up, stiff with pride and rage.

"I have come many leagues," he declared. "I have ridden furiously with my men. I suggested this method for catching the snake when I came here. And now I am insulted by a *gringo!*"

"Señor, señor," Pedro muttered warningly.

"Shut up, Parry," repeated Levine, but the miner was enraged in his turn, and his tongue could be as bitter as any in Mexico for that matter. He shouted out: "If you call me a *gringo,* you greaser puppy, I'm gonna . . . !"

He reached for a gun as he spoke, but an unexpected voice broke in on the debate, not that of Levine or of the followers of Garcías.

It was Speedy, saying cheerfully from the ground where he lay: "Fight it out, boys. When the last of you are dead, I'll be safe enough."

This logic struck Garcías at once.

"That is true. Why should we fight with one another?" he asked. "To please this demon who lies beside us on the ground? We have come to dispose of him, not of one another."

"You'll never dispose of me, Garcías," Speedy corrected. "It's not in the cards for you. Neither for that fat-faced Levine. I know my luck that far away. But don't argue with the *gringos,* as you call them, *Don* Hernando. They have everything better than you have . . . stronger hands, better brains, better guns, better horses to ride on."

Don Hernando groaned with fury. "You say four things and you lie four times," he said. "You are nothing but a lie, a great and complete and horrible lie. We have guns as good, better hands, better wits, better horses."

"You have broken-down, lump-headed, knock-kneed, sway-backed wrecks for horses," said Speedy. "They are the off-casts of the tramps and fourth-rate cowpunchers, who get tired of them and sell them for the price of their hoofs and hides. But they're good enough for you fellows south of the Río Grande. Plenty good enough! You're proud to sit the saddle on brutes like that. You tie sashes about your hips and feed your horses on steel, so that they stumble along a mile or so, and then drop dead. When they die, you have to wait half a year before you can afford to buy another horse fit for the glue factory, and for nothing else."

If there is any tender point with a Mexican of any pretensions to rank, it is the horse that he rides upon. Speedy already had seen the glorious animal that *Don* Hernando usually rode. Although it was not in sight now, he guessed that it must be somewhere near, for it was said that Garcías rode it in all his marauding expeditions.

Don Hernando, in the long flow of insult that poured from the lips of Speedy, was a mere drifting, staggering thing, so did rage buoy and lighten him. At last he managed to say: "Pedro, bring me my horse. Even this lying demon will look on it and gasp. Bring the horse and let him see what a gentleman rides in Mexico."

Pedro went for the horse.

Levine, in the meantime, together with Mike, had carefully propped up the helpless, stiff-lashed body of Speedy against the bank of the mine dump. He and his henchman sat down nearby. Levine said: "Don't get too hot, Garcías. There ain't any use matching words with this here sneak. He's got a vocabulary longer'n his arm, what I mean. Let him go, and we better put our heads together about the best way of getting rid of him."

But here the horse was brought, a fine gray gelding with

black points, gleaming and dancing through the dusk of the day.

The eyes of Speedy, prepared as they were, widened a little.

"Look!" commanded Garcías, "and then tell me what a liar you are. Say it with your own lips!"

"I see what you have there," Speedy said. "You've got a thing that looks like a horse and seems like a horse, walks like a horse and stands like a horse, but it isn't a horse at all. It's only a pretty picture out of a book."

"Ha!" said *Don* Hernando.

Levine began to chuckle, almost inaudibly, behind his hand. He did not object to this badgering of *Don* Hernando. He still owed the man twenty-five hundred dollars—and Levine was not one to love a creditor. One-Eyed Mike, too, was looking on with a grin.

"Only a pretty little picture pony," Speedy repeated calmly. "That's the sort of a pick-up that we give our children to ride. No man would want to be on the back of a horse like that. Take the mare, yonder. She has more brains than you and your men put together. She'll come when she's called, sit down, lie down, fetch, and carry. She'll run faster, and run farther than your gray. She is worth looking at. She has points!"

Don Hernando stared with a fixed passion. Then he said: "You, *señor*, being about to die, already rave. But I would like to show you how the gray would leave the mare behind him. If they ran as far as that rock and back. Then you would see!"

"Bill Parry will ride the mare and make a fool of your horse," answered Speedy. "Bill, show up the Mexican, will you, and his bragging?"

"I'll do it free and willing and glad," said Bill Parry. "It's a good mare and a grand mare to look at. Garcías, I'm ready."

XIII

"The Race"

In all parts of the world, in all times, there have been strange races, but never one under auspices more peculiar than this. Sid Levine was the only one to protest.

"The kid is playing for time," he said. "He's making a fool of us. He may have something up his sleeve. You know that, Garcías."

"What can he do?" answered Garcías. "And what can his friends do? If they come near, we have horses to carry us away, unless we can drive them with our rifles. Before we mount, each of us puts a bullet through the head of *Senor* Speedy. That much is clear. In the meantime, we really have nothing to fear. We have hours before us. The men in Sunday Slough suspect nothing, and we shall kill this man in so many ways that it will repay us everything that we have suffered from him. Also, before that begins, I shall show him that he is both a fool and a blind man, since he cannot judge horses. Manuel, take the saddle of the gray. *Amigo*," he added to Parry, "you ride the mare. I laugh, a little, but I will make you a bet, if you wish."

"I got fifty dollars," said Bill Parry stoutly. "I'll lay it all on the back of the mare."

"I have a hundred," answered the Mexican contemptuously. "I offer you two dollars for one. Are you ready?"

Parry was already mounted, a big, uncouth form on the back of the dainty Betsy. Speedy looked with interest at the short spurs that ornamented the heels of Parry's boots. It was an odd miner who wore spurs at his work.

"Any tricks to her?" asked Parry of the prisoner.

"Sometimes she's lazy," said Speedy. "And if she hangs a little, just warm her up with the spurs. She'll go by the picture horse as if he were tied to a post. Give her plenty of punishment if she hangs fire. There's plenty in her, but she's a little petted and spoiled."

"I'll get the speed out of her," Bill Parry said savagely, "if I have to cut her heart out with the spurs. You can lay your money on that."

"I'll lay my money on her and you, Bill," Speedy said calmly.

"Are you ready, Manuel, you lump?" asked Bill Parry.

"Ready," said Manuel with a sneer of satisfaction.

He regarded the mare with a glance of scorn. He, for one, knew the value of the gelding on whose back he sat.

"I give the word," said the great Garcías. "You are both ready? Remember, to the rock and back to this place, where I draw the line with my toe. Fortune to the deserving. I raise my arm and when I drop it, send the gray on like a demon, Manuel!"

His arm fell, and the two animals shot away, side-by-side.

No! For the gray had a distinct head in front at the very beginning and, running down the very gradual slope toward the big, dark rock that stood on the verge of the trees on the floor of the ravine, with every stride the good gelding shoved farther in the lead, a neck, a half length, a length.

The satisfaction of Garcías knew no bounds. He laughed and shouted. He roared with laughter, too, when suddenly the mare, running still more slowly than before, began to buck. The curses of Bill Parry roared back down the wind to them. Even Sid Levine was laughing heartily. One-Eyed Mike smiled a savage smile.

Swiftly the gray flew on toward victory, and suddenly Bill Parry, for all his riding, flew high in the air, fell, and, as his body thudded upon the ground, the mare cantered easily forward, carrying with her no burden other than the saddle on her back.

That instant, Garcías, with a snarl, observed to his prisoner: "Ha? Is she a return horse? Would she run on into Sunday Slough and bring the warning?" Aloud, he screeched in a voice like the whistling cry of a hawk. "*Hai!* Manuel! The mare, the mare! Stop her, rope her, or shoot her down!"

Manuel heard that far-borne yell and, swinging the gray around, observed the riderless mare swinging down the trail, while the form of her rider lay spread out far behind her. He picked a rope from beside the saddle horn, opened the noose of it, and went for her with a whoop.

She came straight on toward him, only when the rope was flung, underhand, the noose cutting the air like a knife, the heavy, slender rawhide perfectly thrown, did Betsy leap like a dancer to the side. Half of the noose rapped across her back, and down the valley she went in wild flight, as though the blow had been a signal.

"Shoot! Shoot!" shouted the great Garcías.

Manuel, with an oath, drew up the gelding, slid a rifle out of the saddle holster that ran under his right knee, and fired from the shoulder. The light was not good, but he was an expert; he took the head for a target and, at the first shot, she bounded high but went galloping on. At the second bullet, she tumbled head over heels and lay flat upon the trail.

Manuel, putting up the rifle and turning his head to make sure that she was indeed motionless, turned the gray and came victoriously back toward his chief.

"And there it is," said Garcías. "It was not I that wished to do this. It was not I. It was you, *Señor* Speedy. And there lies your horse dead."

"Not my horse," said Speedy. "It belongs to a man who'll follow you and cling to you like a bur. If you manage to do me harm, I know that he'll have your blood later on."

Garcías laughed. "My blood will take care of itself. Welcome, Manuel. It was a good shot. Through the head, I know, by the way the mare fell."

"It was through the head," Manuel said, showing his teeth. "I shot carefully. I clipped her through the brain, just under the ears. The first bullet, it was too far down."

"He knows how to shoot," Garcías said with immense pride. "He could shoot in the dark, aiming at sounds. That is Manuel, a man in one million fighters."

Big Bill Parry, finally managing to get up from the ground, came back to the rest of the group, limping, shaking his bushy head. For he had been badly jarred by the fall, and there was a dimness still in his eyes.

He came to Speedy, and, leaning over him, he shook a fist in his face. "I got a mind to smash you," he said, "and I oughta smash you. I was kind of friendly to you, compared to the rest of these here. But I ain't friendly now. I'm gonna stand by and see them do whatever they wanna. I tell you what, I'm gonna give them a hand in the doin' of it, because I see the snake that you are, Speedy. Yeah, I see it, and I'd put my heel on your head, except that there's ways of making you suffer a lot more than that, before you cash in. You knew that she'd buck like a demon when she got the spur."

"Of course, I knew it," said Speedy.

"You was gonna have her buck me off, and then she'd go into town like a regular return hoss, and start 'em out on her trail, was that it?" demanded Bill Parry.

"Bill," Speedy said, "you have a good, clear-working

brain, after somebody else has pointed the way for you. Except for Garcías, and his man Manuel . . . Garcías who saw what was happening and Manuel who shoots like ten demons . . . she would be well along down the ravine by this time."

Both Garcías and Manuel expanded with pleasure. Praise is always sweet, but never so delicious as when it has been forced from the unwilling lips of an enemy.

"You see now, *gringo,* what it means to cross one of my name?" said Garcías.

"I knew that before, *Don* Hernando," Speedy said. "That was why I hung you like a white flag out a window of your house. I wanted to make sure that you would remember me."

Under the taunt, the Mexican snarled savagely. But he managed to restrain the hand that he had lifted to strike, once more, with the whip. "There is a time," he said through his teeth, "for brave words. But your time has come to be braver still, when the fire answers what you have to say, *Señor* Speedy. My friends, let us sit down and consider, carefully, exactly what should be done to this man. Let us take time, and use much thought. Now there is nothing for us to fear. We may deliberate. Even the tricks of this snake have come to an end."

XIV

"Betsy Comes Home"

It was in the very last light of the day that Manuel had fired his shot and with every moment the gloom increased, shutting in closer and closer upon all within the ravine.

As the men who had captured Speedy sat down to begin

their calculations, like so many Indians around the body of a famous warrior newly taken, Betsy lifted her head, shuddered, and rose to her feet. She had been wounded twice. The first bullet had cut through the chin and that wound was bleeding fast. The second shot had glanced across the top of her neck, behind the ears. It was the shot that was called in the old days a "crease". It was said that the hunters of wild horses, men with a diabolical skill with a rifle, had sometimes brought down the mustangs with a bullet so placed that it nicked, without shattering, the spinal column, just back of the head. So she had been struck and, thoroughly stunned, had fallen as though the bullet had passed straight through her brain.

But when she had gained her feet, she was still able to take the trail. She had been badly hurt, and the blood was running down freely from both her wounds, but the instinct that guided her was as strong as ever, the impulse that had started her down the trail after she had bucked big Bill Parry from the saddle. It was the image of her master that lived in her brain, young Joe Dale, who she had carried through so many dangers and who she loved with devotion. The touch of his hand, the sound of his voice, the very pressure of his knee conveyed to her messages that she understood perfectly as a spoken language.

Now she was in much trouble, badly hurt, and she started on toward him. The trail was not a new one. She had traveled this way many times, carrying her rightful rider, and so she went forward without hesitation, slowly at first, until she made sure of her balance.

So it was that the keen-eared men up the valley did not hear her rise and start off through the shadows. The trees closed behind her, unseen, and now, making sure of herself, she struck into a sharp trot, and then into a sharper gallop.

She grew dizzy. The effects of the blow on the spinal column could not be shaken off at once. She was rather like a boxer who has received a knockdown blow and rises to resume the fight, although with a brain more than half stunned.

So she went through the movements of the gallop, staggering a little, and so blindly that presently she struck a tree trunk with a force that almost broke her shoulder, barking away the skin and knocking her to the ground a second time. She got up slowly, shuddering more violently. But she shook her brave head and then resumed the trail.

It was a strange world that she found herself running through that night. The boulders and the trees were in motion, it appeared, and swayed toward her from either side. When she dodged, the movement of those things that should have been fixed and rooted in the ground became all the more violent. She got on until the lights from the town of Sunday Slough were spread out before her eyes, and then she stumbled, blinded by the swirling illumination. She fell for the third time.

It was not the effort that told upon her so much; neither was it the benumbing effects of the bullet that weakened her. There was hardly strength enough in her head to lift it from the ground. There she lay for a time, the forelegs quivering, braced far apart, but her brave head fixed toward the goal and her ears pointing forward. Something had happened to her that she could not understand.

She strove to rise. Her body heaved, and then sank back. She strove again and this time gained her feet, only to topple over on the right side. She lay for a long moment. A horse, like a man, can be beaten and discouraged before the body is willing to give way. So she lay there, wondering what had happened, and with a chill of actual cold beginning in her body and rising into her soul.

All living things have the sense of death, as it steps toward them, even though without pain. The poor mare knew that greater darkness than the night with its stars was approaching her, but, like all the brave, she was not beaten by two failures, or by three.

Patiently she worked, until once more her head was raised from the ground. Her breathing was harsh and stertorous. She was covered with cold sweat, in streams. She shook violently with every effort that she made. Finally, however, the hindquarters that had failed before reacted to the pressure of her will, and she came uncertainly to her feet. She staggered and almost fell again from the effort, but presently she was able to walk on.

She tried to trot, but it was very hard. The whole landscape immediately became a wavering sea of shadows, mingling with dazzling sparks and long swinging strokes of light. So she had to fall to a walk once more. Before her, the lights separated and spread apart. A chasm of comparative darkness opened, and she entered the main street of the town. That street, as she turned a corner, opened upon many loud sounds of human voices and laughter. There were more lights, blazing intensely, close at hand, half blinding her.

Then a dog ran out and snapped at her head. She almost fell as she strove to rear and strike out at him. The dog ran, and she went on, still staggering. The dust of the street was thick and deep; she slipped in it as though she were wading through swiftly running water, stepping upon rocks as treacherous as glass.

Men came running out to her. Someone cried: "This here is Joe Dale's mare, and look at what happened to her! Look, will you? Somebody's shot her!"

Hands fell on her bridle reins. She shook her head, although the movement cost her pain, and broke into a floundering trot. Down the street, two blocks, she knew that there was a large building, filled with lights, with the sounds of many human voices by day and by night, even, and behind that building there was another of almost equal size where horses were kept and where there was always a cool, sweet savor of hay and of peace.

She thought of that now. And she thought, too, of the long watering troughs that extended before the front of the hotel, three of them in a row, always with the water flowing musically from one to the other, water kept clean and sweet as a mountain stream, with the small, keen faces of the stars deep down in it.

She had been thirsty before, hard-driven down many a mountain trail and under burning suns, but never had she felt such thirst as this, invading the marrow of her bones. She would drink up the very stars that lay like flickering sparks in the bottom of the trough. So she trotted weakly, stumbling, on to the front of the hotel, leaving behind her a swirling train of inquiry. There was the black water, there were the stars a-drowning in it. She plunged her head in to the very eyes, and drank and drank again. She lifted her head, infinitely refreshed.

She was very sick, very weak. All was afloat and shuddering before her eyes. But now she remembered her master more keenly than before. This was where he was to be found. It was into this building that he disappeared at night, and out of it he came every morning. Lifting her head, she whinnied, high and sharp. Even the neigh was wrong. She snorted and tried again, and the old bugle note rang out clearly.

Almost instantly a door slammed and a step ran out onto the front verandah.

"Hello, Speedy," called a voice. "Did you get him?"

It was the voice of her master! She whinnied again, softly,

a note that he would be sure to know, for many a time on night trails she had spoken to him in exactly this manner and he had always known.

He knew now, for he came down the steps with a jump and a lunge. He was at her head. He was touching her wounds. He was crying out in a voice sharp and wild and high, as she, many a time, had heard the voice of a dog, eager for a fight, and snarling at another. So Joe Dale cried out.

He stood with his fists doubled. He groaned with the great apprehension that was in him. Other men ran in about him. "What's happened, Joe?" asked Pier Morgan, among the rest.

"They've murdered Speedy, and they've almost murdered Betsy. She's bleedin' to death," said Joe Dale, "and, when I get them that done this, I'm gonna have the hide off their backs, and put a quirt on the raw underneath. They've gone and got Speedy at last."

The word went like lightning through the town.

There were some who were glad in the bottom of their guilty hearts, but there were many more who were savagely annoyed and these came out, with guns. They offered themselves and their guns to Joe Dale, as the representative of the missing deputy sheriff.

He picked them with care, a stanch dozen men.

He said to the suddenly gathered posse: "I'll tell you what, boys, Speedy was never got by only one man. There's more than one. There's plenty of them that were in on his death. We ain't got much chance to nail 'em. Not hardly any chance at all, because the minute that they killed him, they're sure to've busted loose and run, because they knew that Sunday Slough would go clean crazy about the dirty job. But we'll do our best, and we'll do it on the run."

He turned back to the veterinary who, with shirt sleeves rolled up, was busily laboring over the wounded mare.

"Doc," he said, "you'll do what you can for her. I know that." He himself went to her and laid his hand on her muzzle. Her soft, whimpering answer almost unmanned him.

He heard the doctor saying: "I'll fix her up, old son, so's you'll never know that anything ever happened to her, except the scars. And you wouldn't want to rub them out. The whole of Sunday Slough wants that writing to remain on her, brother, because it'll remind us how she come in and give the alarm, and I only hope that she ain't come too late."

Serious and deep murmurs arose.

There was Bill Turner, the news gatherer, standing with notebook in hand, jotting down his observations of her looks at this grim moment and carefully considering her, biting at his lips for all the world like a man who had started to take down an oral interview from a dumb beast.

Even Joe Dale, no matter how his heart was wrung, could not help a faint smile as he looked at this. He patted her neck for the last time, sprang into the saddle of a gallant roan mustang, and went at a gallop down the main street of the town, heading toward the upper end of the ravine along which the mines were strung.

All of Sunday Slough was out there to see the posse pass and wish them luck, and particularly one huge fellow, very drunk, his long wet mustaches blown out into sails as he bellowed: "Ten thousand dollars for the scalp of the skunk that murdered our Speedy!"

XV

"The Funeral Pyre"

High up the ravine, in their deep consultation, Sid Levine and Garcías worked over the details of their calculations. The ideas of Levine were ingenious.

"Now, I've heard somewheres of a thing like this being done," he said. "I mean to say, they take a lot of men and rope the top of a tree and pull the top down and stake it. Then they pull down the top of another tree, as far as they can get it, and then they take and tie a man spraddling to the two tops of the trees and break the stakes. Them trees start to spring up, and they take and tear the man in two, and, if they ain't too strong, they just do it gradual. Y'understand? They take and rip him like a piece of paper, slow and gradual. I take that to be a pretty good way with Speedy. It might show other nosey fools what happens to 'em when they get between men and their business."

"Sure, it'll show 'em," said One-Eyed Mike. "You got an idea that time, chief."

The Mexican, Garcías, remained in a profound quandary, lost in devoted thought. The faces of his two warriors were turned steadily toward him.

Then he said: "I have given it careful thought. I see, *Señor* Levine, that you are a man with a mind. But, also, I remember hearing of other things. There are very clever Indians in this world. All the brains are not limited to the whites, like you and me. The Indians had some devices. They would stick pine splinters, good resinous pine splinters, into the body of a man, and then light the splinters, that burned down well into the flesh. They had ideas, the Indians."

"Yeah, there's all kinds of ideas in the world," said One-Eyed Mike, "the same as they're all kinds of people. I took a trip over to China once, when I was kind of on the loose and the run, and over there I seen them torture a chink by forcing his joints through pieces of board that was smaller than the bones. Crushed 'em, you see? Them chinks, they got plenty of nerve to stand pain, I know. But that pirate, he just opened his mouth and hollered like I can remember it yet, and feel it yet, too, right down the middle of my back."

"As a matter of fact," said Levine, "we could do several things. There's no use limitin' ourselves. We got the time and we got the means. I've heard tell, somewheres, about lashing of a gent between two boards, and then sawing through the boards and the man. I mean, the boards keep the saw blade working straight. They clean the flesh and the blood out of the saw teeth. It took some imagining to think of that, I say."

"Well," said Mike Doloroso, "for my part, I never knew anything that much beat plain methods, like tying a gent up by the thumbs and putting a fire under his feet so as he gets tired of hanging that way."

"Yes, and I seen a lot of funny things done by just putting a cord around the head of a man," said Levine, "and then twisting the string with a stick. That makes their eyes pop out, and they holler, you can bet."

"He is a singer," Garcías said savagely. "And when he screams, it should be worth seeing and hearing. His face will be good to watch, because it is a handsome face, my friends."

He laughed as he spoke, and the others laughed, also. He thought so much of his remark that he translated it also into Spanish for the enjoyment of Manuel and Pedro, and those worthies grinned from ear to ear.

Pedro said in Spanish: "Take the arm and bend it at the elbow, and then twist. It does things to the shoulder bones. Things to hear and to see!"

Levine suddenly stretched his fat arms and yawned. "We been talking for a long time," he said. "I guess we been here for about an hour, tasting this here without doing nothing. Suppose we start. Start anyway, but make a beginning."

"One moment," said Garcías. "Suppose we ask him what he wishes. *Señor* Speedy, what would you prefer? You have heard us talk of many things."

They had brought a lantern from the mine, and the lantern they now raised to see the face of the victim.

Speedy smiled against the light. "Try anything you want, boys," he said. "If you can be Indians enough to do the things you talk about, I can be Indian enough to stand 'em without squealing, I hope."

"Talking game ain't the same as dying game," said Levine. "We'll get a song out of you before we finish. Curse you. I always hated the look of your mug from the time that I first seen it. Now you're gonna see what happens when you step between men and their work. We're gonna show you."

"Look at the way you're winding up, Speedy," said One-Eyed Mike. "You've had your day, and right now, back there in Sunday Slough, there's plenty of red-eye being drunk to you. They're drinkin' the health of their next sheriff, but he'll be in Hades before ever he'll be in Sunday Slough again. We all know that, I reckon. Oh, Speedy, a fine end you've come to. You'd live your life over again, I guess, if you could do the choosing right now. Speak up and tell the truth."

"Well, I'll tell you the truth," Speedy began. "I've had my fun, and I've had plenty of it. I've been kicked in the face, now and then, but I've been the top dog often enough, too. I've gone where I wanted to go, and when I wanted to go. I

90

have no regrets, and I don't expect that I'll have them when I'm dying here and you fellows play the mischief with me. You can't string it out more than a few hours, at the most, and I can balance a good many free years and happy years against all of that. Go ahead, Levine. Another day or two, and I should have had you."

Levine laughed loudly. "You would've had me," he said, sneering. "But you didn't get me. It was a long game, and you won all the tricks up to the last one. But I'm winning that one, Speedy. You didn't think that I'd reach this far or that I was behind that claim-jumper, did you? You couldn't see that was all a plant?"

"I'd like to know one thing," Speedy said. "Was the other miner in on the deal, too?"

"Him? Oh, no! He's the honest man that was throwed out. I knew that he'd go straight to you. I knew that he'd get you started straight up the valley. I knew that you'd come along, too, because you've built up the kind of a reputation that you don't dare to act like you ever needed any help. I've beat you, Speedy!"

"The simple things will work, now and then," Speedy said calmly. "Nobody can win all the time. But as I die, I'll be thinking of what the boys from Sunday Slough will do to you when they nail you, Levine. And nail you they will, sooner or later. Gray, and Joe Dale, and Pier Morgan, they'll never give up the work until they've cornered you and rendered down some of your fat into lard."

"Bah," said Levine, sneering, "I've matched my brains against theirs more times than I can count. I've always won before, and I'll win again. I know that I'll win. You're the only man in the world that ever bothered me much. I had Sunday Slough in my vest pocket, before you turned up. I had a million or a couple of clean millions in sight, before you appeared. And with you out of the way, I'll go back and get the town in my hand again."

Speedy shook his head. "You're an optimist, Sid," he said. "The town knows you now. The whole town knows what a rotten crook you are. And no decent man will ever be seen with you again. You'll have nothing but muckers like One-Eyed Mike around you, and cheap greaser murderers, like Garcías." He smiled again, straight through the light of the lantern and into the face of Levine.

The latter grew half purple and half white. At last he said: "It's time to commence, Garcías. There ain't any use using up words on him, because words don't mean anything to a dog like him. It needs the whip to make him feel something."

Garcías arose. "We begin, then. Pedro, what's that on the wind? Do you hear anything? Like horses, coming up the valley?"

"I thought that I heard," said Pedro.

"But now there is nothing," broke in Manuel.

"Very well," Garcías said. "My men and I vote for fire, a slow fire built at the feet . . . roasting the feet carefully. When the fire has rotted the flesh off the bones, then move it up higher. A man will live for a long time in flames like that."

"Build the fire," snapped Levine. "You're right, and I should've known before that I wouldn't have ideas worth the ones that you could trot out. Go ahead, then, and start the fire."

The wood was gathered. There was a considerable noise of crackling in the underbrush as Pedro and Manuel broke up the fuel. Then Manuel, with a bit of dry bark, started the fire, heaping the leaves over it and the driest part of the brush-wood, broken short, until the flames had gathered a good headway and showed a brilliant little pyramid of hungry yellow.

"That is enough to roast the meat," said Garcías. "Even enough to char it, unless we keep the joint turning."

He laughed joyously, as he spoke, and Pedro and Manuel laid hands on the prisoner.

Levine, holding the lantern high, leaned close over the face of Speedy. "Can you hold out, now that it's coming?" he asked, sneering. "Beg, you cur. Beg! Promise! Swear! Now's the time for you to talk. Talk us sick. Maybe we'll let you go. Beg for a quick way of dying!"

But, instead, he saw a gradual and deadly smile spread on the lips and in the eyes of the prisoner.

Speedy said nothing at all.

The voice that next spoke was not from anyone about the fire, but from the neighboring brush. It was the sharp, barking tone of young Joe Dale, exclaiming: "Shoot for the legs! We want 'em alive, Garcías and Levine! The rest don't count!"

And rifles spoke like hammer strokes against the ears of the stunned group.

XVI

"Snipe on the Wing"

When snipe, feeding in a marsh, hear the voice of the hunter's dogs in the distance, they will rise staggering into the wind, each on a different course. So, when the cry of Joe Dale was heard, the men of the party gathered around Speedy scattered.

Each went his own way, winged with panic. No doubt every man would have been dropped at the first volley, had not Dale issued his orders. He himself could not understand, afterward, why he had shown such stupidity, except that it seemed to him only fair that the creatures who had been about to torment his idolized friend should taste death for a time themselves before they suffered it.

As it was, his men strictly obeyed his orders, and fired low. But the light was bad. The glimmer of the flames of the fire danced before their eyes and, although every one was a chosen marksman, the execution was surprisingly slow.

Big One-Eyed Mike, with a howl, doubled up as though the first volley had sent a bullet through his stomach, and in this position he ran like a football player, charging the line, straight for the nearest trees opposite to the line of firing. A bullet knocked off his hat. Another sliced through the calf of his leg. But these hindrances did not keep him from running at full speed. He flattened the brush before him like a charging elephant and went on, dashing and crashing.

Sunday Slough saw him no more.

Pedro and Manuel, running in exactly the same fashion, ducked and dodged right and left, heading for the same trees. Pedro reached them without a scratch. But luck was against Manuel. A bullet, flying far higher than the marksman intended, broke the back of his neck and he fell dead on the verge of safety.

Big Sid Levine, screaming like a woman, and like a woman throwing his arms above his head and before him, literally fell forward toward shelter, rushing off in such blind panic that he ran straight into the enemy. A gun butt wielded by Joe Dale with infinite relish struck him fairly on the mouth and knocked out his breath and most of his teeth. He fell down like one who had received a mortal wound. He had fallen in a dead faint, from which he did not recover for half an hour.

Bill Parry, running for safety, stumbled midway in his

course, fell flat, and rolled headlong into tall grass. He had sense enough not to rise again, but crawled away. He would have been taken, had there been any pursuit, but there was none.

Something else was happening beside the fire that attracted attention that way, and all the guns.

For all the men who had surrounded Speedy, intent on snuffing out his young life in the most agonizing possible manner, only *Don* Hernando, in the pinch, remembered the work at hand rather than the preservation of his own life. It was not a blind passion on his part.

The men of Segovia were a part of him, and he was a part of Segovia. He had been shamed in the eyes of all of his people, and he dared not return to them unless he could say that the insulting *gringo* had fallen by his hand.

He was, at the moment of the alarm, the farthest from the scene of the impending torture, surveying it with a calm and well-pleased eye. But the moment that the alarm came, he knew what he had to do, and started to do it. He sprang straight for his victim.

The first hindrance was purely accidental. Big One-Eyed Mike, turning toward his blind side, with his massive shoulder struck the Mexican and knocked the slighter man spinning with his charge.

As Garcias recovered his balance and darted forward once more toward Speedy, young Pier Morgan came plunging in between. He was still very weak. The riding of the last two days and the strain of the excitement had been too much for him, but he could not be kept from the posse that rode out of Sunday Slough to save or avenge his benefactor. So he placed himself instantly between Speedy and danger, standing with his legs braced well apart.

He saw Garcías coming like a tiger, and fired, but missed

with his shaking hand. The second bullet clogged in the revolver. He hurled the weapon itself at the head of Garcías, but it flew wild in turn, and Garcías, holding his own bullet with a terrible fixity of purpose, avoided wasting a shot on the body of poor Morgan, merely knocking him senseless with a blow from the barrel of his gun.

That removed the last screen, and with a frightful cry of triumph, he stood over Speedy, leveling his gun. He wanted to make too sure, or he would have done his work. As it was, he saw the firelight shine into the steady, keen eyes of the prisoner, and, as he was about to pull the trigger that would have banished Speedy from the pleasant ways of this earth, a rifle slug tore through the hips of the Mexican and knocked him down.

He struggled to one elbow and strove to fire again. But Joe Dale, running in like a wildcat, broke his gun arm with a kick.

That ended the battle of Sunday Slough, as it was called from that date henceforward.

Men said that all the credit was due to the brains of Speedy, who had devised the liberation of a dumb beast as a messenger. But they gave the credit, as hero of the encounter, not to Joe Dale, or even to gallant Pier Morgan, who had been willing to die for his friend, but to the beautiful mare, Betsy.

They paraded her through the streets of the town, the next day, decked out with garlands of flowers. For she was of a tough ancestry, and she had not lost enough blood to injure her seriously for long. She was weak, but happy with her master beside her.

As for the prisoners, they brought Garcías, silent and composed, to the town jail, where Marshal Tom Gray took charge of him. With him, they carried the great Sid Levine, fallen forever. He had collapsed completely and had to be carried on a litter, where he lay sobbing out of a broken and bleeding face.

And Speedy?

Joe Dale and Pier Morgan, literally with guns, defended him all the election day from the enthusiasm of the crowds who wanted to break into the sheriff's house.

The election itself was a joke. No man dared to vote against the hero, and in the evening, when the votes had been counted, in the rosy dusk of the day, the whole population of Sunday Slough came trooping to congratulate the hero and make him the center of such a celebration as the Slough had never known before.

Joe Dale went to rouse him from the sleep of exhaustion, but received no answer to his knock. The door was locked. They crawled through the open rear window, and found Speedy gone.

In place of him was a letter which read:

Dear Joe and Pier, and All My Friends in Sunday Slough: Levine is down. My job is ended. My trail is the out trail. If I'm the sheriff, I resign. Good luck to everybody, but I've already stayed too long in one place.

Speedy

That was all of him.

Sunday Slough saw him no more.

His Fight for a Pardon

"His Fight for a Pardon" first appeared in Street & Smith's *Western Story Magazine* in the issue dated June 27th, 1925. It appeared under the George Owen Baxter byline and was one of seventeen short novels by Frederick Faust to appear in *Western Story Magazine* that year. In this story told in the first person, Leon Porfilo, an outlaw of poor beginnings and lowly ancestry, goes up against Jeffrey Dinsmore, a gentleman outlaw born of the privileged class, in an attempt to clear his name and gain a pardon. In it Faust depicts the power of the press to shape public opinion.

I

"Leon Makes a Decision"

When I got down to see Molly O'Rourke, Sheriff Dick Lawton crossed my way with three of his hard-riding man-getters. Every man-jack of them was on a faster nag than my mule, but I kept Roanoke in the rough going, and Dick Lawton was foolish enough to follow right on my heels instead of throwing a fast man out on my course. For he knew what that course was. He had hunted me before, and it was a sort of unwritten law between us that, if I got into the mouth of the little valley where the O'Rourke house stood, I was free.

That may sound specially generous on his side. But it wasn't—altogether. Twice he had pushed his posse up that ravine after me, and it almost cost him his next election. Because that ravine twisted like a snake, back and forth, and it was set out with shrubs and trees as thick as a garden. I simply laid up in a comfortable shady spot, and, when the boys came rushing around the bend, I let them have it. So easy that I didn't have to shoot close to a dangerous spot. I could pick my targets. However, I think that there were half a dozen had wounds in arms and legs. Also, I pulled too far to the left on one boy and drilled him through the body. So, as I say, the sheriff nearly lost his election after that because it was said that he had ridden his men into a man trap.

So far as Dick Lawton was concerned, I knew that valley was forbidden as a hunting ground to him. And, of course, I could trust Dick as far as he could trust me—that is to say, to the absolute limit. Because, except when we were shooting at each other, we were the best friends in the world. I know that Dick never shot extra straight at me, and I know that I never shot straight at him. My guns simply wobbled off the mark when I caught him in the sights.

Well, as I was saying, I kept old Roanoke in the rough where he could run four feet to the three of any horse that ever lived—for the simple reason that a mule's hoofs and skin are a lot tougher than a horse's. By the time I got across the valley, there was a clean furlong between me and Dick Lawton's boys. So I took off my hat and said good bye to them with a wave that was nearly my last act in life. Because just as I put that hat back on my head, a .32-caliber Winchester slug drilled a clean little hole through the brim a quarter of an inch from my forehead.

I've noticed that when a fellow stops to make a grandstand play of that sort, he generally gets into pretty hot trouble. I sent Roanoke into the brush with a dig of the spurs, but the minute I was out of sight, I knew that there was no trouble left.

But I didn't slow up Roanoke. I didn't even stop to roll a cigarette, because I hadn't seen Molly for three months. You see, it was right after the Sam Dugan murder which some fools hung on me. Of course, Lawton hadn't the least idea in the world that I could have done such a rotten, treacherous thing. But they stirred up such a fuss that I didn't dare to try to slip in to see Molly. Because everyone had known for years that I loved Molly and got down to see her once in a while, and, when things were pretty hot, they used to watch her house.

So I slithered up the ravine until I got a chance to squint at the ridge, and there I found a little green flag, jerking up and down and in and out in the wind, on top of the O'Rourke house. I knew that was the work of Molly's father. I think that every day of his life the old man went snooping through the woods to see if the land lay quiet. If it was, he tagged the house with that little green flag—green for Ireland, of course —and then, when someone was laying for me near the house, he would hang up a white flag.

When I saw that green, I dug into Roanoke and sent that mule hopping straight to the house. As I hit the ground, I heard old man O'Rourke singing out inside the screen door of the porch: "Hey, Chet! Here's Roanoke to put up, and sling a feed of barley into him. Hey, mother, come and look at that dog-gone mule! Hey, Molly, there's that Roanoke mule wanderin' around loose in the yard!"

Chet O'Rourke came first, and his old mother at his shoulder, and then the old man came next. I grabbed all their hands. It was like stepping into a shower of happiness, I tell you, to get among people where the feel of their eyes was not like so many knives pointed at you. But I brushed through them pretty quick. I wanted Molly.

"Hey, Molly!" yelped old O'Rourke. "Ain't you comin' to see Roanoke?"

He laughed. I suppose that he was old enough to enjoy a foolish joke like that. I heard Molly sing out from the stairs beyond the front parlor. I reached the bottom of those stairs the same minute she did and caught her.

She said: "Chester O'Rourke, will you take this man away from me?"

I kicked the door shut in Chet's face and sat Molly on the window sill where the honeysuckle showered down behind her like green water, if you follow my drift. It would have done you good to stand there where I was standing and see her smile until the dimple was drilled into one cheek. She began to smooth her dress and pat her hair.

"My Lord," I said, "I'm glad to see you."

"You've unironed me," said Molly. "Just when I was all crisped up for the afternoon."

"Have they nailed the right man for the Dugan murder?" I asked. Because I was as keen about that as I was about Molly.

"They've got the right man, and he's confessed," she said.

I lowered myself into a chair and took a deep breath. "*That's* fixed, then," I said.

"*That's* fixed," she agreed.

"Why do you say it that way?" I asked.

"How old are you, Leon?" she said.

"I'm twenty-five."

"How old does that make me?" said Molly.

"Twenty-three."

"That's right, too. How long have you been asking me to

marry you?" Molly asked.

"Seven years," I said.

"Well, the next time you ask me, I'm going to do it."

"Law or no law?" I said.

"Law or no law."

It made my head spin, of course, when I thought of marrying Molly and trying to make a home for her while a hundred or so cowpunchers and sheriffs and deputies, *et cetera*, were spending their vacation trying to grab me and the $20,000 that rested on top of my head as a reward. I moistened my lips and tried to speak. I couldn't make a sound.

"You know that I've done what I could," I said finally.

"I do. But now things are different."

"What do you mean?"

"William Purchase Shay is the governor, now."

"What difference does that make?"

"He's a gentleman," she said.

"Well?"

"I think he'd listen to reason."

"You want us to go see him?"

"Just that."

"I see myself handing in my name at his office," I said. "I guess he's not too much of a gentleman to want to make twenty thousand dollars."

"Money has spoiled you, Leon," said Molly.

"Money? How come?"

"You're so used to thinking about how much you'll be worth when somebody drills a rifle ball through you . . . that it's turned your head."

"Are you talking serious?"

"Dead serious," she replied. "Besides, you're not the only one that folks have to talk about now."

"I don't understand."

"Jeffrey Dinsmore is the other man."

Of course, I had heard about Dinsmore. He was the Texas man whose father left him about a million dollars in cattle and real estate, besides having a talent for shooting straight and a habit of using that talent. Finally he killed a man where self-defense wouldn't work, because it was proved that Dinsmore had been laying for him. The last heard, Dinsmore was drifting for the mountains.

"Is Dinsmore in these parts?" I asked Molly.

"He showed up in town last week and sat down in the restaurant. . . ."

"Disguised?"

"Yes, disguised with a gun that he put on the table in front of his plate. They didn't ask any questions, but just served him as fast as they could."

"Nobody went to raise a crowd?"

"The dishwasher did, and a crowd gathered at the front door and the back."

"What happened?"

"Dinsmore finished eating and then put on his hat and walked out."

"Good Lord, what nerve! Did he bluff out the whole crowd?"

"He did."

"What's on him?"

"Just the same that's on you. Twenty thousand iron men."

"Twenty thousand dollars?" I repeated.

"You look sort of sad, Leon."

You'll think me a good deal of a fool, but I confess that I was staggered to find that there was another crook in the mountains worth as much to the law as I was. Between you and me, I *was* proud because I had that little fortune on my head.

"Twenty thousand!" I said again.

"Dead or alive," Molly said with a queer, strained look on her face.

"Why do you say it that way?" I said in a whisper.

"Don't you understand?"

Then I *did* understand, and I stood up, feeling pretty sick. But I saw that she was right. Something had to be done.

"I start for the governor today?" I stated.

Molly simply hid her face in her hands, and I didn't wait for her to break out crying.

II

"On the Edge of the Town"

I saw the rest of the family for an hour or so before Molly came in to us. She was as clear-eyed as ever, when she came, but there was something in her face that was a spur to me. I did not wait for the night. I judged that no pursuers would be lingering for me in the valley of this late day, so I slipped out of the house, finding Roanoke refreshed by his rest and a feed of grain. I went away, without leaving any farewells behind me.

I cut across country, straight over the ridge of the eastern mountains. Just below timberline I camped that night—a cold, wet night—and I rode on gloomily the next morning until I was over the crest of the ridge and had a good view of the land that lay beneath me. It was a great, smooth-sweeping valley, most of it, the ground rolling now and then into little hills—but with hardly the shadow of a tree—and so on and on to piles of blue mountains which leaned against the farther horizon. They were a good hundred miles away. Between me and that range lay the city that I had to reach. You will agree with me that it was not a very pleasant undertaking. I had to get myself over seventy miles of open country to the capital of the state. Then I had to get seventy miles back into the mountains once more.

However, there was nothing else for it. That day I went down to the edge of the trees and the foothills, and there I rested until the verge of dusk. When that time came, I sent Roanoke out into the open and heading straight away toward the big town. He could have made the distance before daylight, but there was no point in that. I sent Roanoke over sixty-five miles that night, however, and he was a tired mule when I dropped off his back on the lee side of a haystack. I could see the lights of the town five miles off. Not a big place, you will think, but there were 35,000 people there, and that made it just about five times as large as any city I had ever seen in my life. It was simply a metropolis to me.

The dawn was only a moment away. So I walked away from the stack to a wreck of a shack in a hollow. There I turned in and slept solidly until afternoon.

I was thirsty and tired and hungry when I wakened. Besides that, I had a jumpy heart and the strain of the work ahead of me was telling pretty fast. The worst part of the trip was wasting that afternoon and waiting for the night. The edge of the sun was barely down before I was streaking across open country, and there was still plenty of daylight when I cut down a bridle path near the edge of the town and met an old fellow coming up. He was riding bareback, and I shall never forget how his white beard was parted by the wind.

He gave me a very cheerful—"Howd'ye,"—and I waved back to him.

"Well, stranger," said that old man, "where are you aimin' for, if I might ask?"

"Work," I said.

"Come right along with me."

"What kind?"

He had one tooth in the right-hand corner of his upper gum. He fixed this in a wedge of chewing tobacco and worked a long time at it until he got it loose. All the while he was looking at me with popping pale-blue eyes. I never before had noticed how close an old man can be to a child.

"Well, partner," he said, "young fellers is picky and choosey. I used to be that way myself. But when I come to get a little age behind me, why, then I seen that it didn't make so much difference what a man done. All kinds of work that ever I see gives you the same sort of an ache in the shoulders and an ache in the calves of your legs and in your back. Ain't you noticed that?"

I told him that I had.

He said: "Same way about chuck. I used to be mighty finicky about grub. It don't make no difference to me now. Once a mite of grub is swallered, what difference whether it was a mouthful of dry bread or a mouthful of ice cream? Can you tell me that?"

I could see that he had branched out on his special kind of information. Most old men are that way. They got a couple of sets of ideas oiled up in their old noodles, and, whenever they get a chance, they'll blaze away on them. If they're interested in oil wells, you can start talking about lace and they'll get over to oil wells just as easy as if you started with derricks. I saw that this was one of that brand. However, if he would talk, I saw that he might be of some sort of use to me.

So I said: "I've been back country for a long time. I want to have a try working in town."

He shook his head, very sad at that. "Son," he said, "I live only two mile out, but I have been to town only once this summer. And that time I come home with my feet all blistered up and my head aching from the glare of the pavements. I give the town up. If I was you, I'd give it up, too."

I said nothing, but I couldn't help smiling. The old chap began to nod and smile, too. He was a fine fellow, no doubt of that.

"Well," he said, "you can't expect folks to learn by their elders. If they did, people'd get wiser and wiser, instead of the other way. What you want to do in town?"

"Drive an ice wagon, maybe. I don't care. I never seen the town before."

"You don't say?"

"I guess that's the capitol building?"

"Yes, sir. There she is. That white dome. I guess you seen it in your schoolbooks when you was a kid? There she be. Look here, ain't you been raised right around near here?"

He had sagged a little closer to me while we were looking at the town, and now I caught him batting his bleary old eyes at me behind his glasses. I knew there was danger ahead.

"No," I said. "I've never been in the big town before."

"Oh, it ain't so big. Me, I've been far as Saint Louis. Now, there's a real city for you. It lays over this a mighty lot!"

"I suppose it does. But it hasn't many things finer than the capitol building, I guess."

"Well, I dunno. It's got a lot of banks and things pretty grand with white stone posts around them. And it makes a heap of noise. You can hear it for miles. But you can't hear nothin' here . . . except the scrapin' of a street car goin' around a corner, maybe."

As he finished speaking, out of the distance came the scraping noise just as he had described it—like a rusty violin

107

string, very thin and far. The old man laughed and clapped his hands.

"Well," I said, "I suppose there are other fine big houses there. The governor's house must be mighty fine."

"Him? No, sir. William P. Shay ain't the man to live big and grand. He's livin' in his ma's old house out on Hooker Avenue right alongside the park . . . which has got so fashionable lately, what with the street car goin' out that way, and the park right opposite with the benches to set on. I passed that way once, and I never forget the smell of the lilacs passin' by Missus Shay's house. It was sure a sweet thing."

"I suppose that they're still there?"

"Yes, sir."

"Other folks got 'em, too?"

"Nary a one. Young feller, I can't get out of my head that I've seen you sure, somewheres, sometime."

I knew very well where he'd seen me. It was in some roadside bulletin board or perhaps just a handbill nailed against a post, showing my face and with big letters under it. I knew very well where he had seen me. I decided that I had better go right on into town and get lodgings before it was too dark. But after I had gone a little way, I leaned down as if to fix a stirrup leather and I had a chance to glance back. Old white beard was already over the hill.

I didn't suspect that he had seen too much of me. But when a man has been a fugitive from the law with a price on his head for seven years, it makes him overlook no bets. I recalled, too, that I was riding a mule, and that in itself was enough to make any man suspicious. So I snapped back to the top of the hill, and, through the hollow beneath, I could see the old man scooting along. He looked back over his shoulder, just then, and, when he saw me, he doubled up like a jockey putting up a fast finish down the stretch and began to burn his whip into that old horse he was riding.

I shouldn't have done it, of course. But I couldn't help wanting to make his fun worthwhile. So I fired a shot straight through the air.

I heard his yell come quavering back to me, and after that the horse seemed to take as much interest in the running as its rider did. He hunched himself like a loafer wolf trying to shove himself between his front legs while he beats for cover. It was a mighty funny thing to watch. I laughed till I was crying. By that time the old man had disappeared in the night and the distance. Then I turned around and saw that I had a big job to do and to do fast, because as soon as that old fogy got to a house with a telephone in it, he would plaster the news all over town that Leon Porfilo, on his mule, was heading straight for them, ready to make trouble, and lots of it.

How many scores of men and boys would clean up their old guns and start hunting for me, I could only guess. But right there I made up my mind that I couldn't enter that town on a mule. I put old Roanoke away in a little hollow where there were trees enough to shelter him and a brook in the center to give him water and plenty of long, coarse grass among the trees for provender.

Then I shoved my guns into my clothes and started hiking for the town. It was mighty risky, of course, because, if trouble started, I was a goner. But I decided that I'd be a lot less looked for on foot. You'll wonder, perhaps, why I didn't wait a few days under cover before I went in. But I knew that the next morning a hundred search parties would be out for me, unless I was already in jail.

III

"The Journey Through the Town"

It was not so bad as I had expected. A city of that size, I thought, would be so filled with people that my only good refuge would be in the very density of the crowd, but, when I reached the outskirts, I found only unpaved streets and hardly anyone on the sidewalks saving the few workingmen who were hurrying home late to their suppers. And what a jumble of suppers! One acquires an acute nose in the mountains or on the desert, and I picked out at least fifty different articles of cookery before I had covered the first block.

I started on the second with a confused impression of onions, garlic, frying steak, stew, boiled tomatoes, cabbage, bacon, coffee, tea, and too many other things to mention. Nasally speaking, that first block of the capital town was like the first crash of a symphony orchestra. I went on very much more at ease through block after block with almost no one in sight, until I came to broad paved streets where there was less dust flying in the air—and where the front yards were not simply hard-beaten dirt with a plant or two at the corners of the houses. For here there were houses set farther back. Some had hedges at the sidewalks, but all had gardens, and most of the way one could look over blocks and blocks of neatly cropped lawns, with flower borders near the houses, and flowering shrubs set out on the lawns. There were scores and scores of watering spouts whirling the spray into the air with a soft, delightful whispering. They all had a different note. Some of them rattled around slowly and methodically like so many dray wheels, throwing out a spray in which you could distinguish each ray of water all the way around. There were some singing and spinning and making a solid flash like the wheel of a bright-painted buggy when a horse is doing a mile in better than three minutes. Once in a while a breeze dipped out of the sky and stirred the heavy, hot air of the street, and blew little mists of the sprinklers to me and gave me quick scents of flowers. But always there was that wonderful odor of the ground drinking and drinking.

I felt very happy, I'll tell you. I felt very expansive and kindly to the whole human race. Now and then I'd see a man run down the steps of his house and go out in his shirt sleeves and take hold of the hose and curse softly when the spray hit him and then give the sprinkler a jerk that moved the little machine to another place. Like as not, he jerked the sprinkler straight toward him. Then he would duck for the sidewalk and stand there, wiping his face and hands with a handkerchief and stamping the water from his shoes and "phewing" and "damning" himself as though he were ashamed.

But before they went back into the house, each man would stop a minute and look at the grass and the shrubs, each beaded with water and pearled with the light of the nearest street lamps—and then up to the trees—and then up to the stars—and then go slowly into the house, singing, most like, and stepping light. When those men lifted their heads and looked up into the sky, I knew that they saw heaven.

When one young fellow ran out from his front door, I saw a girl come to the window and look after him, and hurry him with: "The soup will be stone cold, Archie."

I couldn't help it. I stopped short and leaned a hand against a tree and watched him move the sprinkler. Then, humming under his breath, he ran for the house. There were springs under that boy's toes, I tell you. From what I could see of the girl, I didn't wonder. But at his front door, he turned and saw me still standing under the tree, watching, and aching, and groaning to myself: "Molly and me . . . when do we get our chance . . . when do we get our chance?"

He called out: "Hey, you . . . what you want?"

A mighty snappy voice—like the home dog growling at a stranger pup. He was being defensive.

"Nothing," I said.

"Then hump yourself . . . move along!" he snapped.

Perhaps you'll think that I might have been angered by that. But I wasn't. I was only pretty well sickened and saddened. If ever I were caught—and this night there was a grand chance that the law would take me—the dozen men in the jury box would be no better than the fellow—a clean-living fellow, with his heart in the right place—but snarling when he saw a strange dog near his house. Human nature—I knew it —and I didn't blame him.

"All right. I'll move along," I said.

I only shifted one tree down and stopped again. You see, I wanted to watch that fellow go striding into his house and into that dining room and watch his wife smile at him. Sentimental bunk? I know that as well as you do, but when a man has lived alone for seven years with mountains, and above timberline most of the time—seven winters, you know—well, it makes him either a murderer or a softy. I hardly know which is worse. But I was not a murderer, no matter what the world might say of me.

The householder had a glimpse of me again as he swung open his front door, and he came flaring back at me with the running stride of an athlete. I saw that he was big, and big in the right places. He was in front of me in another moment.

"I'm going!" I said, and I turned and started shambling away.

He caught me by the shoulder and whirled me around. "Look here!" he said. "I don't like the looks of you . . . and the way you hang around . . . who are you?"

I shrank back from him against a tree. "A poor bum, mister," I replied. "I don't want no trouble. But I was lookin' through the window. It looked sort of home-like in there."

"You're lying!" he argued. "By heaven, I'll wager you're some second-story crook. I've a mind. . . ." He put his hand on me again.

You'll admit that I'd taken a good deal from him. But it's easy for a big man to take things from other people. I don't know why that is. Little fellows always have a chip on their shoulders. But big fellows learn when they're young that they're always too big for the other boys. But still, I was a bit angry when this young husband began to force his case at my expense. There were two hundred and twenty pounds of me, but down to the very last pound of me I was hot.

Just then the girl's voice sang out: "Archie! Archie! What are you doing? . . . oh!" There was a little squeal at the end as she sighted me.

"You see?" I said. "Let me go. I won't trouble you any. And you're scaring your wife to death, you fool!"

"What? You impudent rat. . . ."

He started a first-rate punch from the hip, but I caught his wrist and doubled his arm around behind him in a way that must have been new to him. He was a strong chap. But he hadn't any incentive, and he hadn't any training.

We stood with our faces inches apart. Suddenly he wilted.

"Porfilo!" he said through his teeth.

"Do you think I'm going to sink a slug in you?" I asked.

I saw by the look of his eyes that he did, and it made me a pretty sick man, I can tell you. I dropped his arm and I went

113

off down that street not caring a great deal whether I lived or died.

I went down that street until it carried me bang up against the capitol building in the middle of a great big square. Off to the right was the beginning of the park. I went off down the street that faced on it. I think I must have passed five hundred people in that square, but I'm certain that not one of them guessed me. It would have been too queer to find Leon Porfilo *walking* through a street. They passed me by one after another—which shows that we see only what we expect to see.

In the street opposite the park, it was easy going again. It was a fairly dark street because there were no lamps except at the corner, and the blocks were long. Lamps on only one side of the street, too—because the park was on the other side and that was a thrifty town.

I walked about half a mile, I suppose, from the central square, and then I found the house without looking for it. It was simply a great out-welling fragrance of the lilacs, just as the old man had told me. There was the yard filled with big shrubs—almost trees of 'em, and in the pool of darkness around the trees were rows and spottings of milk-white lilies. It was a good thing to see, that yard. It was so filled with beauty—I don't know exactly how to say it. It was filled with homeliness, too. I felt as though I had opened that squeaking gate a hundred times before and stepped down onto the brick path where the grass that grew between the bricks crunches under my heels.

Then I side-stepped from the path and among the trees. I went to the side of the house. I climbed up to the window in time to see the ceremony begin. About a dozen people piled into the room, and, when the seating was over, a grim-faced man sat at the head of the table and a pretty-faced girl of twenty-one or so at the other. Then I remembered that the governor's wife was not half his age.

I thought I understood one reason for the tired look on his face. There was nothing for me to do for a time, so I found a bench among the trees and lay down on it to watch the stars.

I waited until the smell of food went through me, and I tugged up my belt two notches. I waited until the humming voices and the laughter that always begin a meal—even a mountain dinner—died off into a broken talking and the noise of dishes. Then music, somewhere. Well, I was never educated up to appreciating the squeaking of a violin. A long time after that, somebody was making a speech. I could hear the steady voice. I could almost hear the yawns.

Somehow, I pitied the pretty girl at the far end of the table!

IV

"Leon Invades the House"

I waited a full hour after that. People began to leave the house, and finally, when the front door opened and closed no more, I began my rounds of the house. I found what I wanted soon enough. It was not in the second story, but a lighted window in the first, and I had a step up, only, to get a view of the inside of the room, and a broad-gauge window sill to hang to while I watched. The window was open, which made everything easier. There was not much chance for me to be betrayed by the noise I might make in stirring about, for the wind was slipping and rustling among the trees.

I was looking into a high, narrow room with walls covered with books and queer, old-looking framed photographs above the bookcases. There was a desk that looked as solid as rock. In front of the desk was the governor. I could have told that it was the governor even if I'd never seen him before, because he had that gone look about the eyes and those wrinkles of too much smiling that come to men who have offices of state. A man like that, when his face is at rest, is simply giving up thanks that he's not offending anyone.

The governor had a man sitting beside his desk—a man who looked only less tired than the governor himself. He was scribbling shorthand while the governor turned over and fiddled at a pile of papers on his desk and kept talking softly and steadily. All sorts of letters.

Well, he had to dictate so many letters, and make them all so different, that I wondered what fellow's brain could be big enough to hold so much stuff, and so many different kinds. I suppose that in that hour he dictated more letters than I'd ever written in my life. I could see new reasons every minute for that tired look. I began to think that he must know everyone in the state.

I heard the secretary ask him if he needed him any longer. I saw the governor look up quickly at him and then stand up and clap him on the shoulder and say: "Go home to sleep. I've not been paying enough attention to you, but forgive me."

I saw the secretary fairly stagger out of the room. Then there was the governor sitting over the typewriter and reading his correspondence on the one hand and picking at the machine with one finger on the other, and swearing in between in a style that would have tickled the ears of any cowpuncher on the hardiest bit of the range.

I didn't hear anyone tap at the door. But pretty soon he jumped up with the look of a man about to accept $10,000,000. He opened the door and the pretty young wife stood there wrapped up to the chin in a dressing gown. She looked him up and down in a way that smeared the smile off his face and left a sick look that I had seen there before. It was an old-fashioned house, and there was a transom over the door. She pointed at the open transom and said half a dozen words out of stiff lips. She didn't say much. Just enough. A bullet isn't very big, either, but, if it's planted in the right place, it will tear the heart out of a man. She jerked about on her heel and flounced away, and the governor leaned against the wall for a minute with all the sap run out of him. Then he closed the door and the transom and went back to the typewriter.

He was pretty badly jarred, though, and he sat there for a moment all loose, like a fellow with the strength run out of him. Then he shook his head and set his jaw and began to batter that typewriter again. I could see that he was a game sort of a man. Mighty game and proud and clean. I liked him all the way through, and yet I felt a mite sorry for the girl wife, too, when I thought of the way the governor's language must have been sliding out through that transom and percolating through the house. I suppose that a real respectable house would take a couple of generations to work language like that out of the grain of it.

I slid a leg against the window and made just enough noise for the governor to stop work and sit with his head up. His right hand went back to his hip pocket—and came away again.

I stepped inside the room and was standing there pretty easy when he turned around. He didn't jump up or start yapping for help or do anything else that was foolish. He just sat and looked me over.

"Well, Porfilo," he said at last, "I suppose that you've tried to work out the most popular spectacular job in the state

117

and decided that the governor's house was the best place for it. Is that it?"

I merely grinned. I knew that he would take it something like that, but it was mighty good to hear him talk up. It sent a tiny tingle through all the right places in me. I just took off my hat and made myself easy.

"What do you want?" he said, frowning as I smiled. "My wallet?" He tossed it to me.

I caught it and threw it back. I had both my hands. Somehow, I hated to show a gun to that man.

"Something bigger than that?" he said, sneering. "I suppose that you'll want the papers to know how you held up the governor without even showing a gun?"

I got hot at that—in the face, I mean.

"No, sir," I said. "I'm not a rat."

"Tell me what you want," he said through his teeth. "There was a time when I served as a sheriff in this state, young man. There was a time when I carried guns. And now the fewer moments I spend with you, the better."

"Governor," I said, "do you think I'm a plain skunk?"

"No," he said, very brisk, and with his eyes snapping. "I should call you whatever you please . . . a purple, spotted, striped, or garden variety of skunk. Never the common sort. Now what do you want with me, young man, if you don't want money? Is it a pardon?"

There was so much honest scorn in the governor's face, to say nothing of his voice, that all the starch went out of me. I could only mumble. "Yes, sir, that's what I want."

He threw up both his hands—such a quick gesture that it made a gun jump out of my pocket as quick as a snake's head out of a hole. I couldn't help it.

He saw the movement and he sneered again. "Porfilo," he said, "I suppose you are going to threaten to shoot me unless

I turn over a signed pardon to you?"

I shoved the gun away in my clothes. I was beginning to get angry in turn.

"I've come to talk, not to shoot," I said. "I've come to play your own dirty game with you."

"Is my game dirty?" he asked through clenched teeth.

Oh, yes, he was a fighting man, that governor. I wished that his young wife could have seen him then.

"Isn't it," I asked, "a lot dirtier than mine? You beg people for their votes."

"Entirely false," he replied. "But I enjoy a moral lecture from a murderer."

"I never murdered a man in my life," I said.

It made him blink a little.

"But you," I continued, jabbing a finger into the air at him, "you get up and talk pretty sweet to a lot of swine that you hate."

He parted his lips to answer me, but then he changed his mind and sat back in his chair and watched me.

"About the murders," I went on. "I never shot a man unless he tackled me to kill me."

He parted his lips again to speak, but again he changed his mind and smiled. "You are an extraordinarily simple liar," he said.

It's a good deal to be called a liar and swallow it. I didn't swallow this very well. I snapped back at him: "Governor, I came here to see you because I was told that you're a gentleman."

"Well, well, Porfilo," he said, a little red, "who told you that?"

"A girl," I answered.

"*The* girl?" he asked.

"Yes."

119

"Good heavens, Porfilo, are you going to try to hide behind a woman who loves you?"

"I don't hide," I replied. "What I ask you to do is to go down the record against me and figure out where I've sunk lead into anybody that wasn't gunning for me. Was there ever a man I sank that wasn't a gunfighter and a crook before he ever started after me? There never was! I've ridden a hundred miles to get out of the way of trouble, when trouble was showing up in the shape of a clean, decent man. But when a thug came after me, I didn't budge. Why should I?"

"Well," he responded, "I'll tell you what you've done. You've made me listen to you. But just the other day Sheriff Lawton had two fine citizens shot by you."

"Leg and arm," I said.

"Yes, they were lucky."

"Lucky?" I said. "Do you think it was luck, governor? If I've practiced hard at shooting every day of my life for the last ten years, at least, do you think that I'm so bad that I miss at forty yards? No, Governor, you don't think that. Nor do you think that I've stood up to so few men that I get buck fever when I have a sight of 'em. No, sir, you don't think that, either."

The governor scratched his chin and blinked at me. But I was pretty pleased, because I could see that he was getting more reasonable every minute.

"I don't mind admitting," he stated, "that I'm inclined to believe the nonsense that you're talking." He grinned very frankly at me. However, I saw that I still had a long way to go.

"Are you armed?" I asked.

"No," he said, "because very often in my official life I have a reason to use a gun. And I'm past the age when pleasures like that are becoming."

"Are you taking me serious?" I said.

"More than any judge would," he replied.

"I believe you," I said, and I couldn't help a quaver in my voice.

V

"Leon's Bargain with the Governor"

I saw that put back my cause several lengths and would make the rest of the running pretty hard for me.

He said in that stiff way of his: "Have no sentimental nonsense, Porfilo."

"I'm sorry," I said. Then I burst out with the truth at him, because I could see that there was no use trying to bamboozle him. "A man can't help feeling sorry for himself when he gets down," I said.

The governor twisted up his mouth, and then he laughed. It did me a lot of good to hear him laugh, just then. "As a matter of fact," he said, "not so long ago I was pitying myself. Now, young man, I think I can say that I like you. But that won't keep me for an instant from trying to have you hanged by the neck until you're dead."

"Do you mean that?" I asked.

"I'm too tired to talk foolishness that I don't mean," he responded. "I'll tell you what, Porfilo. If a petition for your pardon were signed by a thousand of the finest citizens in this state, that petition would have no more chance than a snowball in hell."

He meant it, well enough, and I could see that he did. It made me within a shade of as sick as I'd ever been in my life.

"Well?" he asked.

121

"I'm studying," I said, "because I know that I've got something more to say, but I can't figure out what it is."

The governor laughed, and said: "I come closer to liking you every minute. But why is it that you think that you have something more to say?"

"Because," I explained, "I know that I'm an honest man and a peaceable man."

He laughed again, and I didn't like his laughter so well, this time. "Well," he said, "I won't interrupt you."

"You *know* that I'm a crook?" I asked him.

"About as well as any man could know anything."

"Have you looked up my whole life?"

"A few chunks of it have been served up to me . . . such as the Sam Dugan murder."

"The rest of your information is about as sound as that!" I snapped back at him, thanking heaven for the chance. "The murderer of Dugan has confessed and is in jail now."

The governor blinked at me. "I didn't know that," he muttered.

"Of course, you didn't!" I cried to him. "Every time they have a chance to hang a crime on the corner of my head, that makes first-page news. Every time they don't know who fired the shot that killed, they say . . . 'Porfilo'! But when they find out the facts a couple of days later, it makes poor reading. So they stick the notice back among the advertisements."

The governor nodded. I could see him accepting my idea and confessing that there was something to it.

"Well," I continued, "I ask you to start in and look up my life. It won't be hard to do. One of our secretaries can unload the whole yarn for you in about half a day's work. Then sift out the proved things from the unproved. Give me the benefit of a doubt."

"That sort of benefit will never win you a pardon from me," he said.

"I don't want a charity pardon," I declared.

"What kind do you expect?"

"An earned one."

"Confound it," said the governor, rubbing his hands together, "I like your style. Now tell me how, under heaven, you are going to win a pardon from *me?*"

"You've heard of Jeffrey Dinsmore," I said.

"I have."

"Is he as bad as I am . . . according to reputation?"

"Dinsmore is a . . . ," he began. Then he shut his teeth carefully, and breathed a couple of times. "I should say that he's as bad as you are," he said between his teeth.

"All right," I said. "Here's my grand idea that brought me as close to the rope as the capital city here."

"Blaze away," he coaxed.

"Dinsmore has twenty thousand dollars on his head, same as me."

"I understand that."

"We're an even bet, then?"

"I suppose so, if you want to make a sporting thing out of it."

"All right," I said. "What's better than two badmen. . . ."

"One, I suppose," said the governor. "But I wish you wouldn't be so darned Socratic."

I didn't quite understand what he meant, so I drilled away. "The catching of me has been a pretty hard job," I said. "It's cost the state seven years . . . and they haven't got me yet. But it's cost them a lot for the amount of money that they've spent hunting me."

"Besides your living expenses," said the governor with a twisted grin that hadn't much fun in it.

I caught him up on that. "My living expenses have come out of the pockets of other crooks. I've never taken a penny from an honest man. Look up my record!"

At this, he seemed really interested and sat up, rubbing his fine square chin and scowling at me—not in anger, but as if he were trying to search my character.

"Well," he said, "you are the darnedest crook I've ever heard of . . . with twenty thousand on your head and pretending to live like an honest man."

"For seven years," I said, rubbing the facts in on him.

"Aye," he said, "but will you insist that you've been honest all the time?"

"I helped in one robbery, and then I returned the money to the bank. You can get the facts on that, pretty easy. I had about a quarter of a million in my hands."

"If you have a record like that, why hasn't something been done for you?"

"I was waiting," I said, "for a governor that was a gentleman. And here I am."

"Ah, well," he said, "of course, I'll have to look into this. It can't be right. Yet I can't help believing you. But what is this about earning your pardon?"

"I was saying that the state had spent a good many tens of thousands on me, and there doesn't seem to be much chance of letting up on the expenses right away."

He nodded.

"And this Jeffrey Dinsmore is a fellow with lots of friends and with a family with money behind him. It will surely cost a lot to get at him."

"It will," said the governor with a blacker face than ever.

"I want to show you the shortest way out."

"I'm ready to listen now. What's in your head, young man?"

"Let Dinsmore know the proposition. I say let it be a secret agreement between you and me . . . and Dinsmore . . . that if he brings me in . . . dead or alive . . . you'll see that he gets a pardon, and the reverse goes for me."

The governor stared at me with his eyes enlarged. He began shaking his head.

I cut in very softly—hardly loud enough to interrupt his thoughts. "I can promise you that there'll be no living man brought in. One of us will have to die. There's no doubt about that."

"I know that," said William Purchase Shay. "I believe you, Porfilo. By the way, are you a Mexican?"

"My mother was Irish," I said. "Away back yonder, there was a dash of Mexican Indian in my father's blood."

It seemed to me that his smile was a lot easier when he heard that. Then he got up and took my hand.

"After all," he said, "one gets good laws in operation by hard common sense." He paused. "Is there anything that you need, Porfilo?"

"Wings to get out of this town," I said.

He nodded very gravely. "I don't see how the devil you got into it."

"Walked."

"While they are out looking for a man on a mule! That was the alarm that came in . . . from the old man you shot at. Did you shoot at him, Porfilo?"

"The old scamp was burning up the country to get to a telephone and blow the news about me. So I thought I'd give him a real thrill and I fired into the air. That's all there was to it."

"There's seventy miles between you and the mountains where you are so safe," he said.

"Open country." I nodded. "And seventy miles to

Mister Dinsmore, too."

"Are you sure of that?" asked the governor with a start.

"Why, that's where the report located him."

"The report lied, then. It lied like the devil!"

He said it in such a way that I could not answer him. I held my tongue until he reached out a sudden hand and wrung mine, and his eyes were fixed on the floor.

"Good luck to you . . . the best of luck to you, Porfilo."

I slid through the window, and, when I looked back, I saw him standing just as I had left him, with his eyes fixed upon the floor.

Well, I couldn't make it out at the time, but I figured pretty close, and I was reasonably sure that something I had brought into his mind connected with the idea of his wife, and that was what had taken the starch out of him.

However, I was not thinking about the governor ten seconds later. For, as I dropped from the window for the ground underneath, I saw a glint like that of a star through thin clouds. But this glimmer was among the leaves of some shrubbery, and I knew that it was a touch of starlight on the polished barrel of a gun.

VI

"Facing Guns"

Well, when you hear people speak of lightning thinking, I suppose that you smile and call it "talk"—but between the time I saw that glimmer of a gun in the bush and the instant my heels hit the ground beneath, I can give you my word that I had figured everything out.

If I were caught, people would want to know what Leon Porfilo had been doing in the governor's office. Even if I were not caught, it would be bad enough, because there would be no end of chatter all over the state. But, as a matter of fact, if I wanted to help the reputation of a man who had given me a mighty square deal, the best way for it was to cut out of those premises without using a gun or even drawing one.

I say that I thought of these things while I was dropping from the window to the ground, and I hadn't much time besides that, for, as I hit the ground and flopped over on my hands to ease the shock, I saw a big fellow with two more behind him step out of the brush and the lilacs about five paces away. Five paces—fifteen feet!

Well, you look across the room you are in and it seems quite a distance at that. Besides, I had the night in my favor. But I give you my word that, when I looked at those three silhouettes cut out against the starlit lilac bloom behind them, and when I saw the big pair of gats in the hands of the leader —and the gun apiece in the hands of the men behind—well, I knew in the first place that, if I tried to run to either side, they'd have me against the white background of the house and fill me with lead before I had taken two steps. I turned that idea over in the fifth part of a second while the leader was growling in a professionally ugly way—if you've ever heard a detective make an arrest you'll know what I mean.

"You . . . straighten up and tuck your hands over your head *pronto!*"

"All right," I muttered.

He could not have distinguished the first part of my movement from an honest surrender. For I simply began to straighten as he had told me to do. The difference was in my right hand—a five-pound stone. As my hands flew up, that stone jumped straight into the stomach of the leader.

Both his guns went off, and there was a silvery clashing of broken window glass behind me. One of those bullets was in a big scrub oak. The other had broken the window of the governor's office and broken the nose of the photograph of Shay's granddad—and drilled through the wall itself.

But the holder of the two guns threw out his hands to keep from falling, and in doing that he backhanded his two assistants. One of them started shooting blindly. The other dropped his gun, but he had enough sand and wit to make a dive for me. I clubbed him over the head with my fist, as though it were a hammer, and, very much as though a hammer had struck him, he curled up. I almost tripped over him. By the time I had disentangled my feet, the chief was shooting from the ground.

But he was a long distance from doing me any real harm. The nerves of those three were a good deal upset. I suppose, in fact, that they had not had much experience in trying to arrest men who can't afford to go behind the bars and be tried for their lives.

At any rate, I was lost among those lilacs in a twinkling. At the same time, a considerable ruction broke out in the house. Windows began being thrown up and voices were shouting, and the three detectives themselves were making enough noise to satisfy fifty.

Under cover of that racket, I didn't bolt out onto the street in the direction for which I was headed. Instead, I whirled around, and, under the shelter of those God-blessed lilacs, I tore back down the length of the yard.

I cleared the house—and still all the noise was in the rear and out toward the street. When I got into the back yard, I saw one discouraging thing—a tall fence about nine feet high and a man just in the act of climbing over. He had jumped onto a box, and the box had crumpled to nothing under him as he leaped. However, he had made the top of the fence.

I had to make the same height, without a box to jump from. Still I wondered who was the man who was trying to make his getaway even before me? I didn't stop to ask. I went at that fence with a flying leap and got my hands fixed on the top of it. With the same movement, I let my body swing like a pendulum. And so I shot myself over the top a good deal like a pole vaulter. When I let go with my hands and while I was pendent in the air, falling, I saw that the man who had gone over ahead had stumbled just beneath me, and, like a snarling dog, he was growling at me. He fired while I was still hanging in the air, and the bullet clipped my upper lip and let me taste my own blood.

It's very bad to let an Irishman taste his own blood. It's bad enough to let one who's half Irish do the thing. At any rate, I went half mad with anger. I landed on him. He wasn't big, and my weight seemed to flatten him out.

It was an alley cutting through behind the grounds of the governor's house, and there was a dull street lamp in a corner of the alley. It shed not very much light but enough to show me a handsome-faced young fellow—not made big, but delicately like a watch, you know. A sensitive face, I called it.

Then I started on. One thing I was glad of, and that was that there was a neat-looking horse tethered at the end of the alley, and from the length of the stirrups—as I made the saddle in a flying leap—I sort of thought that it might have belonged to the fellow I had just left behind me.

I cut the tethering rope with my sheath knife from the saddle, and then I scooted that horse across the street and down another alley. I pulled him up walking into the next street beyond and jogged along as though nothing particularly concerning me were happening that night. A very good way to get through with trouble. But the trouble was that there was still hell popping at the governor's house. I could hear their voices—and more than that—I could hear their guns, and so could half of the rest of the town.

People were spilling out of every house, and more than one man who was legging in the danger direction yelped at me, as I went past, and asked where I was going. But that was not so bad. I didn't mind questions. What I wanted to avoid was personal contact.

Here half a dozen fellows on fine horses took the corner ahead of me on one wheel, so to speak, spilling out all across the street as they raced the turn. When they saw me, one of them shouted: "What are you riding *that* way for?"

I knew that they would be halfway down the block before they could stop, and, besides, I hoped that they wouldn't be too curious if I didn't answer. So I just trotted the horse around the same corner by which they had come. But one question unanswered wasn't enough for them. They were like hungry dogs, ready to follow any trail.

"Hello!" yelled the sharp, biting voice of that same leader, to whom I began to wish bad luck. "No answer from that gent. Let's have a look at his face!"

I could hear the scraping and the scratching of the hoofs on the horses as the riders turned them in the middle of the block with cowpuncher yells that took down my temperature at least a dozen degrees.

I was not marking time. I scooted my mount down the next block. The minute he took his first stride, I knew that the race would be a hot one, no matter how well they were fixed with horses. Because that little horse was a wonder! I never put eyes on him after that night, but he ran with me like a jack rabbit—a long-winded jack rabbit, at that. My weight was such a puzzle for him that he grunted with every stride, but he whipped me down that street so fast that I had nearly turned west on the next corner before the pursuit sighted me. But I failed by the stretched-out tail of that little Trojan, and, by the yell behind me, I knew that they were riding hard and riding for blood.

I turned again at the next corner, and, as I turned, I saw that two men were riding even with me. They had even gained half a length in the running of that block. I made up my mind right away. If they had speed, they could show it in a straightway run, because it kills a little horse to dodge corners with a heavy man on his back. So I put my pony straight west up that street, running him on the gutter of the street where dust and leaves had gathered and made easier padding for his hoof beats.

In a mile we were out of the town, but those six scoundrels were still hanging on my rear and raising the country with their yells and their whoops. I could hear others falling in behind me. There were twenty now, shoving their horses along my path. And every moment they were increasing in numbers. Besides, after the first half mile, my weight began to kill that game little horse. He ran just as fast, nearly, as he had before. But the spring was going out of his gallop. Then I was saying to him: "Just hold out over the hill and into the hollow. Just over the hill and into the hollow."

Well, they were snap shooting at me as I went up that hill, and the hill and my weight together slowed my little horse frightfully. However, he got to the top of it at last, and my whistle was a blast between my fingers. Fifty yards of running down that hillside—with my poor little horse staggering and almost dying under me. My heart stood in my mouth, for, if Roanoke were gone, I was a lost man with a halter around my neck.

But, no—there he was, sloping out of the brush and heading full tilt toward me. As I came closer, he wheeled around and began to shamble away at his wonderful trot in the same direction I was riding. So I made a flying jump from the saddle of the little horse and onto the rock-like strength of the back of Roanoke.

VII

"An Unexpected Challenge"

There was not a great deal to the race after that. I suppose that there were half a dozen horses in the lot that could have nabbed Roanoke in an early sprint. But the little gamester I rode out of town had taken the sap out of the running legs of the entire outfit. When I left him for Roanoke, that old mule carried me up the course of the hollow—where water must have stood half the year, by the tree growth—and, after he had run full speed for a few minutes, they began to drop back behind me into the night.

The moment I noticed that, I dropped Roanoke back to his trot. Galloping was not to his taste, but he could swing on at close to full speed with that shambling trot of his and keep it up forever. It did not take long. The hunt faded behind me. The yelling began to grow musical with the distance, and finally it died away—first to an occasional obscure murmur in the wind, and then to nothing.

I think we did thirty miles before the morning sun was on us. Then I put up and spent another hungry day in a clump of trees. But food for Roanoke, not for me, was the main thing at that time. When the day ended, I sent that old veteran out to travel again, and we were soon in the mountains, soon climbing slowly, soon winding and weaving ourselves up to cloud level.

Until I got to that height, back in my own country, I did not realize how frightened I had been. But now that the mischief was behind me, I felt fairly groggy. I sent one bullet through a pair of fool jack rabbits sitting side by side, the next morning, behind a rock. They barely made a meal for me. I could have eaten a hind quarter of an ox, I was so hungry. I kept poor Roanoke drudging away until about noon. Then I made camp and spent thirty-six hours without moving.

I always do that after a hard march, if I can. It is always best to work hard while there's the least hint of trouble in the offing, but, when the wind lets up, I don't know of a better way to insure long life and happiness than by resting a lot. I was like a sponge. I could work for a hundred hours without closing my eyes, but, at the end of that time, I could sleep two days, solid, with just enough waking time to cook and eat one meal on each of those days. Roanoke was a good deal the same way. We spent a day and a half in a sort of stupor, but the result was that, when we *did* start on, I had under me an animal that wasn't half fagged and ready to be beaten, but a mule with his ears up and quivering. My own head was rested and prepared for trouble.

I hit for my old camping ground—not any particular section, though, I knew every inch of the high range, by this time —the whole wide region above timberline—a bitter, naked, cheerless country in lots of ways, but a safe one. For seven years, safety had to take the place of home and friends for me. An infernal north wind began to shriek among the peaks as soon as I got up there among them. But I didn't budge for ten wretched days or more. I spent a shuddering, miserable existence. There is nothing on earth that comes so close to above timberline for real hell! I've heard naturalists talk about the beauties of insects and birds and what not above the place where the trees stop growing. Well, I can't agree with them.

Perhaps I haven't a soul. But those high places make me pretty sick. When I see the long, dark line of trees end that cuts in and out among the mountains like the mark of high water, it sends a chill through me.

But for seven years I had spent the bulk of my life in that horrible part of the world. Seven years—eighteen to twenty-five. And every year before twenty-five is twice as long as every year after that time.

Well, I stayed in the old safe level, as I have said, about ten days. Then I dropped Roanoke five thousand feet nearer to civilization and stopped, one day, on the edge of a little town —right out between two hills where there was a little shack of a cabin standing. I knew that cabin, and I knew that the man inside it ought to know me. I had stayed with him half a dozen nights, and every time I used his house as a hotel, he got ten or twenty dollars out of me. Because that was one of the rules of the game. If a longrider struck up an acquaintanceship with one of the mountaineers, we always had to pay for it through the nose, in the end.

However, I couldn't be sure that old man Sargent hadn't changed his mind about me. I left Roanoke fidgeting among the trees on the hillside, for he could smell the sweet hay from the barn at that distance and his mouth was watering. Then I slid down the hill and peeked through the windows. Everything seemed as cheerful and dirty and careless as ever. Sargent had two grown-up sons. The three of them put in their time on a place where there wasn't work enough to keep one respectable two-handed man busy. There wasn't more than enough money for one man, if he wanted to be civilized. But civilization didn't harmonize with the Sargents. They wanted to live easy, even if they had to live low.

When I saw that there wasn't any change in them, I took Roanoke to the barn and put him up where he could eat all the hay he wanted. Because you can trust a mule to stop before the damage mark—which is a trust that you can't put in a horse.

Then I went to the house and the three of them gave me a pretty snug welcome. Old man Sargent insisted that I take the best chair—his own chair. He insisted, too, that I have something to eat. I had had enough for breakfast to last a couple of days, but I let out a link and laid into some mighty good cornbread and molasses that he dished up to me along with some coffee so strong that it would've taken the bristles off of pigskin.

I said: "How long ago did you make this coffee, Sargent?"

"I dunno," he said.

"He swabs out the pot once a month," said one of the boys, grinning, "and the rest of the time, he just keeps changing the brew, a little. A little more water . . . a little more coffee."

Well, it tasted like that, sort of generally bad and strong—mighty strong. I put away half a cup, just enough to moisten the cornbread that I swallowed.

"Have you come down to get Dinsmore?" said Bert Sargent.

The name hit the button, of course, and I turned around and stared at him.

"Why, Dinsmore has been setting waiting down in Elmira for three days," old man Sargent said.

"Waiting for what?" I asked. "I've been up in the mountains and I haven't heard."

Of course, they were glad enough to tell. Bad news for anyone else was good news for those rascals. It seems that Dinsmore had appeared suddenly in the streets of Elmira. At noonday. That was his way of doing things—with a high hand —acting as though there were no reason in the world why he should expect trouble from anyone. He went to the bulletin board beside the post office and there he posted up a big notice. He had the roll of paper under his arm, and he tacked it up with plenty of nails, not caring what other signs he covered. Well, sir, the reading of that sign was something like this:

Attention, Leon Porfilo!
     I want you, not the twenty thousand. If you want me, you can expect that I'll be ready for you any day between three and four if you'll ride through Main Street. I'll let you know which way to shoot!
                                                      Jeffrey Dinsmore

I don't mean to say that the Sargent family told me this story with so little detail. What they did do, however, was to give me all the facts, among the three of them. When I had sifted those facts over in my mind, I stood up. I was so worried that I didn't care if they saw the trouble in my face.

"You don't like this news so well as you might, partner?" old Sargent said very smooth and swallowing a grin.

I looked down at that wicked old loafer and hated him with all my heart. "I don't like that news at all," I admitted.

The three of them exclaimed all in a breath with delight. They couldn't help it. Then I told them that I was tired, and they showed me to a mattress on the floor of the next room. I lay there for a time trying to think out what I should do, and all the time I could hear whispers of the three in the kitchen. They were discussing with vile pleasure the shock that had appeared in my face when I had been told the news. They were like vultures, that trio.

Well, I was tired enough to go to sleep, anyway, after a time. Then I wakened with a start and found that it was daylight. That was what you might call a real hundred percent sleep. I felt better, of course, when I got up in the morning, and in the kitchen I found old man Sargent with his greasy gray hair tumbling down over his face and his face as lined and shadowed as though he had been drinking whiskey all the night. I suppose that really low thoughts tear up a man's body as much as the booze.

He gave me a side look as sharp as a bird's to see if there was still any trouble in my eyes, but I put on a mask for him and came out into the kitchen singing. All at once, a sort of horror at that old man and at the life I had been leading came over me. I hurried out of the house and down to the creek. It was ice cold, but I needed a bath, inside and out, I felt. I stripped and dived and climbed back onto the creekbank with enough shivers running up and down my spine to have done for a whole school of minnows. But I felt better. A lot better.

When I went back to the house for breakfast, I saw that one of the two boys was not on hand, and I asked where he was. His father said that he had gone off to try to get a deer, but that sounded like a queer excuse to me. I couldn't imagine a Sargent doing such a thing as this, at this hour in the morning. I began to grow a little uneasy—I didn't exactly know why.

After breakfast, as I left, I offered the old rat a twenty-dollar bill, and he took it and spread it out with a real gulp of joy. Cash came very seldom into his life.

"But," he said at last, peering at me hopefully and making his voice a wheedling drawl, "ain't I give you extra important news, this trip? Ain't it worth a mite more?"

I was too disgusted to answer. I turned on my heel and left, and, as I went out, I could hear him snarling covertly behind me.

VIII

"The Town Is Emptied"

However, I didn't like to fall out with the Sargents. I knew that they were swine, but, after all, I might need their help pretty early and pretty often in the next few years of my life.

I went out to Roanoke and sat in the manger in front of him, thinking or trying to think, while the old rascal started biting at me as though he were going to make breakfast off me. I decided, finally, that the only thing for me was to head straight for Elmira and take my chances there, because if I didn't meet Dinsmore right away, my name would be pretty worthless through the mountains. Besides, it was the very thing I had wanted.

But I had never dreamed of a fight in a town—and a big town like Elmira, that had everything in it except street cars. It had a four-story hotel, and a regular business section, and four streets going east and west. There were as much as fifteen hundred people in Elmira, I suppose. It was a regular city, and it seemed a good deal like craziness to try to stage a fight in such a place. As well start a chicken fight in the midst of a gang of rattlesnakes. No matter which of us won, he was sure to be nabbed by the local police right after the fight.

I wondered what could be in the head of Dinsmore, unless he had an arrangement with the sheriff of that county to turn him loose, in case he were the man who won the fight. I decided that this must be the fact, and that worried me more than ever. However, there wasn't much that I could do except to ride in and take my chances with Dinsmore. But one of the bad features was that I had never seen Dinsmore, whereas everyone had had a thousand looks at me in the posters that offered a reward for my capture.

Well, I saddled Roanoke and started down the Elmira trail. The first cross trail I came to, there I saw a board nailed on the side of a fence post and on the board there was all spread out a pretty good poster which said: **Dinsmore . . . twenty thousand dollars reward**.

I made Roanoke jump for the sign to see the face in detail. It was rather a small photograph, but it was a very clear one, and I was fairly staggered when I leaned over and found myself looking into the eyes of the very same fellow who had climbed the back fence of the governor's house a second before me on that rousing night in the capital city. That was Dinsmore!

It wasn't a very hot day, but I jumped out of the saddle and sat down under a tree and smoked a cigarette and fanned myself and did some very tall damning. It was all a confusing and a nasty mess, of course. A *mighty* nasty mess. I hardly dared to think out all of the ideas that jumped into my mind. There had been the anger of the governor when I mentioned the name of Dinsmore. There had been a sort of savage satisfaction when I suggested that the other outlaw and I shoot it out for the pardon. That, together with the unknown presence of Dinsmore at the house—and the pretty face of the governor's wife—well, I was fairly done up at the thought, you may be sure.

I could remember, too, that Dinsmore, though he had always been a fighting man, had never been a complete devil until about a year before—which was about the date of the governor's marriage. I don't mean to say that I immediately jumped to a lot of nasty conclusions. But a great many doubts and suspicions were floating through the back of my brain. I didn't want to believe a single one of them. But what could I do?

The first thing was to throw myself on the back of Roanoke and go down that hillside like a snow slide well under way. Blindly as a slide, too, and the result was that as I dipped out of the trees and came into the sunny, little, open valley below, I got two rifle shots squarely at my face. I didn't try to turn Roanoke aside. I just jammed him across that clearing with the spurs hanging in his flanks, and I opened fire with both revolvers as I went, firing as fast as I could and just in a general direction, of course.

Well, I got results. Snap shooting is always a good deal of a chance. This snap shooting into the blind brush got me a yelp of pain that meant a hit and was followed by a groan that meant a *bad* hit. After that, there was a considerable crashing through the brush, and I made out at least three horses smearing their way off through the underbrush. But what mostly interested me was that the groaning remained just as near and just as heavy as before. So I went in search of it, and, when I came to the place, I found a long fellow in ragged clothes lying on his face behind a shrub. I turned him over and with one look at his yellow face I knew that he was dying.

It was young Marcus Sargent. I knew at once why he had been missing at the breakfast table. They had guessed that I would head straight for Elmira, now that I had the news. So young Marcus thought of the twenty thousand dollars and decided that there was no reason why he should not dip his hands into the reward. He wasn't a coward. He was in such pain that it changed his color, but it didn't keep him from sneering at me in hate. When you wrong a man, hate always comes out of it—on your side. But I didn't hate him, in turn. I merely thanked heaven that he had missed—and I didn't see how he had, because I'd watched him ring down a squirrel out of a treetop many a time.

"How did you happen to miss?" I asked him. "Handshake, Mark?"

The first thing he answered was: "Am I done for?"

I answered him brutally enough: "You're done for. You can't live two minutes, I suppose . . . that slug went through you in the spot where it would do me the most good."

"You're a lucky swine," said Marcus. "Well, anyway, I dunno that life is so sweet that I hate the leavin' of it. But over in Elmira . . . if you should happen to run across Sue Hunter, hand her my watch, will you? Tell her it's from me. You'll know her by her picture inside the cover."

I hated nothing in the world more than touching that watch. But I did it, at last, and dropped it into my pocket.

Marcus didn't want to die before he had done as much harm as he could. He turned on his own family, saying: "It wasn't me alone. The whole three of us talked it over last night."

"Look here, Mark," I said, getting a little sick as I watched his color change, "is there anything I can do to make you more comfortable?"

"Sure," he said, "lend me a chaw, will you?"

But before I could get it for him he was dead.

I didn't like this affair for a lot of reasons. In the first place, I've never sunk lead into a man without hating the job. Although I've had the necessity or the bad luck of having to kill ten times my share of men, there was never a time when I didn't loathe it, and loathe the thought of it afterward. But that was only half of the reason that I disliked this ugly little adventure in the hollow. I had a fair idea that the two or three curs who had ambushed me with young Sargent would now ride for Elmira full tilt and tell the sheriff of what they had tried to do and of where they had last seen me. So, in two or three hours, the sheriff might be setting a fine trap for me in the town.

Of course, I only needed a moment of thought to see that was a foolish idea. No matter how little the people esteemed me, they would not think me such a perfect idiot as to ride on toward the town after I knew that a warning was speeding toward it in the form of three messengers. No, the sheriff was really not very apt to lay a plot for me in the town. Rather, he was pretty sure to come foaming down to the place where I had been seen and try to follow my trail from that point. Well, I decided that, if that were the case, he could pick up my trail if he cared to and follow it right back to his own home town.

In short, my idea was that, when people heard I had appeared so close to Elmira, every gun-wearing citizen would take a turn on his fastest horse and treat himself to a holiday hunting down twenty thousand dollars' worth of "critter". I believed that town would be well cleaned out and that the best thing I could do was to drive straight for Elmira itself, simply swinging a little wide off the main trail. Perhaps nine-tenths of the fighting men would be out hunting me when I reached Elmira, hunting Jeffrey Dinsmore.

Jeffrey Dinsmore, slender and delicately made, and as handsome for a man as the governor's wife was lovely as a girl. Thinking of her and of Dinsmore, I could understand why it was that Molly O'Rourke was only pretty and not truly beautiful. Molly might grow plain enough in the face in another ten years, but the governor's wife was another matter. She would simply become charming in new ways as time passed over her head. There was something magnificent and removed and different about her. She was the sort of a person I wondered any man could ever have the courage to love—she seemed so mighty superior to me. Well, you can guess from all of this that I wasn't in the most cheerful frame of mind in the world until, about two hours afterward, I looked through a gap in the trees and the brush, and I saw about a hundred men piling down the hillside in just the opposite direction and knew that I had guessed right.

IX

"Porfilo Meets Dinsmore"

Elmira had turned out its best and bravest to swarm out to the place where my trail had been found and lost by those three heroes who accompanied young Mark Sargent. They had a long ride before them, and, no matter how fast they spurred back toward Elmira, they were not apt to arrive there until many hours after I had passed through. My chief concern now was simply lest there still remained too many fighting men in the town. But I was not greatly worried about that. I felt that I had reduced the dangers of Elmira to a very small point. The danger that remained was from Dinsmore alone. How great that danger was I could not really guess. It was true that he had established a great reputation for himself in Texas, but before this I had met with men of a great repute in distant sections of the country, and they had proved not so deadly on a closer knowing. Furthermore, when one has picked up another man and dropped him on the pavement, one is not apt to respect his prowess greatly. Which may explain fairly thoroughly why I thought that I could handle Mr. Dinsmore with ease.

I did not think, however, that he would be prepared for me in Elmira. I thought that I probably would be permitted to canter down the street unobserved by Mr. Dinsmore, because, if the entire town was so busy hunting me, it seemed illogical that I should drop into Elmira. I expected to canter easily through the town, with only the danger of some belated storekeeper or some old man seeing and knowing me, for the rest of the town seemed to be out in the saddle.

Of course, I hoped that Dinsmore would not be on hand, because after I had answered his first invitation and he failed to appear, it would be my turn to lead, and I could request him to appear at any place of my own selection. The advantage would then be all on my side.

Outside of the town I stopped for a time. I let the mule rest, and I took it easy myself. I had a few hours on my hands before the appointed time to show myself to little Dinsmore in the town. However, though Roanoke rested well enough, I cannot say that my nerves were very easy. The time was coming closer, faster than any express train I ever watched in my life. The waiting was the strain. Whereas Dinsmore, knowing that the fight might come any day, paid no heed, but could maintain a leisurely look-out—or none at all.

A pair of eternities went by at last, however. Then I swung onto Roanoke and started him into the town. Everything went on about as I had expected it. The town was emptied of men. The first I saw was an old octogenarian with his trousers patched with a piece of old sack. The poor old man looked more than half dead, and probably was. He didn't lift his head from his hobble as I rattled by. The first bit of danger that came into my way was signaled by the screaming voice of a woman.

"There goes Leon Porfilo! There'll be a murder in this town today!"

It wasn't a very cheerful reception, take it all in all. But I pulled Roanoke back to an easy trot, and then I took him down to a walk, because I saw that I was coming pretty close to the place of the rendezvous. When I passed that place—although I wanted most terribly to pass it fast—still I had to be at a gait from which a man can shoot straight—and I've never yet seen anyone but a liar that could come near to accuracy from a trot or a gallop. Try it yourself—especially with a revolver—and see what happens. Even a walking horse is bad enough. It's hard when the target is moving; it's a lot harder when the shooter is in motion.

So I steeled myself as well as I could and reached a sort of mental bucket down into the innards of myself and drew up all the champagne that there was in me. I mustered a smile. Smiling helps a fellow, somehow. I don't mean in any fool way like they have it in ragtime songs and old proverbs. But smiling makes your gun hand steady.

Pretty soon I was right in the midst of the place where danger was to come at me, according to the warning that Dinsmore had sent out. I began to think that the whole thing was just a great bluff and that nothing would come out of it. It was a big play on the part of Dinsmore, and he hadn't the least idea of living up to his promise.

Just as this thought struck me, I heard a calm, smooth voice call out behind me: "Well, Porfilo?"

It was the sort of a voice that comes from a man who doesn't want to call any public attention to himself. He aims to reach just the ear of the man to whom he is speaking. But, at the same time, I knew that was the voice of Dinsmore, and I knew that Dinsmore was mighty bad medicine, and I knew that the fight of my life was on my hands. I spun about in the saddle with the gun in my hand—and I saw that he had not even drawn his weapon. The shock of it sickened me. I couldn't keep from shooting—I was so thoroughly set for that pull of the trigger—but I did manage to shoot wide of the mark. And, just as the gun exploded, I saw my new friend

Dinsmore make as pretty a draw as I have ever had the pleasure of witnessing. One of those snap movements that jump a gun out of the leather and shoot it from the hip.

I jerked my own gun back and fired again, but my hand was mighty uncertain. The whole affair was so infernally unnerving that I was not myself. The idea that any man in the world would dare to stand up to me and give me the first chance of a draw was too much for me. I got in my second shot before he fired his first, but all I did with that second bullet was to break a grocery store window. Then a thunderbolt clipped me along the head and knocked me back in the saddle.

I was completely out—as perfectly out as though a hammer had landed on me—but it happened that in falling, my weight was thrown squarely forward, and my arms dangled around the neck of Roanoke. He started the same instant, I suppose, with that shambling, ridiculously smooth trot of his, so that I was able to stick to his back.

I think that the wild yelling of old men, and women, and children was what brought me back to my senses. Or partially back to them, for my head was spinning and crimson was running over my eyes. However, I was able to sit straighter in the saddle and put Roanoke into a gallop.

I was a dead man, of course. I learned afterward about the miracle that saved me. For the gun of that great expert, that famous Dinsmore, failed to work. The cylinder stuck on the next shot, and before he could get the other gun out to blow me out of this life and into limbo, that wise-headed mule of mine had put a buckboard at the side of the street between himself and that gunman.

Dinsmore had to run out into the middle of the street to get the next shot. But when he saw me again, I suppose that the distance was getting too great for accurate work even for him, and, besides, Roanoke was shooting me along under the shadow of the trees. At any rate, there he stood in a raging passion and emptied that second gun of his without putting a mark upon either the mule or the mule's rider. I suppose that there is no doubt that the fury of that little man was what saved me more than anything else.

But presently I was blinking at the sun like a person wakened out of a dream, and behind me lay Elmira in a hollow. Up and down my head ran a pain like the agony of a cutting knife through tender flesh. Down in Elmira was a man who was telling the world that the "coward had run away from him".

I should like to be able to say that, halting only to tie a sleeve of my shirt around my head, I turned and whirled back into Elmira to find him again. But I have to confess that nothing could have induced me to face that calm little devil of a man-killer on that day. For the moment, I felt that I could *never* have the courage to fight or face him again. I felt that I would take water, sooner.

I found a little hollow about ten miles back among the hills, and there I made myself comfortable, heated some water, washed out my wound, and bound it up. Then I rode straight on to the next little village. On the way, I had to duck three or four parties of manhunters. I didn't have to ask who they were hunting for. I simply wanted to dodge them and get on, for I knew that they wanted either Dinsmore or me.

The next town had not much more than an ugly look—a hotel and half a dozen shacks. But in one of those shacks was an old doctor, and that was what I wanted. The new fangled ideas had taken his trade away from him. But he was good enough for me on that day. I left Roanoke behind his house and went to the back window and saw the poor old man sitting there in a kitchen that was blackened with the shadows of the trees that hung over the place—blackened with time, too, if you can understand what I mean by that. I pitied him, suddenly, so much that I almost forgot the pain of my head. Young men are like that. They pity almost everyone except themselves. I never ride through a village without wondering how people can live in it. Yet I suppose that every one of them is prettier than my home town of Mendez.

I went in, and the doctor looked sidewise from his whittling of a stick, and then back to it. "Well, Porfilo," he said, "I been hearin' that you got licked at last. And a little feller did it. Well, for some things bigness ain't needed."

He stood up—about five feet in his total height. I hung above him, ducking my head to keep from scraping the cobwebs off the rafters.

"I've got my head sliced open. Sew me up, pop," I said.

"Set down and rest yourself, son," he said. "I see you got sense enough to let little men fix you *up,* anyway."

X

"At the O'Rourkes' Again"

I listened to him mumbling and muttering to himself while I set my teeth and snarled at the pain, until the job was done and my head washed and the bandage arranged around it. He gave me a lot of extra bandage, and a salve, and he asked me if I had a good mirror so that I could watch the wound every day. I told him that I had and asked him what the price would be.

"If you're flat busted, the way most of your kind always are," he said, "there ain't no charge, except for your good will. Besides, any young feller has got a reward comin' to him when he listens to an old goat like me chatterin' for a while. But if you're flush, well, for bandagin' the head of an outlaw and a man-killer like you . . . well, it's worth about . . . thirty dollars, I reckon."

I sifted a hundred dollars out of my wallet and put it in his hand.

I was out the door before he had counted it over and he shouted: "Hey, you . . . !" I was on Roanoke, with that fine old fellow standing in the doorway and shouting: "Come back here! You give me too much!"

I sent Roanoke on his way, and the last I saw of him, that poor old man was running and stumbling and staggering after me, waving his glasses in one hand and his money in the other hand and telling me to come back. But I only saw him for a moment. Then I was away among the trees, with Roanoke climbing steadily.

I kept him south through the highlands. When I was far enough away from the last trouble, I made small marches every day, because I knew that a wound won't heal quickly so long as a man is running about too much. While I was lazing around, I worked until both wrists ached over my guns. Because there was fear in me—real fear in me. I had gone for seven years from one fight to another, never beaten, always the conqueror. Now a little fellow had blown me off my pedestal.

I had to get ready to fight him again. I knew that, and I can tell you that I didn't relish the knowing. I had to get in touch with Molly. For she would think, as probably everyone in the mountains thought, that I had either been killed by the after-effects of that wound in the head received from Jeffrey Dinsmore, or else that I had been so thoroughly broken in spirit as a result of that first defeat that I had shrunk away to a new land and dared not show myself in my old haunts.

Well, I thought of a letter, first of all, but then I decided that it would be better to see her, because it might be the very last time that I should ever see her in this world. For, having once witnessed the gun play of Jeffrey Dinsmore, I knew that, at the best, I would need a touch of good fortune in order to beat him in a fair gunfight. And, what with my bulk and my experience, how could I challenge him with any other weapon?

So I drifted farther south through the mountains until I came one midnight to the O'Rourke house and stood underneath the black front of the house—all black, except for a single light in the window of Molly. I called her with a whistle that was a seven-year-old signal between us. She did not open the door and first look down at me, but came flying down the stairs and then out the front door and down the steps into my arms. But, when she had made sure that it was I, she stood back from me and laughed and nodded with her happiness. She told me that she had been sure that I was dead, in spite of other rumors.

"What sort of talk has been going around about me, then?" I asked her.

She shook her head. But I told her that I would have to have it.

"They are fools," she said, but there was a strain in her voice. "They say that you are afraid to go back and face Dinsmore."

Well, I *was* afraid, so I blurted out: "I *am* afraid, Molly."

I saw it take her breath, and I saw her flinch from me. Then she answered very calmly: "However, you'll go back and fight him again."

I was mightily proud of her. You don't find women who will talk like that very often. But Molly was the truest mountain-bred kind—Thoroughbred, in her own way. I spent a single hour with her there in the garden. Then I told her that I was starting back.

"North?" asked Molly.

"North, of course," I said. "You don't think that I'll try to dodge a second meeting?"

"Of *course,* I didn't think so," she said. However, I could feel the relief in her voice. She began to pat the neck of old Roanoke.

"Roanoke," she said, "bring him back safe to me."

So I left Molly and rode north again.

It was a hard journey. I had gone for seven years more or less paying no attention to decent precautions, because they had not been so necessary to me. In fact, I had not appreciated the change in my affairs until I started that northward journey again.

It began in the first house where I put up for a night. Old Marshall's house was a pretty frequent stopping place for me. His family had taken a good deal of money out of my hand, and more than that his nephew, who ran the little bit of cattle land the old man owned, seemed to respect me and to like me because he was always trying to find a better chance to talk to me. But when I came to the house this night, everyone merely stared at me, and then I could hear them whispering and even chuckling behind their hands. People had not done that to me since I was a little boy at school. It made my heart cold, and then it made my heart hot.

But I waited until something came out. With people like that, nothing could be left to silence very long. They had to bring out what they thought and put it into words.

So big Dick Marshall, the nephew, came and lounged against the wall near my chair. "We hear that you been having your own sorts of trouble?" he said.

I lifted the bandage that I still wore and showed him the scar. "I was nipped," I said.

He laughed in my face. "You didn't go back for any more of *that* medicine, I guess?"

I wanted to knock him down. But after a moment I decided that there was no use in doing that. Because he was not a bad fellow. Just a clod. No more cruel than a bull in a herd—and no less. That, and the mischievous, contemptuous smile with which he watched me out of sight the next morning, as I rode away, should have convinced me, I suppose, that there was worse trouble ahead. But when I really found it out, it was merely because four young fellows came bang over a hilltop behind me and tried to ride me down in the next hollow. When they saw that I was making time away from them to the tree line, they opened fire at me.

When I got to the trees, I told myself that I was all right, but to my real astonishment, just as I drew up on the rein and brought Roanoke back to a walk, I heard the whole four of them crashing through the underbrush. I sent Roanoke ahead again, full steam. He was as smooth a worker as a snake through the shrubbery, and the four began to fall behind. I could hear them yelling with rage as they judged, by the noise, that they were losing ground behind me. But all the time I was thinking hard and fast. It wasn't right. Four youngsters like these, not one of whom had probably ever pulled a gun on another man, should not be riding behind Leon Porfilo. By no means.

Well, I decided to find out what the reason was. So I cut back through the forest. The trees were pretty dense, and so I was able to get right in behind the party. I sighted them and found them just as I wanted to find them. They were strung out by the heat of the work, and one fellow was lagging far behind with a lame horse. He had no eyes for the back trail, and he could hear no sound behind him, he was so eager to get ahead. It was easy enough to slip along in a dark hollow and stick a gun in the small of his back. I clapped my hand over his mouth so that I stifled his yell. Then I turned him around and looked him over. He was just a baby. About eighteen or nineteen, with big, pale-blue eyes, and a foolish sort of smile trembling on his mouth. He was afraid. But he was not afraid as much as he should have been at meeting Leon Porfilo. This may sound pretty fat-headed, but you have to understand that I had been the pet dragon around those parts for the past seven years, and I wasn't in the habit of having infants like this boy on my trail.

I said to him: "Son, do you know who I am?"

"You're Porfilo!"

"Then what in the devil do you mean by riding so hard down my trail?"

He looked straight back at me. "There's twenty thousand dollars' worth of reasons," he said as bold as you please.

"Is it a very safe business?" I asked.

He wouldn't answer, but those big pale eyes of his didn't waver. "You can do what you want," he said. "I didn't have no fair chance . . . with you sneakin' up behind like that. No matter what happens, my brother'll get you after I'm dead."

"Am I to murder you?" I said.

"You don't dare to leave me on your trail!"

Well, it sickened me, and that was all there was to it. He actually wanted to fight the thing out with me, I think.

"You're loose," I advised him, and dropped my gun back in the holster.

He jerked his horse back and grabbed for his own gun. Then he saw that I was making no move toward mine, and so he began to gape at me as though he were seeing double.

Finally he disappeared in the trees. But it's a fact that I couldn't have fired a shot at that little fool. This thing, and the talk of young Marshall showed me how far I had dropped in the estimation of the mountain men since they had heard that little Dinsmore beat me in a fair fight. I knew that I would be in frightful danger from that moment on.

XI

"Leon No Longer a Hero"

I knew that there was danger because my cloak of invincibility was quite thrown away. For seven years I had paraded up and down through the mountains, and men had not dared to go out to hunt me except when they had celebrated leaders to show them the way, and when they had prepared carefully organized bands of hard fighters and straight shooters. It had been easy enough to get out of the reach of these large parties. But when the hills were beginning to buzz with the doings of little groups of from three to five manhunters—well, then my danger was multiplied by a thousand. Multiplied most of all, however, by the mental attitude of the people who rode out against me.

For there's only one reason that so many straight-shooting frontiersmen fail when they come to take a shot at a so-called desperado. That reason is that their nerve fails them. They are not sure of themselves. So their rifles miss, and the desperado who has all the confidence that they lack does prodigious things. One hears, here and there, of terrible warriors who have dropped half a dozen men, and gotten off unhurt.

Of course, I was never on a par with these. In fact, my

principle was not to shoot to kill unless I had a known scoundrel up against me. But now I felt that my back was against the wall.

There was only one solution for me, and that was to get at Dinsmore as soon as possible and fight it out with him, and by his death put an end to the carelessness of the fools who were hunting me through the hills. But, in the meantime, how was I to get at Dinsmore himself?

I decided that I must try the very scheme that he had tried on me. I must send him a message and a challenge in the message to meet me at a place and a time of my own choosing. Two days later chance threw a messenger into my path.

I was in a tangle of shrubs on the shoulder of a mountain with Roanoke on the other side, his saddle off, rolling to refresh himself, and playing like a colt, as only a mule, among grown animals, likes to play. While I sat on a rock at the edge of the brush, I saw a pair of horsemen and then a third working up the trail straight toward me.

I was in no hurry. This was rough country of my own choosing, and Roanoke could step away from any horse in the world in that sort of going, like a mountain sheep. I simply got out my glasses and studied the three. As they came closer, rising deeper into the field of the glass, I thought that I could guess what they were—three head hunters, and mine was the head that they wanted. For they were too well mounted to be just casual cowpunchers. Each man was literally armed to the teeth. I saw sheathed rifles under their right knees. I saw a pair of revolvers at their hips. One fellow had another pair of six-shooters in his saddle holsters. They looked as though they were a detail from an army.

I went across the knob of the shoulder of that mountain and I saddled Roanoke. But I didn't like to leave that place. I was irritated again. Four youngsters had been out hunting me the last time. Now it was three grown men. Three! You might say that my pride was offended because that was exactly the case.

I ended by dropping the reins of Roanoke, and the wise old mule stood as still as death in the shadow of the trees, flopping his ears back and forth at me but not so much as switching his tail to knock away the flies that were settling on his flanks and biting deep as only mountain flies know how to bite. I have always thought that Roanoke knew when there was trouble coming, and that he enjoyed the prospect of it with all his heart. There was faith and strength and courage in the nature of that brute, but I am sure that there was a good deal of the devil in him, too.

I left him behind and started down among the rocks until I found exactly the sort of a place that I wanted, a regular nest, with plenty of chances to look out from it with a rifle. I had a fine rifle with me, and ready for action. As for my humor, it was nearer to killing than it had ever been in my life.

The three came up with surprising speed, and I knew by that they were well mounted. As they came, I could hear their voices rising up to me like echoes up a well shaft. These voices and that laughter were sometimes dim, sometimes loud and crackling in my ear. Because in the mountains, where the air is very thin, sound travels not so freshly and easily. And the least blow of wind may turn a shout into a whisper. Have you never noticed that mountaineers, when they come down toward sea level, are a noisy lot? I could hear all the talk of the three, and by their very talk I could judge that they were in the best of spirits.

Then: "Will you keep that damn' bay from jogging around and tryin' to turn around in the trail, Baldy?"

"It ain't me. It's the hoss. It wants to get back to that stable. . . ."

"A hired hoss," said a third voice, "is something that I ain't never rode."

They came suddenly around the next bend of the trail, and I barely had the time to duck down in my nest of rocks. I had thought them at least fifty yards farther away from that bend. I was not quite in time, at that.

"Hey!" yelled the first man—he of the bay horse.

"Well?" growled one of the others.

"Something in those rocks. . . ."

"Maybe it's Porfilo!" laughed another.

"And that's the gent you want."

"Just run up to them rocks and ask him to step out and have it out with you, Baldy."

Baldy said apologetically: "Well, I can't keep you from laughing. But I would've said that the brim of a sombrero. . . ."

I took off my hat and prepared my rifle. As I freshened my grip on it and tickled the trigger with my forefinger, I have to admit that I was ready to kill. I was hot and sore to the very bone. They came laughing and joking on my trail. It was a vacation, a regular party to them. As they came closer, as the nodding shadow of the bay appeared on the white trail just before my nest, I stood up with the rifle at my shoulder.

There's something discouraging about a rifle. About ten times as much can be said with a rifle as can be said with even a pair of revolvers. The revolvers may have a lot of speed and lead in 'em. But they *might* miss . . . they're pretty *apt* to miss. Even a coward will take a gambling chance now and then. But when a rifle in a steady hand is looking in your direction, you feel sure that something is bound to drop. Somehow, there is an instinct in men that makes everyone think that the muzzle is pointed directly at him.

Only one of the three made a pass at a gun. The two boys

behind shoved their hands in the air right *pronto*. But Baldy, up in the lead, passed a hand toward his off Colt. He was within the tenth part of a second of his long sleep, when he did that. I think that there must be something in mental telepathy, because, the moment that thought to kill came into my mind, he stuck both of his paws into the air and kept his arms stiff. His bay turned around as if it were on a pivot and started moving back down the trail.

"Take your left hand, Baldy," I said, "and stop that horse *pronto!*"

He did exactly as I told him to do.

"Now, boys," I said, stepping out from the rocks with that rifle only at the ready, "I suppose that you recognize me. I'm Leon Porfilo. If you want to know me any better, make a pass at a holster. You, Baldy, were about half a step from purgatory a minute ago. The rest of you, turn your horses around with your knees. If you're not riding hired horses, they ought to do that much without feeling the bit. Turn your horses around. I like the looks of your backs better than your faces."

There was not a word of answer. They turned their nags obediently around. There they sat with five arms sticking into the air.

I made them dismount—the rear pair. Then I made them back up until they were near me. After that, I took their hands behind them and tied cords over them—tied them until they groaned.

"You pair of sap heads!" I said. "Sit down over there by that rock, will you? . . . and don't make any noise . . . because I feel restless, today. I feel mighty restless. Baldy, you're next!"

I tied Baldy with his own lariat, and I tied him well. I tied his hands tight behind him, and I tied his feet together under the belly of the bay.

Then I took an old envelope and wrote big on it:

To everybody in general, and Dinsmore in particular: Dinsmore got the drop on me in Elmira. I want to find him. I ask him to come and find me, now. I'll meet him any afternoon between three and four in the Elmira Pass. This holds good for the next month.

Leon Porfilo

I pinned that on the back of Baldy. Then I turned him loose. All that I wanted was to have the world see my message back to Dinsmore to let them know that I was waiting for him.

How that bay did sprint down the hill! There was a puff of trail dust, you might say, and then the bay and Baldy landed in the hollow of the valley below the mountain, and, after that, they skimmed up the mountain on the other side. The bay was certainly signaling that he intended to get to that stable.

Then I went back to the other two. I didn't say a great deal, but they seemed to think that it was worth listening to. I told them that I had gone for seven years, letting people hound me through the mountains and not shooting back. I told them that my next job was to find Dinsmore and kill him, but that, in the meantime, I intended to shoot, and to shoot to kill. And if I met the pair of them again, they were dead men—on the street or in the mountains—it made no difference to me.

I think those fellows took it to heart. Then, because I hadn't the slightest fear that they would overtake the bay, I untied their hands and let them mount and ride back the way that they had come.

XII

"Dinsmore's Crushing Answer"

All in all, I thought that this move of mine was a clever one and that it would reëstablish me a great deal through the mountains. But the answer of Jeffrey Dinsmore was a crushing blow, because that rascal went into the office of the biggest newspaper in the capital city, ten days later, and called on the editor and introduced himself, and allowed the editor to photograph him, and dictated to the editor a long statement about various things.

It was a grand thing in the way of a scoop for that paper. I saw a copy of it and there were headlines across the front page three inches deep. Most of the rest of the front page was covered with pictures of the editor, and the editor's office where the terrible Dinsmore had appeared. In the center, surrounded with little pen sketches of Dinsmore in the act of shooting down a dozen men in various scenes, was a picture of Jeffrey—the picture that the editor had snapped of him.

It showed him as dapper and easy and smiling as a motion-picture hero. He was smoking a cigar, holding it up so that the camera could catch the name on it. That was a cigar that the editor, mentioning the fact proudly in his article, declared that he had given to the desperado.

Altogether, it was a great spread for Dinsmore, the editor, and the newspaper, and a great fall for me. I understood afterward that the editor got three offers from other newspapers immediately afterward, and that his salary was doubled to keep him where he was.

He couldn't say too much about the affair. Dinsmore had appeared through the window of his office, four stories above the street, at nine o'clock in the evening when most of the reporters were out at work on their stories and their copy. The editor of *The Eagle*, being busy at his desk, looked up just in time to see a dapper young man sliding through the window with a revolver pointed at the editorial head and the smiling face of Mr. Dinsmore behind the revolver. So the editor, taking great pride in the fact that he did not put his hands into the air, turned around and from his tilted swivel chair asked Dinsmore what he would have.

"A good reputation," said Dinsmore.

From that point on, declared the editor in his article, **we got on very well together, because there is nothing like a good laugh to start an interview smoothly.**

They talked of a great many things. That editor's account of Dinsmore, his polished manners, his amiable smile, was so pleasant that it was a certainty no unprejudiced jury could ever be gathered in that county. If Dinsmore had murdered ten men the same night, he would have secured a hung jury on the whole butchery. That editor was a pretty slick writer, when you come right down to it. He made Dinsmore out the most dashing young hero that ever galloped out of the pages of a book. And it was almost a book that he wrote about him!

He declared that if Dinsmore were anything worse than an impulsive youngster who didn't know better, he, the editor, would confess that his editorial brain was not worth a damn, and that he had never been able to judge a man. Of course, the chief point in the interview was Dinsmore's own account of his fight with me. That was the main matter, all the way through. Because Dinsmore had called at the editor's office in order to explain to the world why he did not ride back into the mountains in order to answer my challenge.

I won't put in any of the bunk with which that article was filled, where the editor kept exclaiming at Dinsmore and asking him how he dared to venture through the streets unmasked—and how he had been able to scale the sheer side of the building. I leave out all of that stuff. I leave out, too, all that the editor had to say about Dinsmore's family—how old that family was—how good and grand and gentle and refined and soldierly and judge-like the father of Dinsmore had been. How Dinsmore himself seemed to combine all of the good qualities of both of his parents.

So that, said the editor, **I could not help feeling that what this young man was suffering from was an over-plus of talents, of wealth, of social background. His hands had been filled so completely full since his childhood with all that other men hunger for, that it was no wonder that he had turned aside from the ordinary courses of ordinary men. Alas! that he did not live in some more violent, more chivalric age—then his sword and his shield would have won a name.**

The editor rambled on like this for quite a spell. Not very good stuff, but good enough to do for a newspaper. Newsprint stuff has to be a bit raw and edgy in order to cut through the skin of the man who reads as he runs. The whole sum of it was that Jeffrey Dinsmore was a hero, and that he was a little too good for this world of ours to appreciate. Finally Dinsmore told about me.

He had gone up into the mountains to Elmira, he said, because he wanted to find me where I would be at home among my own friends—because he didn't want to take me at a disadvantage.

"But why did you go in the first place?" the editor had asked.

"I'm rather ashamed to confess it," Dinsmore had said

with an apologetic smile, "but when I heard of all the atrocities of this fellow Porfilo, and how he had butchered men . . . not in fair fight but rather because he loved butchery . . . and how helpless the law had proved against him . . . well, sir, I decided that I couldn't stand it, and so I decided that I would have to get up into those mountains and there I'd meet Mister Porfilo, hand to hand, and kill him if I could!"

The editor couldn't let Dinsmore say any more than this without breaking into comment and praising Dinsmore and showing that he was like some knight out of the Middle Ages riding through the dark and unknown mountains to find the dragon.

Well, as I said before, that editor was a good editor, but what he had to say began to get under my skin. I looked again at his picture. He had a thin face and he wore glasses. I wonder why it is that spectacles always make me pity a man?

Dinsmore went on to tell how he had met me, and how I had whirled on him and fired the first shot, while he was waiting to talk. Well, that was all very true. Twenty people could swear to the truth of that, but not one of them had the sense to know that I had fired wide. Then he said that the firing of that first shot showed him that I was a coward and a bully—a coward because I was so very willing to take advantage of another man who only wanted to stand up and fight fair and square.

I couldn't read further in the paper at that time. I had to walk up and down for a time to cool off. Then I looked hurriedly through the paper to try to find a statement by Dick Lawton, or somebody like that, defending me. But there wasn't any such statement. On the fourth and fifth pages of the paper there were opposite accounts of the pair of us. On one page there was the story of Dinsmore, with little illustrations inset, showing the great big house that he had been born and raised in—how Dinsmore looked in his rowing squad at college in the East—how Dinsmore looked in his year of captaincy of the football team, when his quarterback run had smashed the Orange to smithereens in the last two seconds of the game—how he looked on a polo pony—what the five girls looked like that he had been engaged to at various times in his life—how he looked standing beside his father, Senator Dinsmore—how he looked arm in arm with his dear old mother—and how he looked when he rode the famous hunter, Tippety Splatcher, to victory in the Yarrum Cup. Well, there was a lot of stuff like that, with the history of his life written alongside of it. Just like a fairy tale.

On the opposite page it showed the house in Mendez where I was born, and there was a picture of the butcher shop that my father had owned. There was a picture of myself, too, showing my broad face and heavy jaw and cheek bones.

"Like a prize fighter of the more brutal kind," Dinsmore had said.

But there was only a dull account of my affairs—"butcheries", the editor called them. I was made out pretty black, and there was not a word of truth said to defend me. When I got through, I wanted to kill that editor.

I went back to Dinsmore's account. He told how he had decided that I was a swine, and then he had fired after my second shot, and the bullet had wounded me in the head—after which I spurred the mule away down the street as fast as I could. There were plenty of witnesses who could prove that the bullet stunned me and that I did not begin to flee of my own free will. But, of course, none of their statements were wanted. Nothing but the word of the hero.

As for coming back into the mountains, Mr. Dinsmore had said that after standing in the street of Elmira and firing shot after shot "into the air" and watching me ride "like mad" to get away from danger, he had no wish to come back to find me again. He had said that he felt he had fairly well demonstrated that the bully Porfilo was a coward at heart. And he, Dinsmore, feared a coward more than he did any brave man. For a coward was capable of sinking to the lowest devices. He knew quite well that if he accepted the invitation to face the challenge of Leon Porfilo, he knew that he would be waylaid and murdered.

So much for the opinion of Leon Porfilo.

Now, as I read this letter, such a madness came over me that I trembled like a frightened girl. Then I steadied myself and sat with my head in my hands for a long time, thinking, wondering. What I made out at last was rather startling. For it was declared in the paper that Mr. Dinsmore had said that he was in the capital city because he was then engaged in the task of drifting himself rapidly East and that the West perhaps would see him never again. But, as I read this statement, I could not help remembering that I had seen him once before in the capital city, and I remembered, also, all of the nasty thoughts that had gone through my mind at that time.

XIII

"Porfilo's Return to Town"

Perhaps I should hardly call them "thoughts", when they were really no more than premonitions, based upon the prettiness of the governor's wife and the thoughtfulness of the governor—and Jeffrey Dinsmore, gentleman and gunman, climbing the back fence of the governor's house at full speed. I considered all of those things, and the more that I thought of them the more convinced was I that the celebrated Dinsmore was *not* passing through the capital city—certainly not until he had seen beautiful young Mrs. Shay.

So I turned the matter over back and forth in my mind for three whole days, because I am not one of those who can make hair-trigger decisions and follow them. The result of all my debating was that I saddled Roanoke and began to work some of his fat off by shooting him eastward.

We came through the upper mountains, and I had my second view of the lowlands beneath me, silvered and beautified in evening mist. Once more I reached the lowest fringing of trees in the foothills and slept through a day. Once more I started with the dusk and drove away toward the city. Not the city, really, since in my mind there were in it only three people: William P. Shay, his wife, and Jeffrey Dinsmore.

Naturally I passed that last name over my tongue more frequently than I did the other two. Every time it left the acid taste of hate. I was hungry, hungry to get at him. Not that I feared him less than I had been fearing him. Simply that my hatred was too intense a driving force to let me stay away from him.

On the second night I was on the edge of the town, as before, and in the very same hollow where before I had left Roanoke, I left him this time. Only I did not keep a saddle on him because I was hardly capable of doing all of my work in a single evening in the town. I hid the saddle in the crotch of a lofty tree, and with the saddle I left my rifle and all my trappings except a little stale pone, hard almost as iron, but the easiest and most complete form, almost, in which a person can transport nutriment. I tucked that stony bread into my pockets. I had two heavy Colts and a sheath knife stowed handy in my clothes. Then I was ready to take my chances in the city again.

I walked in by the same route, too, except that, when I came through the deserted outskirts of the city, I began to bear away to the right, because I had a fairly accurate idea of where the governor's house was located. As a matter of fact, I brought up only two blocks away from it, and presently I came in behind that house. I had made up my mind earlier, and I put my determination into action at once. The house was fenced, behind, with ten feet of boards as I have said before. But I managed to grip my hands on the upper edge and swing my body well over them by the first effort. I dropped close to the ground and squatted bunched there to look over the lay of the land and see what might be stirring near me. There was not a soul. The screen door of the back porch slammed, and I heard someone run down the steps. However, whoever it was kept on around the house by the narrow cement walk. I heard the heels of that man *click* away to dimness; I heard the rattle of the old front gate, and then I started for the corner stables.

Once that barn had been much bigger. One could tell by the chopped-off shoulders of the barn that it had once extended wide, but now perhaps it was the carriage shed that was trimmed away, and the barn that remained stood stiff and tall and prim as a village church. I didn't care for that. I slipped through the open door of it and stood in the dark, smelling and listening—smelling for hay and finding the sweetness of it—and listening for the breathing of horse or cow—and not hearing a whisper.

So I went a little farther in and lighted a match. It was exactly as I had prayed. There was a heap of very old hay in one end of the mow—perhaps it had been there for years, untouched. The dry, dusty floor of the horse stalls showed me that they had not been occupied for an equally long time. This was what I wanted. I decided that people would not readily look for Leon Porfilo in the governor's barn—no matter how imaginative they might be.

I was a little tired, so I curled up in that haymow and slept until a frightened mouse *squeaked,* half an inch from my ear. Then I sat up and snorted the dust out of my nose and nearly choked myself to keep from sneezing. When I passed out into the night, I found that the lights were still burning in the Shay house.

There was an inquisitive spirit stirring in my bones that evening. The first thing I did was to remove my boots and my socks. I figured that my callused feet would stand about all the wear that I would give them that night. I left boots and socks in the barn. I left my coat with them. I took all the hard pone and the sheath knife and one revolver out of my clothes. Then I rolled up my trousers to the knees. By that time I was about as free as a man could wish, except he were absolutely naked. I felt free and easy and *right.* I could fight now, or I could run. Also, I could investigate that tall old house, and I guessed that there was enough in it to be worth investigating.

First I took a slant down to the window of the governor's little private room. I skirted around through the lilac bushes, first of all. When I had made sure that none of those infernal detectives were hanging about to make a background for me, I drew myself up on the window sill and surveyed the scene inside. It was what I suspected. That was the governor's after-hours workshop—and I suppose that he spent more hours there than in his office. Here he was with a secretary on one side taking shorthand notes, and beyond the door there was the *purring* of a typewriter where another secretary was pouring out copy of some sort. Governor Shay was just the same man in worried looks that I had known before.

I spent no time there. He was not the man I wanted. First I skirted around the house and peered into other rooms until I made out that Mrs. Shay was not in any of them. Then I climbed up to a lighted window in the second story. It was easy to get to it, because there was a little side porch holding up a roof just beneath it. I curled up on that roof and looked inside. There I found what I wanted!

Yes, it was more than I could have asked for. There were all of my suspicions turned into a lightning flash before my eyes. There was Mrs. Shay and standing before her was that celebrated young man of good breeding, Jeffrey Dinsmore, doing his very best to kiss her. But if he were masterful with men, he was not able to handle this slender girl. She did not speak loudly, of course. Her words hardly carried to me at the window. But what she said was: "None of this, Jeffrey. Not a bit of it."

He stepped back from her. I've seen a man step back like that when a hard punch has been planted under his heart. That was the way Jeffrey Dinsmore stepped away. The pain in his face went along with the rest of the picture. He was a badly confused young man, I should say. That was not what he had expected.

Mrs. Shay was angry, too. She didn't tremble; she didn't change color; she wasn't like any girl I had ever seen before in that way. But one could feel the anger just oozing out of her, so to speak. Jeffrey began to bite his lip.

"I didn't think that you would use me quite so lightly," she said. "I didn't expect that."

He said: "I am a perfect fool. But seeing you only once in weeks and long weeks . . . and thinking of you, and breathing of you like sweet fire all the time I am away . . . why, it went like flame into my brain, just now. I won't ask you to forgive me, though, until you've had a chance to try to understand." He said it quietly, with his eyes fixed at her feet.

While he stood like that, I saw a flash of light in her eyes, and I saw a ghost of a smile look in and out at the corner of her mouth. I knew that she really loved him—or thought she did.

"I ought to have time to think, then," she said. "And I'm afraid that I'll have to use it. I am just a little angry, Jeffrey. I don't want to spoil our few meetings with anger. It's a dusty thing and an unclean thing, don't you think so?"

He kept his head bowed, frowning and saying nothing. This wasn't like any mental picture of him. I thought he would be all fire and passion and lots of eloquence—buckets full of it. Then I saw. He was taking another rôle. He was being terse and very plain—that being the way to impress her, he thought.

"So you'd better go," she said.

He answered: "I'll go outside . . . but I'll wait . . . in the hopes that you'll change your mind."

"Good bye," she said.

I expected him to come for the window. Instead, he opened the door behind him and quickly stepped out into a hall.

I was down from the roof in a moment, and I began to rove around the house, waiting for him to appear. For five or ten minutes I waited. Then I realized that there must be more ways of getting in and out of that house than I had imagined. There might be half a dozen cellar exits and ways of getting from the second story to the cellar. It was a time for fast thinking, and this time I was able to think fast, heaven be praised.

What I did was to swing up to the roof of the porch and get back to the window where I had witnessed this little drama. Mrs. Shay was lying on a couch on the farther side of the room, and her face was buried in a cushion. Her shoulders were quivering a little. However, I had no pity for her, because I was remembering the face of the governor. I simply slid through the window and stood up against the wall. The floor *creaked* a couple of times under my weight.

"Yes?" she said.

I suppose she thought that it was someone at the door, tapping.

"There is no one there," I said.

XIV

"Enemies Face to Face"

Oh, she was game. She didn't jump and squeal, but she looked around slowly at me, fighting herself so hard that, when I saw her eyes, they were as cool as could be. But when she managed to recognize me, she went white in a sickening way, and stood up from the couch, and crowded back into the corner of the room. She said nothing, but she couldn't keep her eyes from flashing to the door.

I said: "I have that door covered, and I'll *keep* it covered. No help is coming to you. You're in here helpless, and you'll do what I tell you to do."

Still she was silent, setting her teeth hard.

I went on: "First of all, I'm going to wait here to make out whether or not Mister Dinsmore was outside and saw me come through the window. If he saw me, I think he's man enough to come after me."

There was a flash of something in her eyes. A sort of assurance, I think, that it would be a bad moment for me when her hero showed up. But still she wouldn't talk. Oh, she was loaded to the brim with courage. She was meeting me with her eyes all the time. I liked her for that. But that was not enough. There was something else for which I hated her. It was boiling in me.

I went on to explain: "When I saw him leave the room, I went down to the yard and tried to find him as he came out of the house. But he must have vanished into a mist."

At that the words came out quickly from her: "Were you watching when he left the room?"

"Yes," I said, and I looked down to the floor, because I didn't care to watch her embarrassment. But, in a moment, I could hear her breathing. It was not a comfortable moment, but, sooner or later, I had to let her understand what I knew.

"And if Mister . . . Dinsmore . . ." she said, and stopped there.

"If he doesn't come back," I said, "I don't know what I'll do . . . yes, I have an idea that might pass pretty well."

So we waited there. That silence began to tell on her and it told on me, too, partly because I was waiting for Dinsmore's step or voice, and partly that just being with that girl in that room was a strain. It was not that she awed me because of the fact that she was the governor's wife, but just because she was a lady, and this was her room, and I had not a right in it. It was full of femininity, that room. It fairly breathed it. From the Japanese screen in the corner to a queer sort of a vase of blue stuck in front of a bit of gold sort of tapestry—if you know what I mean. Well, everything in the room was that way.

When a man fixes up a room, he puts in rugs to walk on— chairs to sit in—a rack to hang something on—a table to get your legs under—and a table that will hold something. Maybe what he puts in happens to be good-looking. Maybe it doesn't. But you can bet your money that it will stand wear, and a lot of it. In a man's room, you can heave yourself at a couch and make sure that you won't go through it and wind up on the floor.

172

But when a girl fixes up a room, you would think that the folks that live on the earth are sort of spirits, maybe, or something like that. You'd figure that a chair didn't have any more weight to bear than somebody's eye turning around the room. You'd figure that paper pictures were as good as canvas, and the older the rug the better. Why a girl all fresh and crisp and dainty should figure that she needs to surround herself with raggy-looking furniture I can't understand, unless it's for the sake of contrast.

Well, I stood in the corner of that room with the ceiling about an inch above my head, and, as I stood there, I was conscious, I'll tell a man, that my feet and legs were bare to the knees from my rolled-up trousers—and I knew that my shirt was rolled up, too, to the elbows—and that my hat was off and that the wind had blown my hair to a heap—and that I was sun-blackened almost to the tint of an Indian. I was a ruffian. And I had a ruffian's reputation. Yonder was the governor's wife looking like the sort of a girl that painters have in their minds when they want to do something extra and knock your eye out.

No, I wasn't extra happy as I stood there, and neither was she. So the pair of us were waiting for the sound of his feet.

Then she said: "Do you think that I'll keep silent when I hear him . . . if he comes?"

"You may do what you want," I said. "But if you make a sound, he won't be the only one that hears." No doubt about it—a gentleman couldn't have said such a thing. Well, a gentleman I cannot pretend to be. I said: "You'll make no noise. You'll sit tight where you are."

She looked quietly up to me and studied me with grave eyes. How cool she was. Yet I suppose that this situation was more terrible to her than a frowning battery of guns pointed in her direction.

"Do you imagine," she said at last, "that I shall permit you to murder him?"

I answered her quickly: "Do you imagine that I wish to murder him?"

Her eyes widened at me.

"I understand," I said. "Dinsmore has filled your mind with the same lies that he has published in other places. It is going to be my pleasure to show you that I am not a sneak and a coward, even if I have to bully you now . . . for a moment."

Then she said: "I almost believe you." She looked me up and down, from my tousled head of hair and my broad, ugly, half-Indian features, to my naked toes gripping at the floor. "Yes," she said, "I do believe you."

It was a great deal to me. It almost filled my heart as much as that first moment when Molly O'Rourke said that she loved me.

"But if he has not seen you? If he is not coming?" Mrs. Shay said.

"Then you will make a signal and bring him here to me."

She shook her head. "What would happen then?"

"You guess what will happen," I responded. "I have no mercy for you. I have seen the governor. I think he is a good man and a kind man."

"He is," she agreed, and dropped her face suddenly in her hands.

"If you will not call Dinsmore back, I shall go to the governor."

"You will not!" she gasped, not looking up.

"I shall."

Then she shook her head. "I have no right for the sake of my own reputation . . . or what. . . ."

"Listen to me," I said, standing suddenly over her so that my shadow swallowed her, "if you speak of rights, have you a

174

right to touch Governor Shay? This thing would kill him, I suppose."

She threw back her head and struck her hands together. Just that, and not a sound from her. But, I knew, that was her surrender. Then she stood up and went to the window, and I saw her raise and lower the shade of the window twice. Then she returned to her place, very white, very sick, and leaned against the wall.

"I'm sorry," I said.

But she made a movement of the hand, disclaiming all my apology. "There will be a death," she said huskily. "No matter what else happens, I shall have caused a death."

"You will not," I said. "Because after two men such as Dinsmore and I have met, we could not exist without another meeting. Will you believe that, and that our second meeting must come and bring a death?"

She cast only one glance at me, and then I suppose that there was enough of the sinister in my appearance to give her the assurance that I meant what I said.

"Because," I went on, "one of us is a cur and a liar. And I hope that heaven shows which one by the fight. You are going to be standing by."

"I!"

"You are going to be standing by," I insisted.

She dropped her head once more with a little gasp, and so the heavy silence returned over us again. It held on through moment after moment. I thought that it would never end. Perspiration began to roll down my forehead. When I looked to the girl, I could see that her whole body was trembling. So was mine, for that matter.

But, at last, no louder than the padding of a cat's foot, we heard something in the hall, and we did not have to ask. It was Dinsmore. As if he had been a great cat, I could not avoid dreading him. I wished myself suddenly a thousand miles from that place.

His tap was barely audible, and the voice of Mrs. Shay was not more than a whisper. The door opened quickly and lightly. And there was Dinsmore standing in the doorway with a face flushed and his eyes making lightnings of happiness until his glance slipped over the bowed figure of the girl and across to me in the corner, dressed like a sailor in a tropical storm. Then he shut the door behind him as softly as he had opened it.

He stood looking from one of us to the other, and there was a fighting set to his handsome face, although the gaiety and the good humor did not go out of it for a moment. I felt, then, that he was invincible. Because I saw that he was a man unlike the rest of the world. He was a man who *loved* danger. It was the food that he ate, and the breath in his nostrils.

He only said: "I thought it was only a social call . . . I didn't know that there was work to be done. But I am very happy, either way."

XV

"The Duel"

Even the *sang-froid* of this demi-devil, however, could not last very long, for, when his lady lifted her face, he saw enough in it to make him grave, and he said to me: "You could not stand and fight, but you could stay to talk, Porfilo."

Then I smiled on this man, for somehow that touch of malice and that lie before the girl gave me a power over him, I felt. So I said to him: "We are going down to the garden, the three of us. The moon is up now, and there will be plenty of light." For the electricity in the room was not strong enough to turn the night black. It was all silvered over with moonshine.

"What's the trick, Porfilo?" said Jeffrey Dinsmore. "Are you going to take me down where you have confederates waiting? Am I to be shot in the back while I face you?"

"Jeffrey!" said his lady under her breath.

It made him jerk up his head. "Do *you* believe this scoundrel?"

Her curiosity seemed even stronger than her fear, for she sat up on the couch and looked from me to Dinsmore and back again to me, weighing us, judging us as well as she was able. "Every moment," she said, "I believe him more and more."

"Will you go down to the garden with us?" he asked. "Will you go down to watch the fight?"

"Leon Porfilo will make me go," she said.

"He and you," said Dinsmore, "seem to have reached a very perfect understanding of one another."

"You will lead the way," I stated.

"Are you commanding?" he said with a sudden snarl, and the devil jumped visibly into his face, so that there was a gasp from the girl.

"As for me," I said, "I had as soon kill you here as in the garden. I am only thinking of the governor's wife."

He bit his lip, turned on his heel, and led the way out of the room. I saw at once what the secret of his goings and comings was. This was a dusty little private hallway—and it connected with what was, apparently, a disused stairway. Perhaps at one time this had been the servants' stairs and then had been blocked off in some alteration of the building. At any rate, it led us winding down to the black heart of the cellar, where I laid a hand on the shoulder of Dinsmore and held him close in front of me with a revolver pressed into the small of his back.

"This is fair play, you murderer," he said.

"Listen to me," I said. "I know you, Dinsmore. Do you think that your lies about me have *convinced* me?" This was only a whisper from either of us, not loud enough to meet the ear of the girl.

We wound out of the cellar and stood suddenly behind the house. There was a very bright moon with a broad face, although not so keen as her light, in the high mountains. Enough to see by, however. Enough to kill by.

"Now," said Dinsmore, turning quickly on me, "how is this thing to be done?" I could see that his hand was trembling to get at his gun. He was killing me with his thoughts every instant. Then he added: "How is this to be done with a poor woman dragged in to watch me kill you."

"I needed her," I said, "to make sure that you would fight like a gentleman. Also, I needed her to see that, when I kill you, I shall kill you in a fair fight. Otherwise, she might have some illusion about it. She might think that her hero had died by treachery and trickery. Besides, I wanted her here because, as the time comes closer, she will have a better chance of seeing that you are a cur or a rat. The devil keeps boiling up in you continually. She has never seen that before."

"Will you step back among the shrubbery?" he said to her.

"If I go," she said, "I shall only be turning my back on something that I ought to see."

"You will see me dispose of a murderer, and that is all."

"If he were a murderer, he could have shot you in the back . . . and the people who heard the sound of the shot would have found you lying dead . . . in my room . . . at night. The governor's wife."

"You remember *him,* now," Dinsmore said, his voice shaken.

"I remember him, now," she said, "and I hope that I have always remembered him a little . . . if not enough."

He clapped his hand across his breast and bowed to her. "Madam," he said, "I see that you are cold."

"Are you spiteful, Jeffrey?"

"Spiteful?" He stepped backward, after that, and he faced me with a convulsed face. I could see, now, why she had been shrinking farther and farther away from him. She was having deep glimpses of the truth about this gentleman of good breeding and of an old family.

"Are you ready, Porfilo?" he said quietly.

"Ah, God, have mercy . . . ," I heard the girl whisper. But I saw that she did not turn her head away. No, not even then.

"Do you know the time?" I asked.

"I do not," answered Dinsmore.

"Do you, Missus Shay?"

"It is nearly ten . . . it is almost the hour."

"I have heard the big town clock," I said. "At the first stroke, then, Dinsmore."

"Good!" he said. "This ought to be in a play. At what distance, my friend?"

"Two steps . . . or twenty," I replied. "You can measure the distance yourself."

"Jeffrey!" cried the poor lady. "It is not going to happen . . . you. . . ."

"It means something one way or the other," I said. "It has to be decided. And there is a witness needed."

Now, as I said this, I looked aside, and I saw, through the shadows of the trees and dimly outlined at the edge of the moonlight, the tall, strong figure of a man. I hardly know how I knew him, but suddenly I saw that it was the governor's self who stood there. It made my heart jump, at first, but instantly I knew that he had not come on the moment. He had been there from the first—or at least for a space of time great enough to have heard enough to explain the entire scene to him. Yet that did not make my nerves the weaker. After all, it was his right to know. I really thanked heaven for it, and that he should realize, if I died in this fight, it was partly for his sake as well as for my own. Or, if the other fell, it was also for his sake as well as for my own.

Then, crashing across my mind, came the *clang* of the town bell, and I snatched at the revolver. It caught in my clothes and only came out with a great ripping noise. I saw the gun flash in the hand of Dinsmore and heard its explosion half drown the scream of Mrs. Shay. But he missed. Almost for the first time in his life, he missed. I saw the horror and the fear dart into his face even before I fired.

He was shot fairly between the eyes, turned on his heel as though to walk away, and fell dead upon his face. The shadow among the shrubs reached him and jerked him upon his back. It was the governor. He did not need to tell me what to do, for I had already scooped up the fainting body of Mrs. Shay and was carrying it toward the house. There, close to the wall, he took her from my arms.

"Ride, Porfilo!" he said. "I shall keep my promise. God be with you!"

But I did not ride. I went back and stood beside the body of the fallen man until the servants came tumbling out of the house and swarmed about me. I tried to get one of them to come to me and take me a prisoner and accept my gun. But they were too afraid. One of them had recognized my face and shouted my name, and that kept the rest away.

At length, one of the secret service men who were presumed to keep a constant guard about the house of the governor came to me and took my gun. Then he marched me down the main street of the town to the jail. A crowd gathered. Perhaps it would have mobbed me, but it heard the great news that the brilliant Dinsmore, the great gunfighter, was dead, and that numbed them.

XVI

"Acquittal"

When the doors of the jail closed behind me, and when I was hitched to irons in my cell, I decided that I had been a fool and that the wild life in the mountains had been better than such an end to it. But when Molly O'Rourke came up from the south land and looked at me through those bars, I changed my mind. After all, it was better to live or to die with clean hands.

I began to discover that I had friends, too. I discovered it partly by the number of the letters that poured in to me. I discovered it partly by the amount of money that was suddenly subscribed to my defense. But I did not want a talented lawyer at a high price. What I felt was that the facts of my life, honestly and plainly written down, would be enough to save me and to free me. I wanted to trust to that. So I had Father McGuire, who had been my guardian up to the time that I broke jail and became an outlaw, and who was one of the first to appear, select a plain, middle-aged man.

He was staggered at the fine fee offered him. He was staggered also by the importance of this case that was being thrust into his hands. So he came to me and sat down in the cell with me and looked at me with mild, frightened eyes, like a good man at a devil. He wanted to assure me that he knew this case would make him a fortune by the notoriety that it would give him. He wanted to assure me that his wife begged him with tears in her eyes to accept the task. But he had come in person to assure me that he was afraid his conscience would not let him take a cause which, he was afraid. . . .

I interrupted him there by asking him to hear my story. It took four hours for the telling, what with his notes and his questions. Before the story was five minutes old, he said that he needed a shorthand reporter. There was no question about him wanting the case after that. He took down that entire report of my life, from my own lips. A very detailed report. I talked for those four hours as fast as I could and turned out words by the thousand. When it was all ended, he said: "I only wish that I could make people see the truth of this, as you have told it to me. But seven years have built up a frightful prejudice."

"Give it to the newspapers," I told him.

He was staggered by that, at first. To give away his case into the hands of the prosecution? But I told him that I would swear to every separate fact in that statement. So, finally, he did what I wanted, and against his will.

I suppose you have seen that statement, or at least heard of it. The editor of the local paper came to see me and begged me for a little intimate personal story to lead off with—an interview. I asked him if he were the man who wrote up the statement of Dinsmore. He said that he was, and apologized, and told me that he realized since I had beaten and killed Dinsmore in a fair fight, that there was nothing in what Dinsmore had said. He begged me to give him a chance at writing a refutation. Well, I simply told him at once that he did not need to ask twice. He was the right man in the right place, and I told him to do his editorial best to give me journalistic "justice".

He did. He began with the beginning and he finished with the end. He made me into a hero, a giant, almost a saint. I laughed until there were tears in my eyes when I read that story. Molly O'Rourke came and cried over it in real earnest and vowed that it was only the truth about me.

However, the editor was a great man, in his own way. He didn't really lie. He simply put little margins of embroidery around the truth. Although sometimes the margins were so deep that no one could see the whole cloth for the center. That great write-up he gave me saved my skin, at the trial.

But while the trial was half finished, another bolt fell from the blue when the governor announced that, no matter what the jury did, he intended to give me a pardon after the trial was over. From that point I had the governor's weight of authority so heavily telling in my favor that the trial became a sort of triumphal procession for me. There was no real struggle, for public opinion had begun to heroize me in the most foolish way in the world. I was still a prisoner when people began to ask for autographs, and I was still in jail when a boy scout came in to have my name written on the butt of an air rifle.

You know how it goes when the newspapers once decide to let a man live. The jury itself would probably have been lynched if it had so much as decided to divide on my case. They were only out for five minutes. When they brought in a verdict of acquittal, the real joke about that matter was that they were right and not simply sentimental, because, as I think you people will agree who have followed my history down to this point, I had not as yet committed a real crime. The cards had simply been stacked against me.

Three great factors fought in my behalf—the governor's word first—the honesty of my stupid lawyer—and the genius of that crooked editor. I don't know which was the more important. But what affected me more than the acquittal was the face of Molly O'Rourke in the crowd that cheered the verdict.

Peter Blue, One-Gun Man

Although the majority of Frederick Faust's Western stories were published in Street & Smith's *Western Story Magazine*, "Peter Blue, One-Gun Man" appeared in Street & Smith's *Far West Illustrated*, in the issue dated June, 1927. Two of Faust's serials for that year were also published in *Far West Illustrated*. It was Faust's intention for the story to be titled "Barnegat, Barnegat", after the song sung by various characters, but it was changed by the magazine to the name of the story's protagonist, Peter Blue, the infamous gunman. The storyline reflects one of Faust's favorite themes, the redeemed outlaw.

I

In every sunny day, there is one golden moment which lasts just long enough to fill a man's heart. One cannot find the proper instant on the clock, and it will never come at all if one remains indoors, but, if you go out in the late afternoon with no purpose except to live and breathe and see, certainly with no expectation of magic, the golden moment will come upon you by surprise. It may be any instant after the sun has lost its burning force, when it may be looked on without blindness in the west, and it will be before the face of the sun turns red and his cheeks are blown out as he enters the horizon mists. It may be that you walk through the town and suddenly come on a street down which flows a river of yellow glory, and then one cannot help turning toward the light, for it seems a probable thing that heaven lies at the end of that street, and, if one hurries a little, one may pass through the open gates.

It was not through the narrow vista of any street that Sheriff Newton Dunkirk and his daughter saw the perfect moment on this day. They had before them the great bald sweep of the Chirrimunk Hills—to what lofty spirits of the old days were those grand summits merely hills?—and, as their horses cantered on around a bend, suddenly they saw the Chirrimunk River running gold, and all the west before them was blended with golden haze, and above the haze was a golden sun hanging out of a dark blue sky.

Horses can understand, I think, and that pair of mustangs slowed to a walk that there might be no disturbing creak of saddle leather or clatter of hoofs, while father and daughter lifted their heads and smiled first at the beauty of this world and then at one another as their hearts overflowed.

But when the mustangs had climbed to the top of the next rise, the golden moment had passed. There was lavender, green, and rolling fire in the west; the sun was half in shadow and half in flames. But the magic was gone, and Sheriff Dunkirk looked across the foothills and pointed.

"Who's in the Truman shack?" he asked.

"Nick and August, perhaps," said Mary Dunkirk. "They live there when they're trapping along the river, you know."

"It ain't time for Nick and August," the sheriff contradicted. "It's some tramp, more likely. I'll have a look."

Mary, with a shadow in her eyes, looked again at the smoke that lolled out of the crooked smokestack above the Truman shanty. All manner of danger to her father might wait under that sign of habitation, but she had learned her lesson long ago and never allowed her protests to reach her lips. The folly of her mother had taught her this wisdom.

She caught the reins that Dunkirk threw to her as he dismounted near the hut, and, as her father neared the shack, she saw a tall man step into the doorway, but whether he were young or old she could not guess, only by the darkness of his face she knew that he was long unshaven. She saw her father pause to speak, then pass inside, and the doorway was left black and empty. Perhaps he never would come out again alive—and only a moment before they had been so happy.

Inside the shack the sheriff was saying: "I'm Sheriff Dunkirk of this county. What's your name, stranger?"

"My name is Tom Morris."

"Ah! Are you Tom Morris from over Lindsay way?"

"Did you know him?"

"Did I? Well, that's right . . . he died last year. And what are you doing here, Morris?"

"I'm looking around."

"For what? Work? There's plenty on the range. Old man Bristol wants hands. I know he needs two 'punchers. Have you tried him?"

"No," the tall man said slowly. "I haven't tried him."

"And you don't expect to?" suggested the sheriff curtly. His eyes wandered around the shack, touched on the patched and sagging stove, and the table that was kept on its feet by being wedged tightly into a corner. "No traps," resumed the sheriff. "Not a trapper, then. You're only looking? Enjoying the view, I suppose?"

A horse snorted in the adjoining shed, and Dunkirk pushed open the connecting door. He saw two blood horses, big, magnificently made, that threw up their heads and stared at him with a childish brightness. One was a deep bay, and one a black chestnut with a long white stocking on the near foreleg.

The sheriff whirled sharply around, a frightened but determined man.

"You're Peter Blue!" he said. "You're Peter Blue, and that's your horse Christopher . . . that black one."

"Not black," corrected Peter Blue. "Black chestnut. Step in and look at him more closely, if you wish. Then you'll see the leopard dapplings."

The sheriff looked into the inscrutable eyes of Peter Blue and remembered that the horse shed was very narrow and crowded, and the arms of Peter Blue were very long. He shook his head with decision. "I've seen enough," he said. "We don't want you in this county and we won't have you, Blue. You needn't talk. I know you."

"Very well," said the other patiently. "Tell me first what law I have broken?"

"Law? I understand. You're a slick operator, Blue, and you've never done anything wrong in your life . . . only had to defend yourself quite often. But I can find the law to fit you. Vagrancy. We have a vagrancy ruling in this county, and I enforce it when it needs enforcing. Is that clear?"

"Dunkirk," Peter Blue said, "I've heard that you're a straight man and a fair man. I intend to make no trouble here, but I want a few weeks of quiet."

"You've always wanted quiet," said the sheriff. "I've known a good many of your kind and they've always wanted peace and rest, but trouble comes and hunts them out, at last. Come, come, man. I've spent years in this county and those years have turned me gray . . . you're not talking to a fool. I'll be riding this way tomorrow, and I'll expect to find the Truman shanty vacant. That's final." He paused in the doorway. "I'd like to know a thing, though. You're a smart fellow, Blue, whatever else they may say about you. Then why the devil don't you drop your horse, Christopher, and get another just as good? You're always spotted through that nag. Is he your good luck, maybe?"

"No," Peter Blue replied, touching the holstered gun on his hip. "He's not my good luck, but I keep him because there would be a difference between Christopher and another just as good."

"Yes," said the sheriff grimly. "It would be hard for any man to get away from that long-legged devil, I suppose."

"Or," the other picked up, "to put it another way, it would be hard for a man to catch that long-legged devil. Besides, Christopher was made for the bearing of burdens . . . and I'm a heavyweight, as you can see for yourself." As he said this, his eyes seemed deeper and darker than ever, and the sheriff frowned.

"You're mocking me, somehow, Mister Blue," Dunkirk declared, "but that don't bother me. All I want is to see this shack empty tomorrow. So long. But wait a minute. If you wanted to sell that Christopher, I might find you a buyer. Would you sell him?"

"Oh, yes," said Peter Blue. "I'd sell him, of course. But," he added rather dreamily, "not for money. No, no, not for money."

"For what, then?"

"I don't want to keep you here too long," said Peter Blue.

The sheriff frowned again, hesitated again, and his face lighted beautifully. "I understand," he said. "You love 'im, eh? Well, so long, and good luck to you, Blue."

He held out his hand and the other made a gesture to meet it, but the sheriff stepped back with a little muttered oath.

"I've never taken the left hand of a man in my life," he said, "and I don't intend to begin with you, my friend." So saying, he backed slowly down the steps, and into the path, and walked sidling toward his horse, looking back. He even kept his eye on the blank doorway while he was mounting, and, as he spurred away, Mary saw him shudder strongly, like a child who has escaped from darkness into the light of another room.

"What is it, Dad?"

"I don't know," murmured the sheriff. "Nothing, I guess."

She was glad to change the subject by pointing toward a meadow near the river edge, where an old man held the staggering handles of a plow that was drawn slowly by two oxen.

"There's Uncle Harry. He puts in a long day, doesn't he? Poor old man." She added: "Who takes care of him?"

The sheriff turned a little and cast another glance down the road, as though to make sure that he was not being followed. Then he answered rather briefly: "Uncle Harry? Those old codgers don't need care. The more they wither up, the tougher they get."

The oxen were drawing their furrow up the hill, and the sheriff drew rein a moment to await the plowman. For, after all, men never are too old to vote. But Uncle Harry turned the corner of his land with deliberation before he stopped his team and saluted the two with a formal lifting of his hat. His long white hair flashed in the evening light.

"How are you, Uncle Harry?"

"Never no better, folks. And how's yourself?"

"What do you hear from Judy and Dick?"

"Well, you and Judy was right fond of each other, Mary, wasn't you? I got a letter from her last month. Her boy has had the chicken pox, but they're getting on pretty good. I ain't heard from Dick for a spell. Not since he headed for Utah."

"Why, Uncle Harry, wasn't that six months ago?"

"Let the young 'uns rove and ramble, and, when they get slowed up a mite, then they'll remember the old 'uns, I always say."

"Dear Uncle Harry, you never come over any more."

"Well, honey, when I go to your place now, I miss your grandpa a tolerable lot. I dunno but your front porch looks sort of empty without him setting there with his pipe."

"I'm going to bake you a big mince pie, one of these days, and bring it over."

"You jes' bring yourself, dearie, and don't you bother about no pie!"

They turned their horses down the road again, for it was growing late, and, glancing back to Uncle Harry, the girl saw him reeling at the handles of the plow as he ran furrow.

"Poor old fellow! How does he manage?"

"Don't you go getting sad about him, Mary. Those old ones, they don't have the same feelings young folks do. When they sit quiet, they ain't thinking so deep as you guess. They ain't thinking at all. When they smoke their pipe, all they're seein' is the white curling of the smoke. They get like babies."

"I wonder," said the girl.

II

In the Truman shanty, as the sheriff rode away, Peter Blue went back to his interrupted work. At that rickety corner table, on which the last western light was falling, he placed a little square mirror against the wall and sat down before it with a paper and pencil. He began to write with intensely knitted brows, and there was reason for his clumsiness, for he was looking not at the paper but into the mirror, guiding his pencil by the image that he saw. What made the matter worse was that he was using his left hand. He worked until the sweat stood on his forehead, and he stopped only when the fading light made the image in the mirror a blur.

Even though he knew what the sentence should be, he could hardly decipher this crazy scrawling: **The quick red fox jumps over the lazy brown dog. The quick red fox jumps over the lazy. . . .**

Then, with an impatient exclamation, he shifted the pencil to his right hand and attempted to write. He made but a single stroke, a wobbling, jerking, unmanageable stroke that ran off the side of the paper, and, with that effort at nervous concentration, his entire right arm began to quiver and jump. He dropped the pencil with a faint exclamation and with his left hand gripped the other wrist hard as though by sheer strength he would crush the senselessness out of his right hand and restore its old cunning.

However, it was only the petulance of a moment, which he mastered with a grim effort and went to the door to breathe the crisp night air. He could see the blurred outlines of two oxen and a man coming up from the river toward another shack, not half a mile away, and Blue sighed and turned thoughtful. For in the old days he would have scorned a spirit so pedestrian that it enabled a man to work at the plow behind oxen from dawn to dark. He felt no scorn now, but only a profound, sick envy of all in this world who suffered under a lesser curse than that which weighed him down.

A rabbit, bound home for the warren late, scampered across the trail—a tidy bit of fresh meat for his supper—and the old instinct made him sweep the Colt from its holster. It came clear of the leather, but slipped through his nerveless fingers and crashed upon the floor; the frightened rabbit turned into a dim streak across the field. It was a moment before he picked up the gun—with his left hand, and, reaching clumsily across his body, he dropped the weapon back in its sheath, but he remained a little longer leaning against the doorjamb, for a deeper darkness than that of the night was spinning across his brain.

At length, however, he went to the stove and made a great rattling in shaking down the ashes and freshening the fire, for the blaze was cheerful and gave him heart to fry bacon for his supper, boil strong coffee, and complete his meal with heavy, soggy pone. After that, all of the evening was before him, and he prepared for it by taking a candle from the pack that lay open on the floor and lighting it so that he could resume his work.

But before he began, he opened again the little book that he had read so many times before. The leaves parted at a well-thumbed place, and he read: . . . **but the chief requirement is great patience, endless patience. From the cradle a man lives by his right hand. It wields the hammer, draws the knife, strikes the blow, swings the racket, and above all it performs the cunning intricacies of writing. Man's forceful gestures are made with his right hand; by his right hand he lives; and by it we may almost say that he thinks, for thought, after all, is sometimes executed by the mechanical movements of the body, and sometimes it is inspired by the sense of physical power and craft. Therefore, it is apparent that he who has performed the most delicate work will be robbed most vitally by the loss of the right hand, and, although it is the purpose of this book to teach the series of mechanical exercises through which the left hand may be taught to do the work of the right, nevertheless, in all honesty, it must be confessed that in the end something may be lacking. One may learn to work with the left** hand, to write with it, etc. But the cabinetmaker, the draftsman, and others will find it difficult to *think* with the left hand, as they have been accustomed to think with the right. But for rougher labor, and for those whose livelihood does not depend upon a delicate craft of hand. . . .

Peter Blue raised his eyes from the book. Not his livelihood, but his life was concerned, and the book said nothing of such men as he. Then, as his habit was, he laid on the table before him his naked Colt, picked up the pencil, and returned to the dreary labor of forcing his hand to trail out the letters by staring at the image in the mirror.

His attention began to flag. He had worked many long hours this day, and now in spite of himself his thoughts began to slip away into dreams—right-handed dreams. He saw himself as he had been before that fatal bullet tore through his right forearm, and, whether with cards or dice or guns, it was always his right hand that played and always the right hand that won. It had made him famous up and down the range, that good right hand. He had the fame still. The awe of other men surrounded him wherever he went, but he no longer had the skill to maintain his reputation. The day must come when he would be challenged by the friend of some enemy of the old days, and, when that challenge came, he must go down unless he could transfer to this childish, awkward, blundering, laggard left hand a moiety of the skill that had lived in its mate. He was almost tempted to let the world know the truth, that the old Peter Blue was dead. But he knew that the instant his weakness was revealed, there would be a host of bullies and cowards to find and kill. So one of them might wrap himself in the ghost of a reputation.

Who was it, in the end, that would be able to say: "I killed Peter Blue!" Would it be some gay cavalier of the range, bent on adventure? Would it be some swelling braggart and bad-man? Would it be some cool-headed old fox? He had known many of all these kinds, and now he let their portraits pace swiftly across the eye of his mind.

A rising of the wind called him out of his musings. He found the room was cold, and, when he went to the open door, he saw the night sky was crystal clear, so flooded with moonlight that only a scattering of stars showed faint and small. The Chirrimunk curved through the hollow in a broad sweep of polished silver with the trees along its banks raising their dark heads against the brightness.

On such a night as this he had stood under a certain window in Juárez and played his guitar and sang. . . . Was there music in a left hand? On such a night as this, he and Christopher had descended upon Lindley Crossing. . . .

He went hastily into the shed, and the two horses stood up in the darkness and whinnied anxiously to him and reached for him with their soft muzzles. He took Christo-pher into the open and threw a saddle on his back, and on the back of the stallion he was almost a king again. The wind of that wild gallop blew some of his melancholy away, and so he came past the neighboring shack with a sweep and a rush.

A little distance past it, he reined in and looked back. No smoke rose from the chimney into the glistening moonlight, and yet the night was so cold that his gloved fingers were turning numb on the reins. One faint light had been burning in the cabin, which proved that the dweller was in the place. Then why not a fire?

That small thing turned Peter Blue back. He left Christo-pher with thrown reins fifty yards from the cabin and went to investigate. Not a sound, not a sound from within, so he knocked at the door.

The voice of an old man called: "Hey, hey, who's there?"

Peter Blue pushed the door open and looked in at a neat little one-room cabin, swept and dusted with a scrupulous care, and all in good order. On the table stood a lantern, turned low, and near it were scattered a few fragments of hardtack, and a tin cup half filled with . . . water. No soiled pans stood on the stove. Yonder on the table lay the remains of the supper that had been eaten in this shack. All these details were seen in a single flicking glance that steadied on the old man, who sat by the table with a blanket huddled around his shoulders. In spite of that, his lean face was lined and shadowed with the blue of cold. Yet he smiled at Peter Blue.

"Come in, stranger," he said. "Come in and rest yourself. You're in the Truman house, I reckon?"

"How did you guess that?" asked Peter Blue.

"Well, when you get old, you get long-distance eyes. Your hand may miss its hold on something right under your nose, but far off things you can see pretty well, y'understand? Besides," he added with a deliberate and admiring survey, "it ain't so many that have your outline ag'in' the sky, even a half mile off. Sit down, won't you?"

Peter Blue sat down.

"Sheriff Dunkirk knows you, don't he? I seen him stop at the Truman house for quite a spell this evening. Now I ask you, ain't he an honest man . . . young Newt Dunkirk? But you know him, don't you?"

"Yes. I know him."

"He's give us a quiet county," said the old man. "There ain't been a man stuck up or a gunfight for close onto six months now. By the way, what might your name be?"

"My name," said the visitor, looking instantly at Uncle Harry, "is Peter Blue."

The other started and blinked at his guest.

"Peter Blue? Peter Blue?" he said. "I know that name . . .
somehow . . . I've met up with it somewhere. It's streaked
across my mind sometime as bright as lightning. But I
disremember. When your eyes get long distance, your
memory gets long distance, too. The nearby things, you
fumble at them and forget them, and they slip through your
fingers like your brain was numb with cold. But the far away
things . . . you see them like looking through the small end of
a field glass . . . small but clear. All drawed together with distance. So's you can hold ten of the old years in the palm of
your hand and talk about 'em. And if I'd known you in those
times, I sort of reckon that you would have been pretty big in
my eye. Reach yourself that jug behind the door, will you? It's
old stuff. Good, too. The pure quill. Help yourself, Mister
Blue . . . it's a mighty cold night!"

III

Peter Blue took the big earthenware jug and tilted it to his
lips by bending it over the crook of his left arm. As he put
it down—"Left-handed, and what a hand!"—said the old
man. "Marty McVey, he was left-handed. And even Marty
couldn't have handled that jug more easy."

"Will you have some? You haven't told me your
name."

"I won't have any, thank you. I'm Uncle Harry Barnes. I
only keep that liquor for friends, when they drop in. But me
. . . it addles my head and sets it singing . . . plumb foolish.
Hold on, have you had your supper?"

"Have you had yours?" asked Peter Blue.

"Oh, yes. My stummick was a-ragin' lion, once. Oh, I

could eat for two. But the lion has turned into a lamb. A few crackers do me as good as a steak and onions, just. Which is an advantage of bein' withered up and light, like I am now. But at your age, I was always hungry."

"I've had my supper," said the younger man. "But I can see that you're able to save a pretty penny, working your farm, and living so carefully. The bank must be glad to have your account."

"There's my bank." Uncle Harry laughed, pointing to an old boot that hung on the wall. "I turn my money into silver and dump it into that old boot. As long as there's money in the heel of it, I know that I can get through the winter easy. But when I got to reach into the toe, then I know that I'm getting low. But having my coin in the boot bests a bank all hollow. It's more fun."

"Yes." Peter Blue nodded. "But sometimes your silver must overflow from the boot. When you get the crop from that piece of land by the Chirrimunk, for instance. . . ."

"If it was all for me, yes. But my girl Judy didn't marry money, and I have to help them along."

"Her husband is sick, perhaps," suggested Peter Blue.

"Not him. But he's young, and one of the boys. Pay day means a party to him. But what's a grandfather good for? If I didn't have my Judy to work for, I might settle down to trapping and hunting, same as Nick and August. Just plain lazy. You look cold, Peter Blue. Wait a jiffy while I fix up a fire."

"Not for me."

"Are you sure now?"

"Yes, I'm warm enough. But I might say you look a little chilly yourself, Uncle Harry."

"Do I, now? Cold is good for an old man. I've seen some huggin' the fire and drowzin', but I say . . . live like a man, and

198

not like a house cat. Besides, I got to save my strength. Time was when I thought nothing of laying in a store of wood and everything needful. But now it's different, and I got to put in my handwork where it will count most. Suppose I was to build the most ragingest fire that ever you seen. Would it warm Judy and her children away off beyond the mountains? But the work that I use in that ground, it comes back to me in dollars, and dollars put a fire in Judy's stove, and pays the doctor, and helps for clothes, and such. Here, son, you ain't sat down. By the Lord, you *are* cold. Here . . . I'll start a fire snorting. . . ."

"Let me do it," said Peter Blue. "You sit quiet."

He went out to his horse and galloped back to the Truman shack. There he took bacon, coffee, and pone and returned to the other house. In the moonlight, he saw the axe by the pile of lot wood, and he dismounted there and commenced to labor mightily. They were awkward strokes that seldom found the mark, but even in the left hand of Peter Blue there was more power than in all the body of most men. Presently he carried a vast armful into the shack.

"Ha!" cried the old man. "That was what the ringin' of that axe meant, then? No, no, Peter Blue. You keep that wood for yourself in your own shack. If you're in my house, you got to burn my wood. Why, what would folks be sayin' of me? Man, man, drop that wood right there. . . ." He started from his chair, filled with excitement and trouble, but Peter pushed him firmly back.

"Now, you keep in your place, Uncle Harry. Tush! You think only of yourself."

"Now what might you mean by that?" Uncle Harry asked coldly.

"You'd have me strip the clothes off the backs of Judy's children, and take the food out of their mouths. Not a bit of

199

it. Sit there . . . and watch this fire roar, will you?"

Roar it did, in another moment, with all the drafts open and the flame hurtling up the chimney in such masses that the whole shack trembled a little. A glow crept across the cabin and the pain left the face of the old man. Then the sizzling of bacon sang in his ears.

"Hold on, Peter Blue!" he cried. "Lord, Lord, what are you doin', man, to shame me? Cookin' your own food in my house?"

"Did you ask me to supper?" Peter Blue said.

"Yes, yes, lad."

"Is there a bit of bacon in this house?"

"I could fix you up . . . ," began Uncle Harry.

"Tush!" said Peter Blue. "You've asked me to supper, and here I am. It's my right to bring what I want."

"It's wrong," said Uncle Harry, grasping futilely at the great shoulder of his guest, rubbery with muscles. But then the delicate fragrance of coffee reached the nostrils of the old man and he sighed and shook his head. "It ain't hospitality, Peter," he said.

"No," Peter Blue said, "it's food and friendship. Shall I eat bacon up there in my lonely shack? And you stay down here and eat crackers in yours? Nonsense! You're an old, wise, and dangerously crafty man, Uncle Harry, but you can't drift me against the wind like that."

"Besides," said the other, "you've ate already, Peter."

"I? I haven't touched a thing since morning."

"You was lying, then?"

"Smaller lies than some you've been telling. Sit down at that table and look some of this pone and bacon in the face . . . and here's the coffee."

"I got no appetite," said Uncle Harry. "I've ate already."

"Like a parrot or a hen," said Peter Blue. "But now you

can eat like a man."

"Son," said the veteran, "it's kind of you, but enough is enough, and I can't touch a bite. Lord, Lord! Your food and in my own house."

The forefinger of the giant leveled like a gun. "Then," he said, "I'll write to Judy and tell her that you're starving yourself to put clothes on the backs of her youngsters."

"Not that, Peter! You wouldn't be doing that. Then I see you're going to bully me into it, so I'll take a mite."

They faced one another at the table, and presently, as he ate, the eyes of the old man were going up and down, from the loaded plate to the face of his guest. "Ah, Peter," he said, "you're a good lad."

"If you won't eat any more," said Peter, "why not tune up that old guitar and give me a song while I do the dishes?"

"Me sing? My throat has forgot all my songs, boy. The singin' muscles have forgot their business complete." But he picked up the guitar. "What shall it be?"

"You know McVey?"

"Yes."

"Sing that one of McVey's fight with Barnegat."

"Lemme think. Now I remember. Hey . . . how it rolls back the years!" He leaned back in his chair, his eyes closed, a smile on his lips, and he sang in an infirm but pleasant tenor voice:

> **Barnegat, Barnegat, belt on your gun,**
> **For Marty McVey is a-comin',**
> **He's ridin' to hell or to heaven for fun**
> **And the wind in his hair is hummin'.**

The bass of Peter Blue, softened that it might not drown the leader, chimed in with the chorus:

Marty McVey, Marty, McVey,
Barnegat's gun will talk today.
Barnegat, Barnegat, gimme your hand,
For he's galloping up the river.
Barnegat, Barnegat, take your stand,
For I feel the ground a-quiver.

Marty McVey, Marty McVey,
Barnegat's gun will talk today.
Barnegat, Barnegat, that's my name,
And who the hell are you, sir?
Barnegat, Barnegat, you're to blame
When I. . . .

The voice of the singer died away.

"Go on, Uncle Harry."

"It's clean popped out of my mind."

"Wait a minute and it'll pop in again."

"No, not tonight. You can't force an old man's mind. It's like a young horse. Whipping only makes it balk all the more. Now, I could tell you about that fight, though."

"The devil you could! You've heard about it?"

"I saw it."

"The fight between Barnegat and McVey? I thought it was only a story."

"No, sir. I seen McVey come ragin' into the town with the wind blowin' through his long, bright hair. And I seen Barnegat take his stand in the middle of the street, with a gun in each hand. McVey had a big Colt poised with its nose in the air, and he rode straight down the street. Barnegat, he dropped one gun level and fired, but McVey come right on. Barnegat dropped his other gun level and fired, but still McVey galloped at him with his own Colt hanging in the air,

202

ready to shoot. Barnegat was a crack shot, y'understand? But I suppose that shooting at McVey was too much for him. It whittled the manhood out of him. He give a yell, dropped his guns, and turned and ran for it. McVey rode right on down that street, just laughing. Seems McVey had bet that he would make Barnegat run without firing a shot. One of them two bullets slipped right straight through the body of McVey, but that didn't keep him from laughing. He'd won his bet."

"Ah," Peter Blue said, his head raised and a smile on his lips, "there was a man, that McVey."

"Not a man, but a lion. They don't make his kind any more. Big and foolish, and simple and wild, and kind and cruel . . . they don't make his kind any more." Here his eyes narrowed at the younger man and he added thoughtfully: "Except now and then, maybe."

IV

The sheriff had two guns newly oiled and freshly loaded when he walked up to the door of the Truman shack the next day. In the doorway he paused to look in at big Peter Blue, who was seated studiously at a table, facing a little mirror, with a gun before him. The sheriff paused abruptly. In such a mirror, so placed, Peter Blue might be able to see the open doorway. At his hand lay the ready revolver. For such a trickster with weapons, such an uncanny marksman, would think nothing of snatching up his Colt and taking a snap shot over his shoulder.

The sheriff forgot his own two guns. "You're still here, Blue?" he said.

The other turned sidling in his chair. "Still here, Sheriff. Have they traced any rustled cows my way, as yet?"

"Set and grin," said the sheriff coldly. "This day is your trick, because I ain't going to arrest you. I'm here in this county to enforce the law, and not to commit suicide. But I'm coming back with enough to handle you. Mark that, Blue."

He backed away, regained his horse, and galloped for the town. A little shame mixed with his anger, and, accordingly, his horse dripped with black sweat before Dunkirk gained the town. Then he let his mustang fall into a dog-trot that dusted him and his rider with white. The sheriff took no heed of a little dirt, however, for, as he jogged the horse down the long, winding main street, his glances were busy prying at the houses on either side and making mental notes.

He wanted picked men. He could have a hundred rough-and-ready riders, rough-and-ready fighters, in five minutes, but what chance would they have on the trail of Peter Blue and Christopher? No, for such work as this he needed the finest horses and the keenest men, so he dismissed the inhabitants of each house as he swept by. In front of the hotel he drew rein, for here he must find someone.

Suddenly he cried out and waved a violent hand. For he saw a tall man leaning against one of the wooden pillars, rolling a cigarette—a tall man with nobly developed shoulders and a long pair of sandy mustaches, grown after an outworn fashion. "Livernash! Livernash!" he called. He fairly flung himself from his horse and ran to the hotel steps. There he checked himself under the stare of a pair of cold blue eyes.

"What's on me?" Livernash asked calmly. "What you want of me, Dunkirk?"

The sheriff laughed. "You're wrong this time, Steve," he said. "I want to use you, not to jail you."

Livernash breathed a long sigh. "Have the makings," he proffered kindly.

"I'm talking, not smoking, Steve. I'll finish the job today," he continued rather wildly. "God or the devil must have planted you on this porch just in time for me." He added abruptly: "Is that your horse?" He pointed to a down-headed mustang that stood in front of the porch near the watering trough.

"That's mine," Livernash said, nodding.

"Not good enough. Not half good enough," said the sheriff. "But you can have the pick of my string. For this job, it will be more important to mount you well than to have me on a racer."

"And what's the game?" Livernash asked.

"I'll tell you later. Wait here. I want to collect half a dozen more. Be back here in a few minutes. . . ."

"I ain't making a long stop," Livernash advised. "I got important business. You better tell me now."

"No matter what your business is, it's not as important as this."

"What's important to you and me might be a speck different, Dunkirk."

"Today, my business is yours. Trust me for that."

He started down the hotel steps but Livernash called: "Sorry, Sheriff! I can't wait. My job is pressing."

So Dunkirk unwillingly turned and frowned at this interruption. "Every minute that you hold up the posse," he said, "the rascal will be putting miles behind him. I give you my word that you want to do this job even more than I do, Steve."

"Who is it, then?"

"The first man in my life that I didn't try to arrest single-handed," said the sheriff. "Told him yesterday to leave the county. Came back today and found him in the same place . . . and he simply smiled at me, but I swallowed that and came to town." He repeated what he had said before on this day: "I'm here on the range to enforce the law, not to commit suicide."

"Ah," Livernash said, more and more interested, "I got a funny idea that maybe your trail is mine, old-timer."

"I tell you it is! Take my word for it. How many times have you fought, Livernash? Never mind. I know. And you were beaten only once."

"Wait, wait," said the tall man. "I know the time you mean. Ain't the whole world been grinding that one time in on me? But I swear to God that what beat me was a new gun. I hadn't had a chance to file off the sights. And it stuck in the leather . . . it stuck in the leather. I didn't even fill my hand that day."

"I believe it," said the sheriff, "and I know that you want to get at Blue again."

"Want it?" Livernash said, drawing in his breath as though the air were wine. "Want it? I'll tell a man I want it, Dunkirk."

"You'll have your chance, then, if our horses can bring us up with him today. That's why I don't want to waste any more time. I'll round up a party in ten minutes, Steve, and. . . ."

A long arm shot out and a lean-fingered hand fell on the shoulder of the sheriff.

"Us?" he said. "Party?" he echoed.

"To get Pete Blue."

"No, old-timer. Not me. I'm not in no party to get Peter Blue."

At this, Dunkirk bit his lip. "That other time made you a little down-hearted, Steve," he suggested coldly. "But I thought that just now you was raving to get at him."

"Not with a posse," said the other. "What posse did Blue have behind him when he dropped me that day in Juárez?"

"Ah," said the sheriff, able to smile suddenly. "You mean you want to play a lone hand?"

Livernash brushed his long mustaches with painful care

and then spoke with deliberation. "Five months ago I started north," he said. "I missed him by a week in Phoenix." He checked off the item on one finger. "I was two weeks behind him at the Colorado. He left Carson one day before me. But then he put on one of his damned bursts of speed and I was eight days late at Butte. I bought two new horses and twisted back south on his heels. I dodged him into Idaho and back to Montana. I trailed him to Kansas City when he took a fling East. I doubled back on his heels, one train late, and nearly nailed him in Denver. Then two weeks out in the mountains. I had him in the circle of my glass once when he was going up one divide while I was on the top of the next one. I was out of range. Damned if that didn't near break my heart. Then I came down here, and you tell me that he's in reach. And you want me to join up with a posse . . . a posse!" He parted his mustaches and spat far into the street.

The sheriff, in the meantime, had grown darkly thoughtful. "I know you, Steve," he said. "I got a lot of trust and faith in you."

"Leave that be," interrupted Livernash harshly, "and tell me where this hound might be."

"Just a moment, Steve. I say that I have a load of faith in you. But now we're talking about Peter Blue."

"Bullets won't sink into him, maybe?" Livernash asked with a sneer.

"Sometimes these fellows don't like to face the same man twice," declared Dunkirk. "If you've followed him so long . . . why, man, it almost looks as though he was running away, doesn't it?"

"Running away? If I knowed that he was in front of me, didn't he know that I was behind him? Why did he slide from Carson to Montana as fast as those long-legged horses of his could snake him along?"

"I never heard of fear in Peter Blue," declared the sheriff thoughtfully.

"There ain't any use for talk," Livernash said. "Lemme do something besides wag my jaw, will you? Where does he camp?"

Dunkirk made up his mind. "After all," he admitted, "he would run away from more than one or two. And if he ran, what can catch Christopher? Follow this road straight out of town. Never leave it. When you cross the first creek, there's a big trail bearing to the left. Don't take it. Head straight, leaning always toward the river, when you're in doubt. Finally you'll come in sight of the Truman shack, standing on a hill, without no trees around it . . . so's he can keep on watching the road, I suppose. You'll find him there, living quiet and studying up some sort of hell-fire. So long, Livernash. Good luck to you and. . . ."

He let his words die away, for Steve Livernash had flung himself on the back of his mustang and rushed down the street. He disappeared; the muffled beat of hoofs trailed rapidly into a faint pulse of sound and a great cloud of dust floated in the windless air.

"It's wrong! It's wrong!" the sheriff cried suddenly, as his second thought came strongly home to him. He hurried to his own pony and was about to put foot in the stirrup when he saw the beaten condition of the mustang. Before he could change mounts, Livernash would be far out of reach. So Sheriff Dunkirk came wearily back toward the verandah steps. "Maybe he'll have the luck, though," said the sheriff. "You never can tell. Sooner or later they all get theirs. Sooner or later the greatest of 'em go down." He sank into a chair and tilted it back against the wall of the hotel, but although his body was at rest, his brow was still furrowed. "Hey, Dunkirk,"—came a voice from the hotel door—"have you heard about Christy's new house he's gonna build?"

"But not Peter Blue," said the sheriff.

"What's that?"

Dunkirk pushed a hand across his knotted forehead. "Don't talk, man. My brain's overcrowded now!"

V

It was not more than an hour after the sheriff brought his warning to Peter Blue that his daughter rode on the same trail, but with a different destination, for she turned in at the shack of the old man which, as has been said, stood about half a mile from the Truman house.

There she found Uncle Harry busily sweeping out the cabin with a broom made of a thick twist of straw fastened on a stick. Some dried apples were stewing on the stove and filling the place with a delicate fragrance as though a sort of faded spring had been restored to the world. Uncle Harry's pipe was in his teeth, however, and he was puffing forth clouds of strong tobacco smoke that usually drowned the perfume of the fruit entirely. Through the back door of the cabin, the girl saw a deer hung up on the branch of a tree.

"Ah, Uncle Harry," she said, "what a jolly place you keep here, and you have everything so comfortable that I'm almost ashamed to bring you this bit of cake." She laid it on the table, a fine fruit cake, the brown-baked crust of which was raised or broken here and there by the crowding nuts and raisins that filled it.

"Hey," cried Uncle Harry, "he'll be glad of that now! God bless you, dearie, but he'll be glad to put a tooth in that cake."

"Who will?" asked the girl rather anxiously.

"Who but Peter Blue, of course? I ain't got any other

neighbors that I know of."

"Ah," the sheriff's daughter said. "I've come to talk to you about him."

"Nothin' I'm gladder to talk about," said Uncle Harry. "Excepting my Judy, of course, and my boy," he added with a rather guilty afterthought. "What you going to say, Mary dear?"

She was rather abashed by this enthusiasm on the part of the old man. But she went on gravely: "Do you mean to say that he'll come here and eat with you?"

"Why not?" said Uncle Harry. "Ain't it his right to come here and have a meal . . . him and me both being lone men?" He added: "Hold on a minute!" He hurried to the door of the oven and opened it, pulled out a broad roasting pan, and basted several big grouse that were browning beautifully. The steam and the delicious aroma of the roast poured into the room, and he said as he slammed the oven door again: "Peter'll be set for those by noon, I reckon."

"Peter?" she cried. "Peter Blue, do you mean?"

"Aye, Peter Blue."

"Oh, the rascal! To live on the charity of a. . . ."

"Tut, tut, honey. No charity. Except on his side. He shot these here birds."

She stopped, the next words dying on her lips. "He shot them?" she said more faintly.

"Aye, he did. He shot them. Left-handed, Mary. And them on the wing. I seen it. We walked out in the dawn, him and me. He's learning to shoot left-handed, y'understand? God knows how fine he could shoot with his right, but he says that everybody had ought to have two hands, instead of just one. So he's going to forget that he has a right hand, and try to train his left hand until it catches up with his right. Now, ain't that a rum idea, Mary darlin'? Them kind of ideas, he's full of. He won't touch his right hand to nothing. He eats and sews and rolls cigarettes and sweeps and shoots, all left-handed. Only been doing it a short time, he says, but, girl, it's a wonderful thing to see how good he manages. Now and then he spills things, of course. He missed the first deer that we spotted. But he got the second one." He pointed exultantly through the open door. "Look at it hanging there, Mary."

She looked, and shook her head. "Uncle Harry, I see that you're fond of him."

"Fond of him? I have roved and ranged up and down this here world for nigh onto seventy-five year or more, honey, and I never before seen young man or old, or boy or woman, that ever fitted into my mind as fine and quick and snug as Peter Blue does. I ain't knowed him hardly at all. Not a day, hardly, but if my own son was to stand here in the shack beside him, dog-gone me if I would know which I loved the most of the pair of them."

The sheriff's daughter bowed her head a little.

"Are you doubting me, Mary?"

"Oh, no, Uncle Harry, but I'm only wondering whether it's right for me to tell you what I know about him? If you like him so well. . . ."

"Oh, well," said Uncle Harry, "I suppose that a gent has got to hear gossip about a friend, now and then. I might as well hear it from you, Mary, as from somebody else."

"Not gossip . . . but facts," she said.

"Everything that's living is changing," said the old man. "Peter is tolerable much alive. There ain't no facts but dead ones, my dear. You ain't going to poison my mind ag'in' Peter."

"Look," said the girl, "you are setting yourself hard against me, and yet I can tell you things that will simply tear your faith in Peter Blue to pieces."

"Try it," Uncle Harry said with a faint smile. "You jes' sit down and try it, honey."

She said earnestly: "He's dangerous company for you or for any man, Uncle Harry."

"Tut, tut. I'm too old to worry about danger, Mary."

"Do you know why he's learning to do everything with his left hand?"

"Well, you can tell me."

"Because he isn't satisfied with the number of murders that he's done with his right alone, and he wants to be able to slaughter with two guns at once!"

She said it with fire and seriousness, and Uncle Harry blinked at her a little.

"Do you mean to tell me," he said, "that Peter is a gunfighter?"

"Oh, Uncle Harry, the most low, despicable sort of a gunfighter, a true safety killer."

"One of them that shoots from behind a hedge, maybe?"

"No, no, I don't mean that. I mean a man who has so much skill with a gun that no other person has a chance against him. He picks fights, and lets the other fellow grab for a gun first . . . and Peter Blue always gets in the first shot, and the first shot always kills."

"A gunfighter. A gunfighter," Uncle Harry said, blinking a little again. "I dunno that I like that idea. I seen old Tom Leicester killed by a crooked gunman from El Paso. I always hated the professional gunfighters ever since that day. Because what chance does an ordinary gent stand against them? What chance?"

"None at all," said the girl. "Not a bit of chance. While you're here cooking and getting a meal ready for that scoundrel, he's probably up in that other shack, practicing with guns and getting ready for more murders. Oh, Dad has told me all about that sort of a person."

"Practicing murders? I dunno." Uncle Harry grinned. "Except that my old Dan and Dandy would sometimes get a gent pretty mean and ornery in disposition. But, otherwise, it don't look like the preparings for a murder, do it?" He stepped to the front door and pointed across the trail and down the long, soft slope toward the river where the slow oxen were running the furrow—and a man held the handles of the plow behind them.

"I don't understand," Mary said, staring.

"Peter Blue," said Uncle Harry. "Is that murder, my dear?"

She turned around and faced the old man with a frown. "It's very odd," she said, her voice fainter than before.

"Ain't it?" Uncle Harry said. He took out a tobacco pouch and refilled his pipe

"What a beautiful bit of old pigskin," Mary observed. "Like amber . . . but so rich and dark."

"It ain't bad," admitted Uncle Harry. "It would have to be pretty good, because Peter give it to me . . . along with the tobacco in it. And Peter, he don't give away no cheap things. Not him."

She half closed her eyes. "I was going to warn you to have nothing to do with that terrible man-killer, Uncle Harry. Why, he's famous for the list of men he has killed. But it seems to me as though . . . as though . . . well, as though I must be wrong." She opened her eyes and looked rather wildly about her, at the steaming apples on the stove, at the deer that hung on the tree outside, and listened to the sizzling of the baking birds in the oven. Although she no longer faced the fields, across the back of the brain she could feel the two patient oxen toiling, and the hands of the warrior gripping the handles of the plow.

"Shooting of men," Uncle Harry stated, "is a pretty bad thing, though I suppose that the reason that more of it ain't done is that there ain't many folks with the courage to take the chance. Besides, honey, suppose that a horse has the knack of running extra fast, are you going to blame that horse for liking races . . . and are you going to blame him for winning the races when he starts?"

She sighed, hunted for words, and found that she could do nothing but stare. That lonely little cabin on the roadside was always a burden on the minds of the sheriff's entire family. In the old days, when Uncle Harry came over to visit Grandpa Dunkirk, they could feed the visitor well, and take his socks for patching, and send him back equipped with anything from an old coat to a side of bacon. But since he no longer visited, it was hard to know how to handle him. He was not a beggar, and rank charity could not be offered to him. So, each time they passed the shack, the sheriff and his people bit their lips, and felt a burden fall upon their consciences. And here was the cabin converted by a magic touch and filled with such warmth of good cheer that her heart was melted.

She heard Uncle Harry saying: "He's coming up from the field for lunch right now. You'll have a chance to see him."

"I don't want to," said the girl. "I wouldn't look into the face of that brutal. . . ."

"Brutal fiddlesticks!" Uncle Harry laughed. "I'll tell you what, Mary darlin', now that I look at you close and hard, I can see that you're pretty near good enough to stand up beside him. You're almost nice-looking enough to be Missus Peter Blue."

"What a *silly* way to talk," the girl said, crimson.

"Ain't it?" The old man grinned. "Tolerable silly and tolerable true."

"Do you think," she asked, "that I would ever look at a vagabond assassin who . . . ?"

"Look at him?" He laughed softly. "When you see Peter Blue, you're just gonna ask yourself . . . 'Could God please make this here man love me?'"

"Uncle Harry, you almost make me mad . . . you do."

"When you see Peter, you'll forget all about me, dearie. When you see him standin' up there, fillin' that doorway, big and grand and a sort of a sad look in his eye, honey . . . a sad look, because I suppose that it grieves him considerable that there ain't any more men in the world that will stand up to him and give him a fight . . . I say, when you see him standing up there, you'll just get weak in the knees."

"As if I haven't seen men before," Mary cried, rosy and laughing.

"No," he said, "you ain't. You've seen folks, that's all. But here's your chance to see a man, if you'll stay to lunch with us. You'll see your first real man, my dear. It will sort of scare you, but it'll make you terrible glad that you stayed."

"I must go, Uncle Harry. I really must. . . ."

"Hey? If you start now, it'll be plain that you're runnin' away from him. Would you be doin' that? Listen! He's takin' pot shots with his Colt as he comes up from the field. Left-handed pot shots at birds or rocks or twigs . . . he don't care what. And . . . well, you'll stay, I see. There's the sparkle in your eye, dearie, and I know that you're thinkin' of him."

VI

Mary Dunkirk stayed for lunch. She felt a vague excitement, and a peculiar sense of guilt, and a delicious sting of delight, because, before Uncle Harry finished his talk, she had never wanted to see any man as she wanted to see this same Peter Blue. She saw him take the span of oxen to the watering trough. She saw him place them at the feed rack. She saw these things by glimpses, so she flew here and there about the cabin, opening the stove, putting in more fuel, examining and basting the roasting birds, but now and then she could catch a glance through a window and see a stalwart back or a vaguely distant form.

"You keep fussin' around and workin', honey," said Uncle Harry, "and he'll never figger you got excited about seein' him. He'll just take it for granted that you been all heated up by the cookin'. You keep right on, Mary, because I'll tell you that there ain't nothin' that opens up the heart of a man so quick as to see a pretty girl in a kitchen . . . if I only had a white apron to tie around you, I'd just about guarantee you to fetch him. Dog-gone me if you ain't a lovely girl today, Mary Dunkirk."

"Uncle Harry . . . you're simply maddening! Why, he's going up the hill."

"Now, now . . . don't you worry and fret . . . he'll come back."

"Nonsense. How you *will* talk. I don't worry or fret about him. I never even think of him."

"If lyin' was shootin'," said the old man, "you'd sure leave more dead behind you than ever Peter Blue done. Peter's gone up the hill to fetch his horses out to water. And you watch him come rarin' down the hill with 'em."

"Ah," said the girl, "I hear that he has two fast horses . . . and nothing else to call his own. Who but robbers and thieves need such fast horses, Uncle Harry?"

"He has two legs and two arms and two hands that will break other men in two . . . look at this bare piece of firewood, honey, and see how he slashed it with one cut of the axe. He's

216

got the finest head that was ever set on a pair of shoulders, and the grandest heart that ever beat in a man's breast. That's what he's got, and what has any man got more? As for his fast horses . . . well, he wants 'em for the glory of ridin' fast and far. Besides, would any common nag match him, I ask you? Wait . . . listen! Now you come look."

He caught her by the arm and dragged her to a window so forcibly that she could afford to hold back and pretend that she did not wish to go. There from the window she saw Peter Blue come out of the Truman shack with a span of horses, and she saw him throw himself on what seemed a black horse with a white foreleg. . . .

"It's Christopher!" she cried.

They galloped madly down the slope, Christopher leading in spite of the weight of his rider, and the bay racing a close second. They flashed into a closer sweep of her eyes. She saw Peter Blue for the first time as he was in action.

"Look at him racin' and tearin' along!" cried Uncle Harry. "Oh, see if God ever made another like him. Nothin' so fine, so wild, so careless, so free, so plumb beautiful. Nothin' so big, so strong, so terrible fierce and so brave!"

"Oh, they'll crash into the fence!" Mary worried.

"Not them. No, open your eyes."

She opened her eyes, and she saw Peter Blue and Christopher hanging in the sky—so it seemed—then shooting forward across the fence. The bay followed. So they rushed to the watering trough, and Mary hurried back to the oven.

"Come back here," said the old man. "He won't notice that you're spyin' on him. He wouldn't care if he did. There ain't nothin' spoiled or mean or low about him. He must have had admiration around him all of the days of his life. So you come and look again, honey, and don't you fear that he'll notice."

"I wouldn't have come the first time," she said angrily, "if you hadn't pulled me to the window."

"But I didn't hold you there," he said, cackling. "Oh, Mary, you young beauties was made to fool the boys, but never to fool the old fellows. You could fool maybe even Solomon, when he was young. Maybe when Peter comes in, he'll think that I got an angel in here cooking for me. I'll tell you what, honey, if you're real good, I'll keep you here to wash the dishes, and make Peter stay, so's you can see something more of him."

"I won't listen to another word!" she cried. But she felt a little dizzy, and her hand fumbled twice as she burned the tips of her fingers before she found the knob of the oven door.

Then someone was whistling in the distance, and coming closer. It was he! Aye, and a grand bass voice suddenly struck up:

> Barnegat, Barnegat, belt on your gun,
> For Marty McVey is a-comin'. . . .

It seemed to the girl that it was a marvelous organ music that reached to her heart of hearts.

A moment later, the shrill treble of the old man joined the chorus:

> Marty McVey, Marty McVey,
> Barnegat's gun will talk today.

> Barnegat, Barnegat, gimme your hand,
> For he's galloping up from the river,
> Barnegat, Barnegat, take your stand. . . .

Into the doorway came the lofty form of Peter Blue, his

lips still parted with his singing and his great voice thronging through the cabin and throwing strong, sharp echoes back from the walls, so that Mary Dunkirk felt as though the very ground were trembling under her feet. Then he saw her and took off his hat, and his grave, dark eyes looked straight into hers.

She had expected someone boisterous, gay, wild, ignorant —and, as she met him, at last, she felt quite at sea. She was glad, for the first time, of the chattering of old Uncle Harry, as he made the big man welcome, and talked of the plowing, and asked how the oxen had pulled through the tough ground farthest from the riverbank, and how the blackbirds had followed the plow.

Then the men were at the table, and she served them with her own hands, and she heard old Uncle Harry saying: "Now look at the brown of them birds, Pete, will you? It takes a woman, to cook like that! Just slice into 'em and see the juice run, will you? That's Mary's touch. Now, dog-gone me if she ain't going to make a wife for a king, one of these days. Then why not for you, Peter?"

She felt as shamed and as helpless as a child, and stamped her foot. "Uncle Harry!" But then she met the mild, amused eyes of Peter Blue. He was not in the least embarrassed.

"He's old enough to talk like that," Peter Blue said to her. "Don't let it bother you. Aren't you going to sit here? Do you know that Uncle Harry hasn't told me your name?"

"I'm Mary Dunkirk."

"You're the sheriff's daughter?"

"Yes."

Once more those dark, keen eyes looked at her with quiet understanding, but without malice or scorn or amusement. Even more than when she had seen him sweeping down the hill on the back of Christopher, she knew that he was a very strong man.

She really dared not sit down. For she felt that, if she did, she would be foolishly aware of her feet and her hands, and that she would never be able to meet the eyes of this tall fellow about whom she had come to warn Uncle Harry. So she made it her business to wait on the table, and always found something to do.

"She's her mother's daughter," Uncle Harry said when Peter protested. "Let her wait on the men, if she wants to."

But, after a time, she grew a little more comfortable and more at ease; she could look at them both; she could enjoy the merry eye of Uncle Harry and the handsome face and the prodigious appetite of Peter Blue. All the time a great happiness was growing in her—greater than could be believed, almost. It swelled her heart and made her smile. She felt a strange sense of possession and kindliness, which enveloped the entire world of her knowledge.

Then, as the smile grew out on her lips, she heard the rapid hoofs of a horse in the distance, the beating, insistent, hurrying hoofs of a horse driven up the trail by some hardhanded rider. She listened, and the smile went out, for she felt that calamity was drawing close, and the charm that held this circle in such an enchanted happiness would suddenly be snapped.

VII

She turned at last from the stove to the window, in time to see a flying horseman rush up the trail and drive straight at the door of the Barnes shack. The wind of his gallop furled the brim of his hat above his eyes and parted his streaming, pale mustaches. He was out of the saddle the instant the pony he rode came to a halt, and, as it stood with hanging head, the tall fellow strode into the doorway of the shack, saying: "Is there anybody here that knows where I can find a hound by the name of Peter Blue that has been living up the road in the . . . ?"

Here he stopped himself and finished his sentence with a sweep of the hand that brought out a revolver. He covered Peter Blue, where the latter sat at the table, half turned toward the newcomer.

"And here you are, Steve?" Peter murmured to the tall stranger.

"Fill your hand, you low skunk!" bellowed Steve Livernash. "You ain't gonna talk yourself out of this hole, Blue. Fill your hand and lemme see you fight, if you can."

Mary Dunkirk had shrunk to the corner of the room, but now she sprang into action, for she knew that the process of "filling a hand" was a most perfunctory matter. It was a little flaw in the code of Western honor, which declared that it was quite permissible in a pinch to kill any man, so long as that man had a gun in his hand and was facing the enemy. It mattered not if the victor covered a victim with a steady rifle on a rest and bade the other grasp a weapon. As long as the hand was "filled", shooting became legitimate. So, knowing this, Mary Dunkirk sprang straight back into the line of fire between Livernash and Peter Blue. As she came between them, she felt as though death were already reaching for her.

"Fair play!" cried Mary Dunkirk, and she faced the stranger magnificently with her head high.

"Get out of the way!" yelled Livernash, and he sprang to get to one side of her.

She moved on the inside of the arc, and still cut him off, and the next instant he found himself facing a double-barreled shotgun, securely gripped in the withered hands of Uncle Harry, whose old eye squinted down the sights.

"I'll take a hand in this," said Uncle Harry. "Mary dear, you've done real fine. But now you go sit down and cry, because I know that you must feel like it. You go over there and sit down. Now, stranger, if you got any talking to do, I'll talk to you. What is it that you want to say?"

Mary Dunkirk turned and threw a frightened glance at Peter Blue.

He had not yet filled his hand. No, this lightning gunman had not swept a weapon from his holster, but he was rising slowly from his place, and then he took her arm.

"You'd better do as Uncle Harry says," he suggested. "You're a tremendously brave girl, Mary Dunkirk. If your father could have seen you do that, he would wish that you were a boy."

"Oh, oh!" gasped Mary. "Is it all over?"

"Yes," he said.

"There's no more danger . . . you're not going to be murdered?"

"Certainly not . . . thanks to you."

She would always feel that it was chiefly because Uncle Harry had suggested tears that she began to weep bitterly. Peter Blue brought her to a chair and kneeled beside her and dried her tears with his handkerchief.

"I'm ashamed," said Mary, choking.

"You're a dear," Peter Blue insisted. "There's nothing to be ashamed of."

"You'll despise me," said Mary.

"No, I shall not."

There was so much honesty in his voice that she began to control herself. It was hard to lift her eyes from the floor to his face, but, when she managed to do so and saw him smiling faintly, she could not help breaking into laughter.

"I've been a perfect idiot," Mary Dunkirk announced.

In the meantime, the would-be assassin had been backed out the door and held with his hands above his head by old Uncle Harry Barnes.

"You step right out there in the open," said Uncle Harry. "I ain't going to get you killed there on my floor. I been working for a week whitening up that floor, and here you'd be spoiling all my work for me. If you got your heart right set on dying, why, Peter'll kill you right here. And we'll bury you wherever you say, stranger."

"You damned old fool," Livernash said, his hands in the air, but his eye was bright and as dangerous as ever, "I'll have the pleasure of twisting your neck for this, one day."

"Son," said the old man, "don't you go talkin' foolish. You better be sayin' any prayers that you can remember. Think about the friends that might be needin' messages from you. Because I would jot them down and send them through the mails."

"You be damned, will you?" Livernash yelled.

"Hey and hello," said Uncle Harry. "Ain't the man wild, though. No friends? No religion? No nothin'? Leastwise, you might be thinking over where you would like to have us put you away. I'd suggest that rise, yonder. It faces south and gets the winter sun. And the first flowers, they come out there in the spring. What would you say to that, Steve? Or then, there's the bank of the river, down there. If you're special fond of rivers and such, we could bury you there in the shade and that would keep you cool. Or right out there in the garden patch, maybe you'd rather be planted for fertilizer, because there's some that likes to be useful, living or dead. I reckon that you're that kind, Steve."

Steve exploded in a violent assortment of curses.

"Hushaby, honey," old Harry said. "The girl'll be hearin' you and she ain't old enough to quite appreciate such language as you got in your deck. Just tie up that tongue and leave it behind you when you come to call again, Steve. Well, here's Peter come to settle you."

"Aye," said Livernash, half hysterical with fury. "By God, I've run him over half the continent in the last six months, and now I'm double-crossed and murdered by an old thug and a damned cowardly. . . ."

"Steady, steady," Peter Blue said, and smiled. "Have you really been chasing me for six months, Steve?"

"You know it!" cried Steve.

"I know it?"

"Aye, and you've been sneaking through the mountain like a whipped puppy."

"Steve," said Peter Blue, "I understand why you felt like this. You've never got over the last time we met. After that, you had enough time to think things over in the hospital, and you should have learned some sense. But it seems that you haven't. Go back to town, Steve, and think this over. After-wards, I'll meet you wherever you wish . . . with people to see what's happening. But I don't want to kill you today. Uncle Harry, just see that he gets away down the road, will you?"

He turned deliberately back into the house, while Uncle Harry said: "Climb onto your hoss, young feller. It seems that you ain't going to be planted today, after all. Now, I'd call that downright generous of Pete. But I'll tell you something more, on my own part. If I see anybody skulkin' around here, I got such poor eyes that I might take 'em for a coyote sneakin' around, and then I'd be apt to take a pot shot. And I don't often miss with a rifle, old son!"

The other had remounted his horse with his mind in a whirl. He did not speak again, but favored Uncle Harry with one murderous glance, and then rode down the trail toward town as slowly and with as little spirit as he had come with speed and fire.

Uncle Harry went back into the cabin and found the girl putting on her hat. She was excited and trembling and felt that she should go home at once.

"And after not touching a bit of nothing," said Uncle Harry. "Well, if you got to go, I suppose that you'll be seein' her home, Peter."

"No, no," Mary said.

"Yes, yes!" said Uncle Harry.

Peter left the room.

"I don't want an escort," she insisted. "And . . . I can't wait."

"But you will, though." Uncle Harry grinned. "Hey, it ain't every day that a girl has Peter Blue to ride across the hills with her. Oh, you'll wait for him, Mary. I was proud to know a girl like you this day. Dog-gone me it was a fine thing to see you come sashayin' in between the murderin' gun of that varmint and my Peter! Another split part of a second, and there would have been a killing."

She covered her eyes with her hands. "He would have murdered Peter Blue," she said.

"Him? Him?" snorted the old man. "Don't you fool yourself, honey. Peter didn't have no gun in his hand, but what's that to Peter? Quicker than a wink he would have filled his hand and finished off that gent. And then what would've happened? Why, he would have had to ride out of the county, and maybe I would never have laid eyes on him again. That was why I got my gun and marched that Steve gent out of the shack. But, Lord, wasn't our Peter fine and easy and grand?"

"Yes," Mary agreed, smiling faintly as she looked back on the memory of all that had happened. "Wasn't he?"

"You could see that he had the thing in hand all the time. He wasn't bothered none. Oh, I tell you what, you could lay ten men together end to end and six deep, and they wouldn't make up the bigness of Peter Blue. 'Go back to town and think it over, Steve,' he says. 'I don't want to kill you today!' Well, think of it, Mary. Think of havin' the life of a man in your hand like that. Think of bein' insulted the way that our Peter was, and then bein' calm and cool and forgivin' the way that he was. Don't it warm your heart, honey?"

They heard the distant tramp of a horse.

"I must go!" cried Mary.

"Aye," said the old man, "you hurry along, now, so's you won't keep Peter waiting, because here he comes."

The color rushed into her pale face at that. "I had no such idea, Uncle Harry, and you know it," she declared.

He wagged a forefinger at her. "You go fix your hat," he said, "and make yourself pretty. Dog-gone me if you ain't almost got him already. And if you let him see you smile a couple of times on the way home, who can tell if you won't have him landed before you see your house? Hurry, honey, and I'll go out and talk to him."

He rambled from the door of the house to where Peter waited, holding his tall Christopher and the pony of the girl.

"Ain't she wonderful, Pete?" he asked. "Ain't she a girl in a million? Aye, you don't have to answer me. Your pride, it don't fool no one. Because I know the kind of a girl that fits into the heart of a man as snug as a nut into its shell. And, hey, Peter, lean down your ear, will you?" When he had been obeyed, he whispered: "I got an idea that she likes you a little, son. Just a mite. Be kind to her. And keep her smiling. Who knows but you might land her before even you see her house today."

Mary came out and was given a hand into her saddle. Then off they went, side-by-side, with Mary looking back, at last, and waving with a sudden joyous laugh to Uncle Harry.

"Oh, Lord," said Uncle Harry, "ain't they a picture, now? Ain't they a picture, I ask you?" He went back to the door of the shack and watched them out of sight. He began to laugh a little, and rubbed his thin hands together. "What a day's work for me," he said. "What a bang-up, full day's work. I dunno that I'll waste time plowin' this afternoon."

All the time that he was washing the dishes and the tins, his high, uncertain tenor was never still, but wavered through one after another of the old ballads of his youth.

Now and again, too, he would step to window or door and scan the skyline with a careful glance, but that skyline showed no threatening form. Steve Livernash had not come back as yet.

VIII

The gloom with which Livernash started on his disappointed way back to town lasted all the way to the village. Not once did he lift his head, not even when a stag broke cover out of a little copse and dashed across the trail just fifty yards before him. The killing of a deer meant nothing to Livernash now, because his heart was filled with much greater concerns.

He knew not who to reproach. As for himself, he felt that his work had been flawless. He had found his man and taken him by surprise and secured the drop on him. Then what had happened? Two perfectly negligible quantities began to operate on him. A girl sprang before his gun, and then an octogenarian covered him with a shotgun. Such things could not be foreseen, and therefore Steve began to feel rather grimly comforted, and decided that he would place the blame with fate.

He was troubled, too, by something more than his mere

failure, for the manner in which he had failed was of great importance. He had had victory within his grasp. But he could not understand the sluggishness of big Peter Blue. There had been no move on the part of Blue to defend himself, and Steve felt that this could be explained in only one of two ways. Either Blue had been frightened out of his wits, or else he despised the danger too greatly to give it the slightest attention.

In spite of himself, Livernash felt that the latter explanation was apt to be the more accurate one, and, although he gritted his teeth with rage at the thought that he had been merely despised, yet he made sure that this had been the case. He vowed, of course, that one day he would teach Peter Blue to respect him thoroughly. But in the meantime, it would pay him to practice with his guns every day. For he felt more assured than ever before that Peter was no common man.

This was the humor of Livernash, partially chastened, partially infuriated, and wholly sulky, by the time that he reached the village. There he rode down the main street and encountered the sheriff before he met another soul. Dunkirk drew up with an exclamation.

"You didn't find him!"

"The hell I didn't," Livernash snapped, and he rode straight on.

"Wait a moment."

He turned grimly and faced the sheriff. "Why didn't you tell me that he was out there livin' with an old fool and his granddaughter?"

"Hello?"

"I say, a withered old goat. . . ."

"Uncle Harry Barnes, you mean? But Harry has no granddaughter."

"There was a girl there. That's all I know. A damned

pretty one. Well, Blue always had his way with the women. The rattleheads. A solid man, he ain't got no attraction for the skirts. But a damn' good-for-nothin' like Blue. . . ."

"Steve, tell me what happened."

"I missed him in the first shack. I seen the other place up the trail and headed for it, and, when I got there to ask if Blue was around, there he sat havin' lunch. I had him covered like that."

"My God, man!" breathed the excited sheriff.

"Don't count up the money before it's paid," the other said. "Fact was Blue knew that he was a goner, and he didn't make a move, not even when I told him to fill his hand."

"That's hard to believe, old fellow."

"Don't call me a liar, Sheriff. I've stood for a good deal today. But I won't stand for that. Just as I was about to drive a bullet through the gizzard of that crook and end my long trail, a bit of calico stepped in between me and my target. . . ."

"You mean that the girl jumped between?"

"Quick as a wink. Blue gets all the girls so crazy about him that they're all glad to die for him. This little fool, she was no different from the rest. She stood there lookin' like it would please her a good deal if I was to send a bullet through her heart."

"Who could that girl be?" Dunkirk exclaimed, biting his mustache. "How did she look, Steve?"

"Too damned pretty to be good, was how she looked. But to hell with her. I'm talkin' about Blue. I say, I was about to yank that fool of a kid out of the way and ram a yard of lead down the throat of Blue, when the old goat that was there . . . Barnes did you call him? . . . he brought down a shotgun, and took a bead on me, and walked me out of the shack."

"Uncle Harry did that, eh?" murmured the sheriff. "Well, he was always an old fire-eater and a grand old chap."

"A grand old chap, eh?"

"Go on, man. What did Blue do?"

"He stayed behind to tell the girl that it was lucky she didn't get killed, and to hear her say that he was worth dyin' for, I suppose. Anyway, he finally come out and he says that he didn't want to kill me today . . . was how he put it . . . and so he would wait for a better time, and would I please to let him know when I wanted to die, because then he would be glad to oblige me."

Livernash, in the excess of his fury, quirted his own horse heavily across the shoulders, and then sat the beast with gritted teeth and wrenched at its jaw as it bucked. When it was quiet again, he said: "So I'm gonna wait, and maybe you would like to name the time and the place where I'm to kill Blue?"

"No," Dunkirk responded, "he'll be on his way out of this county even now, Steve. And you'll have another six months of trails to find him."

"Do you think that?"

"I know it."

Livernash considered, and then he shook his head. "It's plain that you ain't seen this kid that's so sweet on Blue," he said.

"Eh?"

"Because she's a beauty, old fellow. A plain beauty. I tell you, she's a girl that could make a whole town fall in love with her in ten seconds. That there girl, Dunkirk, heard Blue promise that he'd meet me when I was ready. No, he'll never run out on me. If she was a mite less of a corker, he might beat it, but I figger that even a varmint like Blue had rather die than to have this here girl turn up her nose at him."

"Who could it be?" the sheriff wondered with a grunt, and he frowned at the ground. Then he added: "The important thing, Steve, is that I cannot wait until you're ready to polish off Blue. I simply can't wait. It's a matter of honor with me."

Livernash gaped. "It's a matter of honor with you, eh?"

"It is."

"Why, hell, man, and what is it to me? Ain't I swore that I'd find him and kill him?"

"Tell me how you'll go about it, Livernash?"

"If I can't think of a better way," he responded, "I'll write out and invite him to come into town and settle this here deal with me in the main street."

"Would he do that?"

"The girl'd shame him into it. And the old man . . . what was his name?"

"Barnes."

"Barnes? I'm familiar with that."

"You may have met his son."

"Aye, maybe I did. What's Barnes to Blue?"

"God knows how Blue wormed himself into the confidence of the old man, but he seems to be there. So far as I know, they're strangers to one another."

"Barnes?" the gunfighter said to himself, and he frowned at the sky, heedless of the voice of the sheriff, who was stating: "I'll tell you what, Steve. If you think that you have a ghost of a chance with Blue . . . a ghost of a chance to make him fight it out with you, I mean . . . I'll wait for you, because I know that you've set your heart on that meeting. But my duty really is to run him out of the county *pronto*. I'll think it over."

Dunkirk turned his horse and started off, and still the other remained in the saddle, staring at the sky. Finally Livernash started on slowly down the street, lost in his brown study, and, when he arrived at the hotel and had put up his horse, he said to the proprietor: "You know old man Barnes down the road, yonder?"

"Uncle Harry, you mean?"

"Yes. He has a son, eh?"

"Yep."

"By name of what?"

"By name of Dick."

"Ah," Livernash murmured, a glint in his eye. But he went on slowly: "A sort of an ornery-lookin' gent, eh?"

"Sort of."

"With a scar in the holler of his cheek?"

"Oh, that's him, all right."

"By God, then," said Livernash, "it fits in, after all."

"Fits into what?" asked the hotelkeeper.

But Livernash was already striding off.

IX

Altogether, the sheriff felt that it might be as well to let this complicated affair rest as it was. If he directly rode out with a posse to catch the gunman, Peter Blue would range swiftly away on his matchless horses. If he went alone to make the arrest, he would fall under the bullets of the man of battle. But if he left the matter in the hands of Livernash, the latter would be sure to execute his revenge or else die in the attempt.

Absolute insistence upon the course of duty was not in the heart of the sheriff. He was accustomed to handling each affair as it arose and in a special manner. All that he cared about was to finish off the career of Peter Blue, so far as that county was concerned. But if in addition the life of Blue were actually ended, the sheriff had not the slightest doubt that it would be for the good of society. He wanted no government warrant to encourage Livernash in the latter's earnestness for revenge.

His heart was now lighter than it had been for some days, and he rode home that evening, singing softly to himself. As he drew closer to his house, he heard the sweet voice of Mary singing the very song that was on his lips, and the sheriff reined in his mustang and listened. She sang well. To the sheriff, it seemed that she sang perfectly. Above all, because he could remember the day, long years ago, when he had taught her that same song.

He put up his horse and went into the little house through the kitchen door, where his wife was busy with her cookery. "Mary's fair busting with song tonight," he observed with much satisfaction.

"I wish that she'd bust songs, instead of dishes," said his wife. "She's smashed a plate and two glasses, setting the table tonight."

"Aw, let her be, let her be," Newton Dunkirk murmured. "What's a dish or two in a girl's life?"

"Me?" the housewife cried sharply. "Are you going to marry her off to a millionaire, maybe?"

"Ain't she worthy of it?" asked Dunkirk.

"A fine chance she has to take up with one," Mrs. Dunkirk replied, heated with the stove and her work. "A fine, fair chance that girl has, after we've spread ourselves on her education and all. No, but she'll be picking up with some low-down, ignorant, good-for-nothin' cowpuncher, and then slave the rest of her life away the same as other women have done . . . that I could tell you about!"

The sheriff felt the imputation and bit his lip. But he never struggled against the will of his better half when he found her in such a humor. Instead, he went obediently out of the room and found his daughter in the dining room putting the last touches to the table in the form of a bunch of wildflowers in a flat glass dish.

"Hey and what?" the sheriff grunted, grinning broadly. "What young gent is comin' for dinner tonight, honey? Is it maybe Jeff Dixon?"

"Stuff!" said the girl. "Jeff Dixon is hardly more than a baby."

"It's Bud Loomis, then," he declared.

"Bud? Poor Bud. He's just a youngster."

"Look here, Mary, those boys were your best friends just around the corner of yesterday, and what's made you grown up past them, so quick?"

"Shall I tell you, Dad?"

"By the Lord," the father said, "I think that you're going to tell me something worth hearing."

"I am! Something that'll surprise you a lot. I've met a man."

The sheriff looked deeply into her shining eyes and felt a chilly sense of loss. But, after all, every daughter must marry someday. So he braced himself and smiled back at her. "An honest-Injun hundred percent man, Mary?"

"An honest-Injun one. Really! There's only one trouble."

"And what's that?"

"He's a man that you don't like."

"Ah, I got the pleasure of knowing this gent before, have I?"

"Yes, you have. It makes it rather hard to talk to you about him. Because you've seen him in the wrong way."

"Going or coming, do you mean?"

"I mean he's the man that you've always written down as a rascal and a bad fellow. But he isn't at all."

"I'm glad to know that," the sheriff stated more grimly. "Well, I'll guess who it is."

"No, you never could."

"It's that spindling, squint-eyed, hard-headed Casey Langhorne!"

"No, no, no! How horrible."

"Horrible, eh? Why do you say that? Is this man you're talking about the one that you're going to marry?"

"Yes, if he'll have me."

"*If?*"

"He hasn't asked me."

"Hold on, now, Mary. Are you makin' a joke of me?"

"No, not a bit."

"Have you been losin' your heart to a gent that ain't even looked at you favorable?"

"I have."

"My God, honey, what do you know about him?"

"Nothing at all. I never saw him before today."

The sheriff sat down suddenly. He felt weak and rather old and useless in this dizzy world of youth.

"You never seen him before today?" he echoed.

"Never." And she laughed at him joyously.

"But you know that you love him, of course?"

"Of course I do."

"So much that you put flowers on the table in honor of him, even though he ain't coming to dinner?"

"Exactly."

"Maybe he's a married man, honey?"

"Maybe he is."

"Confound it, Mary, doesn't that make any difference?"

"Not a bit, really."

"Hey?"

"I couldn't help it if he were married, could I?"

"You could forget about it if you had to, though."

"No, I couldn't."

"Then you tell me what you could do, young lady!"

"Why, I'd just take him away from his wife, of course. I mean, I would if I could."

"You would, eh? You'd run off with a married man?"

"I would in a minute."

"With a wife and kids at home?"

"I'd never give them a thought."

"Mary, if I didn't know that you're lyin' to me, this here would make me pretty sick."

"I can't help laughing, because I'm so happy," said Mary. "But as a matter of fact, I'm terribly serious."

"I believe you," Dunkirk said gravely. "So now you go ahead and tell me something more about this gent that you're going to run away with, and leave his wife and his babies at home. How long is he gonna keep on loving you?"

"Forever, I hope. But if not, it's worthwhile to have him even for a day or a week. . . ."

"Dog-gone me if I'm not paralyzed the way you talk, Mary. It ain't because it's so indecent, but because it don't sound like you. Your voice has changed, even. If I was in the other room and overheard you, I wouldn't recognize that it was my own girl talking to me."

"I *have* changed, Dad. He changed me in two minutes."

"I'd like to find out the name and the address of this here philanderin' married man," the sheriff hissed through his teeth. "Because if he's got a temporary home, maybe I could give him a permanent address."

"Do you mean in town?"

"I mean in hell!"

She merely laughed again. "Dear Dad," she said, "he's not that kind of a man."

"What?"

"I mean he's such a wonderful man that no one would ever dare to stand up to him."

"Where did you meet this here wonderful lion?" asked the sheriff with a sneer.

"In old Uncle Harry's house today."

The sheriff leaped from his chair and caught his daughter by the arms. "Lovin' God!" said the sheriff. "You ain't meaning what you say, Mary?"

"Why do you act like this, Dad? Why shouldn't I go to poor old Uncle Harry's house?"

"It was you!" the sheriff cried hoarsely.

"I who did what?"

"Who jumped in front of the gun of Livernash and saved the life of Pete Blue."

"Oh, that? I'd almost forgotten. Yes, I did stop that big, ugly man. Not that Peter needed saving. He could have blown Mister Livernash off the face of the earth, if he hadn't been so kind-hearted."

"Mary, Mary, stop babblin' and laughin', will you, and listen to me, before I go mad!"

"Of course, I'll listen, but I simply can't stop laughing. Only tell me . . . is Peter really married?"

"Damn Peter! Eternally damn and blast him! How do I know? But I do know that he's a renegade man-killer, a professional life-taker, and a butcherin'. . . ."

"Dear old Dad, you just don't understand. Why, you should see the way Uncle Harry loves him, and he's just like a son to Harry. You've said yourself that Uncle Harry never makes a mistake about a man."

"The miserable blind old idiot is in his second childhood. *Knows?* He knows nothing. Mary, Mary, Mary, are you meanin' what you say? You ain't jokin' with me? You ain't laughin' at me to make me mad? But for God's sake tell me that you don't mean that you've fallen in love with that devil of a man, Peter Blue."

"Sit down again, and I'll tell you everything, of how I rode over to warn Uncle Harry against him, and of how I first saw Peter, and how I came to know him, and how he rode home with me, and how I loved him, and how he didn't so much as speak to me, hardly, all the way here . . . and yet I'm so happy that I hardly know myself!"

X

Newton Dunkirk was not a man to be overthrown by a single shock, and, although he had never before been so staggered as he was now by the outburst of his daughter, he listened gravely to all that she had to say. Not that he changed his opinion of Peter Blue, but because it was important for him to understand the exact viewpoint of Mary. As he listened, he felt that he could understand why Peter Blue might have tried to fascinate the girl. He, the sheriff, had threatened to drive the gunman from the county, and was it not more than probable that, with malicious craft, Blue was striving to wound the man of the law in his most vulnerable spot?

The problem of Dunkirk grew more and more complicated, for now he must adjust his plans in another fashion. Merely to drive Peter Blue from the county would be worse than useless, from his own point of view, because the girl would continue to worship this new idol at a great distance. Death is an ugly word, but the sheriff felt that it might be the only one that could supply the solution for this difficulty. He had thought of meeting the gunfighter with foul play, but he was determined to overwhelm Peter Blue by the force of the law.

That night, after dinner, he wrote a batch of telegrams directed far and near and confided them to one of his ranch hands to carry to the telegraph office. Those telegrams were inquiries directed north and south and east and west to officers of the law who would be apt to know something concerning the past life of Peter Blue. Not about the crimes of Blue did the sheriff ask, but concerning the record of the famous gunfighter with women. For on that score he hoped to dig up a scandal or two that might daunt Mary in spite of her professed carelessness.

When he had dispatched these telegrams, he felt more at his ease, and, coming into the sitting room, there he found his wife with her knitting. Her resolute thriftiness forbade her to keep a servant, and the one quiet hour in her day was this just before bedtime, when she sat with her lap filled with knitting, crooning a little song and oblivious of the world.

The sheriff, looking at her time-marked face, wondered how she could be the mother of Mary Dunkirk, whose gay song was floating from her room, dimmed by distance but not made less joyous. Yet he was fond of his wife. Her pressure had turned him from a careless, rollicking youngster into a settled man of middle age, with a prosperous ranch, and a chance to take out his restless love of adventure in the work of his paid office as sheriff. He admired her foresight. He respected her courage. But his affection was tempered a good deal by fear. Yes, if the truth must be known, the sheriff was afraid of his better half.

He picked up a paper, tried to read it, and then crumpled and tossed it to one side.

"Sally."

The humming continued from the knitter.

"Sally?"

"Aye, Newt."

"Do you know what you're singing?"

"I don't know. Was I singing?"

"You was. You are now."

"Newt."

"Well?"

"Mister Fitzgerald came back today to have another look at that stack of barley hay."

"Did he?"

"I told you that he'd be back. He looked it all over. 'I'll give you fourteen and a half a ton,' he said. 'Don't you talk to me,' I said back. 'I'd let you have that hay in a minute, but my husband, he holds out steady for sixteen.' "

"I don't, Sally. Fourteen and a half is a grand price! Twelve would be good enough for that unbaled stuff. Why should you make a Jew out of me?"

"Because you'll get the pleasure of the money, and why shouldn't you take the blame for the bargaining, can you tell me?"

"Did he leave then?"

"He offered fifteen, told me to tell you about it. I know he'll be back to give the sixteen, though, before the week's out. He wants it bad. I told him that the Marshall brothers had sent out a man to look at the hay."

"But they didn't!"

"What difference does that make? If the Marshall brothers was real businessmen, they *would've* sent out a man."

Another pause.

"Sally, will you stop that damn' singin'?"

"Was I singin', Newt?"

"You was. What song . . . d'you know?"

"I can't guess. It was in my throat, but not in my head, Newt."

" 'Little Brown Jug'. Dog-gone me if I ain't listened to that song every evening for these twenty years . . . and still you will keep on with it to drive a man mad. Sally! You're at it ag'in."

She made a slight pause in her knitting and looked at him over the rim of her glasses. "What's on your conscience, Newt?"

"On my conscience? Nothin'."

"Oh, yes, there is. There's always something on a man's conscience when he acts the way that you're acting. Come out with it."

He glared at her. He felt bitterly triumphant to find her wrong, for this once. "My conscience is as clean as the palm of my hand," he said.

"Soap and water is good for the skin, an' repentin's for the conscience," she advised.

"But I ain't got nothin' on my conscience, woman!"

"Lord, Lord," said his better half, "the more a man talks, the more he gives himself away."

There was a pause. Then: "Damn it, Sally, will you stop that singin' or do you want me to leave the room?"

"It's a tolerable bright, soft night, out," Mrs. Dunkirk commented. "Mary's happy, tonight, ain't she?"

The voice lilted in the distance, and the music flowed softly through the house.

"And d'you know why?" he barked.

"Why, then?"

"She's found a man."

"She's comin' to the age," Mrs. Dunkirk said.

"Woman," cried the indignant sheriff, "you ain't got no nacheral feelin' in your heart for your girl! You don't even care who the man is."

"You mean this last one?" said Sally Dunkirk.

"Yes."

"Peter Blue?"

"Hey? Has she told you?"

"Of course. First thing."

"And you don't care?"

"What good does carin' do?"

"You'd let her go off and marry that scoundrel?" the sheriff asked bitterly. "You wouldn't be bothered none?"

"I ain't even thought about it."

"After her sayin' that she's in love?"

"What good does lovin' do?" she asked. "Marryin' is what counts."

"Suppose he's married already, I ask you?"

"Time and tide take care of all things, Newt."

"Damn the time and damn the tide! Double damn it! D'you know what kind of a man Peter Blue is?"

"I've heard tell of him, I think."

"A gunfightin', man-killin' hound!"

"Them things," Mrs. Dunkirk said, "will sort of bring a girl's eyes on a man."

"Will you stop that knitting and talk sense?"

"I don't think very good unless I got my hands busy," she said.

"You're gonna throw your girl away on him, are you?"

"Is he so bad?"

"I've told you what he is!"

"Man-killin'?"

"Ain't that bad enough?"

"What counts," she said, "ain't what he is to men, but what he's gonna be to his wife? Has he got no eddication?"

"Maybe he can read and write, I dunno. He can shoot, that's what the world knows about him."

"Read, write, and shoot," murmured Mrs. Dunkirk. "What more could you do when I married you, Newt?"

He leaped from his chair. "Badgerin' me is always what you're keen on," he declared. "Mary, she don't count."

The knitting ceased. The hands of the knitter folded

one on top of the other.

"Do you know something, Newt?"

"Not according to you!"

"I tell you, all our talkin' and strivin' wouldn't change that girl no more than it would keep the wind from blowin'."

"I'll see about that. I'm her father."

"Don't you go tryin' it. She's different from us. She's plumb different from us, and she always was, and she always will be."

"Ain't she our flesh and blood?"

"I was a pretty girl," said her mother, "but I never had the eye that Mary has. And you're a strong man, Newt, but you never had the strength of our Mary."

"I dunno about that."

"I've seen her put you down a hundred thousand times. If she don't handle you with a frown, she'll handle you with a smile. But she's always got something left that you and me can't guess at. The best plow in the world can't follow a racer, Newt."

"So you're gonna fold your hands and let her go?"

"I am."

"And take no care for her? Woman, ain't you got no shame?"

"I can pray for her," said the other. "But handle her I can't. Nor can you."

"We'll see what happens!" the sheriff hissed, more and more savage.

"What will you do?"

"All that a gun *can* do!"

"Aye," said the mother, "but a six-shot brain ain't enough to handle Mary."

XI

In the faint light of the early dawn, Peter Blue left the Truman shack and stood with a Colt fifty paces from a slender sapling. He fired three shots in one minute—three deliberate careful shots—and then he walked closer to investigate. He had chosen as a bull's-eye a little lump on the side of the tree, and he saw that it was quite blown away, and a treble hole, the inner edges of which almost touched, driven through the heart of the sapling. He stood back with a smile.

That was not bad. Even right-handed shooting could not surpass this very greatly. As he walked back to his distance again, he told himself that the painful hours he had spent working before the little mirror with pencil and paper had not been wasted. They had keyed up his motor senses in the fingers of that hand and made it closer to a real organ for action.

But such slow target work was, of course, useful for hunting but very little use, indeed, for fighting. Fights with men, according to his experience, did not happen after that fashion. Two men did not face each other and take deliberate aim. Instead, it was a chance encounter as one swung around a corner, or it was a single angry word of insult that caused the explosion, or it was the slamming of a door—and one turned to face a foe. Or perhaps one wakened in the night and heard a stealthy stir through the darkness, or it might be that a quiet foot stole up behind one—then, with tensed nerves, to whirl and fire from the hip. Not in a third of a minute. Not even in a second. But to move so that one's movement almost overtook one's thought, to think the bullet home, and actually to drive it to the spot. That was what a man might do, and without that power for action, accuracy was nothing whatever. Particularly to Peter Blue, surrounded as he was in this quarter of the world with enemies of the heartiest fashion.

So you may understand that his lips were tight as he stood with his back to the sapling, the gun in its holster—on his *left* hip. He tensed body and nerves, then, at a mental signal, he whirled and snatched at the revolver and fired. . . .

Fast enough, you would say. And look! the bullet has clipped the rim of the sapling. But Peter Blue beat his numb right hand against his forehead.

"Dead, dead, dead!" he said aloud with a groan. "Dead as I turned. Dead before the gun was clear of the leather . . . and even in the finish, I missed the heart."

He nerved himself once more. Again, again, and again he fired before he gave the thing up with a groan. He had not touched the sapling with any of the last three shots, and in addition each shot had been got off more clumsily than all that preceded.

He went back slowly to the shack. The early morning darkness in the little house was too much for him, and he went into the horse shed and leaned his head against the mighty shoulder of Christopher. There he was sure of consolation, no matter what else. So he stayed until the day was brighter outside, but although the day grew brighter, his heart did not grow more bright, you may be sure. He had failed, and he knew that his failure was practically complete.

Shoot left-handed he could, but he knew that he could never think with the sinister hand, and that was what he needed. To forget that he had such a thing as a right hand when the time came for critical action, that was what he needed. He pondered this gravely, steadily, meeting the truth with open eyes. His right hand could never recover. He had been told so by a doctor who never missed in his judgments any more than Peter, in the old days, had missed with a gun.

Nothing but the left remained to him, and with that left he knew that he could never attain to the old heights of skill.

He mastered himself with a great effort, but, as he walked out through the hills, he wondered what he could do. In a wave of weakness, he wished to let the world know of his stricken condition. Very shame might then hold back his enemies. No, the hundred faces looked suddenly in upon his mind—dark eyes, sneering lips, keen, cruel faces, as merciless as the faces of wolves. They would never forget and they would never forgive, and they would pity him no more than the wolves pitied a failing moose, caught in the snow.

When he had come to this decision, he discovered a rabbit flying across the hillside before him, and he downed it, not from the hip as his old custom had been, but with one of these deliberate, careful shots. The rabbit fell, but it had been almost out of effective shooting distance before he could pull the trigger, and he told himself with a bitter smile that a human fugitive could have filled him with lead during the interval.

Such was the conclusion of Peter as he turned down the hill again and saw the smoke rising above the roof of Uncle Harry's cabin. He stopped and smiled in a different fashion. Ah, if he could change some of the old wild days and ways for a little of the quiet happiness that might be had in that same shack with that same old man—but he shrugged the idea behind him. What is impossible is impossible, and he determined that he would say farewell to Uncle Harry that same morning.

So down he marched to the cabin with the rabbit for breakfast, and he found the stove shimmering with heat, the floor freshly swept, and Uncle Harry busily skimming a thick, stiff layer of cream from a pan of milk that stood in the window.

"Hey, Peter!" cried the old man, "come look at this, will you? Never seen cream standing so thick in my life. The old cow, she must be comin' into good days again!"

He turned and gestured with the dripping skimmer. Peter could hardly recognize him as the wan old meager-faced man who he had first seen only a few days before. There was color in that face, and there was life in the eyes, and the body was held straighter, and the hand trembled no longer. So much meat and drink had done for him, and, more than that, happiness which fills the heart of old age as well as ever it filled the heart of youth. He examined the cream and praised it. It was due, perhaps, to the change of the cow from the long grass to the short. Long grass always made thin cream, said Uncle Harry.

"Or maybe it's due to you, Peter. You bring so much luck along with you."

They had breakfast shortly afterward, facing one another across the old table, which Peter had braced until it stood strongly on its legs as in the times of its youth.

"Are you plowin' or studyin' this morning?" asked Uncle Harry.

Now was the time to break the news, but as Peter hesitated before answering, old Uncle Harry broke in: "No, no, lad . . . there's no plowin' for you, unless you want to do it. For me, I'm never happier than when I see the loam turnin' before the share. I want to tell you something that I been turning over in my head, the same as the grass turns before the plow. Peter, look out the window, and you tell me what you can see."

"I can see the river, on the right," Peter said patiently. "And then the meadows between us, with the strip of the plowed ground . . . how that strip's growing! And then the rolling ground that goes up from the meadows toward the hills."

"You see all of that?"

"Yes."

"Anything on that ground?"

"Some good oak . . . and some fine pine groves up on the hillside."

"Now I'll tell you something, lad. All of that ground that you see there, it belongs to me. Every peg and leg and stitch of it belongs to me."

"Hello!" said Peter. "Then you're a rich man."

"Someday I will be," the veteran agreed with fiery eyes rolling over the landscape, "if I could get anyone to go in with me and help at the work and bring some of that land under cultivation. Why, man, there's five thousand acres of farm land out there . . . and fifteen hundred acres that could be irrigated from the river in a dry spell."

"Yes," Peter said. "I believe that."

"I wanted my boy to stay," said old Uncle Harry. "If he had stayed here to work the ground with me, we could have got in a little the first year, and a little the next, and every year sunk back the profits in buying more tools, more horses to work the ground . . . and finally we would have been working the whole lay of the land. But he wouldn't do it. I tried to get the sheriff interested, but he thinks I'm too old to have sense. And nobody believes that anything will grow on this land, except by the edge of the river. But I've tried. I've dug up bits of ground all the way to the ridge of the hill and planted the spots with grain and everything . . . and it all prospered fine. Though not like a garden, the way that it is in the hollows. I tried to tell my boy all of this, but he was always lookin' away across the hills. Boys is like that. They figure that a happy day is waiting for them . . . maybe tomorrow. If they only shift scenes often enough, they'll get to a paradise where everybody is rich, including themselves. They always raise their eyes fixed far off. But as a matter of fact, you can't see so far toward the skyline. Stand anywhere on the face of the earth, Peter, and the longest distance you can look is straight up over your head. It's all the same. Why should you travel? The gents that you meet is no different from your neighbors at home. They ain't any kinder, braver, meaner, or wickeder. They're just men. If I'd seen that myself before I was past sixty-five, I would've had all of this here land blossoming around me. D'you believe that?"

"I believe that," Peter answered gravely. He felt that he would have to postpone his departure until the afternoon. He could not break in upon this rosy dream.

"But you and me, Peter, could do wonders. I know that the bank would start me with a loan, if they was sure that I had a good partner . . . and, with that, we'd begin ripping the ground open . . . now, Peter, what do you think of the idea?"

"Why," Peter said, "it might be a wonderful thing."

"In two years," said Uncle Harry, "we'd have a fine big house built there on the hill. Dam the creek beside it and make a fine little lake, and then you and Mary could live up there like a king and a queen, and, every Sunday morning, you could come down here and have a breakfast of broiled trout. Now tell me if that ain't practical, son?"

"Why . . . ," began Peter.

"A half interest to each of us, y'understand?"

"Uncle Harry . . . take a half interest in your land?"

"The only question is . . . could you settle down? Could you be content to live right here . . . with Mary to keep you sort of entertained, say?"

"Could I be happy?" Peter Blue closed his eyes. "God . . . yes!" he said at last. "Couldn't I . . . just!"

XII

The imagination of the old man flowed fast and free, after this. He saw the fences built, the ground enclosed, the timber cleared, the soil plowed and seeded. With a few sentences he crowded the rich pastures along the hills with fine cattle and with blooded horses, and with a few more he built corrals and barns and sheds. But it required some time for him to pour forth his fancy upon the subject of the house on the hill, in all its wide-armed magnificence and to describe Peter Blue riding forth on his Thoroughbreds, with his children on ponies beside him.

"And what of your son?" Peter asked, willing to humor the old man in his daydreaming.

"He'll come back," Uncle Harry announced. "The finest lad that ever laid a foot in a stirrup, my boy! You'll know him and you'll love him. Goes six months without writing a letter, but that doesn't matter. Some of these days he'll turn up . . . pray God."

He added the last two words with a sudden wistfulness, and Peter Blue could tell that this was the most weighty sorrow of Uncle Harry's life. He had his doubts about the career and the reappearance of that young man. But he would not for this world discourage his older companion.

Uncle Harry went out to the plow, and Peter, waving good bye to him, knew that he had not enough courage to say farewell to him face to face. Instead, he would write a little note.

He washed the breakfast dishes first, smiling at the conscience that urged him on. Then he sat down to write, but words would not trickle swiftly from the end of his pencil. He sat for some time chewing the base of the pencil, and he looked up from the meditation to see a horseman clattering toward the door of the cabin.

"Uncle Harry!" called the stranger. "Hey, this is for Uncle Harry," he continued when he saw that Peter was alone in the shack. "I brung it up from the mail box for him."

Peter followed to the open door and squinted hard at the letter. Letters were not over-frequent in the days of Uncle Harry, he knew, and, if this were word from the son or the daughter of the old man, he would want to have the news at once.

However, it was a great distance from the shack to the farther corner of the meadow beside the river, and Peter raised the letter to the sun, squinting shamelessly into it, in the hope of descrying some telltale word through the envelope. Like all Western horsemen, he hated a long walk. He could make out several words at once, for the envelope was thin and the writing was in a powerful, broad, heavy hand. But the words that interested him most came at the bottom of the sheet. They were the signature: **Stephen Livernash**.

All indecision left Peter Blue, at that. He held the envelope in the dense cloud of steam that issued steadily from the spout of the kettle on the stove until the mucilage of the flap was softened. Then he pulled the flap open and extracted the contents, twisted them open, and read:

Dear Mr. Barnes,

When I was out at your place the other day, I didn't have the chance to look things over very well, so you may remember that I was kind of hustled away before I could do much talking . . . or shooting. But when I come back to town, I found out that you're the father of Dick Barnes, which made me kind of wonder how come that you are still the friend of Peter Blue. But then I asked around, and I found out that nobody out this way has got the news, yet, about the death of Dick, which I thought that it was only right I should sit down and write to you about it. I was personally myself in the room in Eutaw Corners when your boy Dick Barnes come into the place and I seen Peter Blue pull out a gun and shoot him down. Dick died without having no chance to defend himself. He didn't even have a chance to get his gun out.

I ain't going to say nothing to nobody about this, but, just the same, I would like to know what you figure on, and how Peter Blue comes to be a friend in your house? It looks to me as though the explanation must be that you ain't ever heard the facts about what happened that day in Eutaw Corners.

If that's the case, then maybe you'll be aiming at some sort of a revenge, when you get a chance. I suggest that you keep Blue on quietly in your shack without letting him know nothing, and then the rest of us, maybe a dozen or so, will go out and arrange a little necktie party and string him up for the murdering of your boy. Let me know what you think.

Stephen Livernash

When Blue had finished with the letter, he tapped his fingers thoughtfully on it for a long moment. It was almost as much of a shock to him as it would be to Uncle Harry. He could remember that evening in Eutaw Corners when the raw-boned youth, heated with liquor, had entered the room where he was sitting at cards. Perhaps moonshine whiskey had crazed the brain of Dick Barnes—if that was his name. At any rate, he certainly had not tried to fight fair, and probably he might have killed Peter Blue on that night had it not been for the fire in the eyes of the youth when he looked at Blue on entering. That glance had been warning enough, and, like a cat, Peter had watched the other stride down the room until he was at the side in a most effective position. There the voice of the youth had bellowed—"Blue, you devil!"—and a gun had gleamed in his hand.

Only a snap shot from the hip from beneath the table enabled Peter Blue to drop the would-be assassin. Barnes pitched on his face and was dead when they picked him up. What had caused him to make the attempt was a mystery, for Peter had never seen him before, but there are many reasons why ambitious youngsters should strive to sink a bullet in Peter Blue. Just as there were reasons, in the old days, why young men often picked quarrels with famous duelists in the hope that some of the settled fame of the older fighters might be inherited by their slayers.

At any rate, that was the true story of the killing of the young man at Eutaw Corners, an attempt so exceedingly rank that Peter had not been even questioned by the sheriff. Now Livernash was striving to falsify the facts enough to poison the mind of the old man against him.

The hot blood rushed into the brain of Peter Blue and a temporary madness seized him. He controlled himself with a great effort and forced his mind to clear. After all, he could no longer surrender to the old, wild, fighting impulses. His deadly tools were blunted. But what a dastardly thing it was! He had not realized, before this, how much Uncle Harry meant to him. To others, he was the reckless, bloodthirsty desperado, Blue. To Uncle Harry, he was all that was desired or desirable in human character. Now, with a single lie, Livernash could blast his good name and leave him an object of eternal hatred to the old fellow.

All of this Peter Blue considered. But what was he to do? If he fled and destroyed the letter, Livernash would simply write another, and the news would be believed because Peter had fled in the meanwhile. What possessed Livernash, however, to use such underhanded means? He had never been a coward. No man in the world had more ample confidence in himself than had Steve Livernash, and yet now he was working with the craft of a lowly, secret poisoner. The only explanation, in the eyes of Peter, was that Livernash felt his enemy was entrenched among friends in the shack of Uncle Harry. He wished to blast Peter out of the trenches with this letter as with a bomb, then he would catch and fight his foe in the open. Perhaps that was the way that Livernash had worked the thing out, which did not diminish the dastardly nature of the lie in that letter.

Peter sat down by the window and looked across the pleasant slope, misted with brightness of the morning sun, and, as he sat there humming "Barnegat, Barnegat!" to himself, he turned the letter back and forth in his mind. He might slip away from this snare. But other snares awaited him. Sooner or later, they would corner him and they would down him. Why not now, then, as well as later? Suppose that Livernash kept his word and said nothing to anyone until he heard from Uncle Harry . . . suppose that his lie was kept to himself . . . why, then, if he, Peter Blue, could kill the liar, the tale would never reach the lips of Uncle Harry. Could he not kill the man? He would have to die himself in order to do the trick. For he could never shoot straight enough with that left hand to down Livernash before Steve fired, and, when he fired, Steve fired straight. Yet, even with two or three bullets in his body, a man could still maintain a battle. Or, at least, a man could rouse himself for a single death effort.

So said Peter Blue to himself, his eyes glaring out the window and the muscles of his jaw tense. Time to concentrate on the firing of one shot was all that he asked. Given the time, he did not doubt that even his left hand could shoot straight enough. He would pay for that time with a dozen death wounds, if necessary.

That plan was vaguely forming before the eye of his mind, and yet he paused again and again to shake his head and sigh. Suppose the very first bullet from the gun of Livernash should be through head or heart. . . .

A rattle of hoofs outside the door—and there was Mary Dunkirk leaning far off to glance inside, calling from the saddle: "Uncle Harry! Uncle Harry!"

Peter walked out to her.

"Hello!" she said. "Where's Uncle Harry?"

"In the field, plowing," Peter answered. It seemed to him rather odd that she should have ridden down the road without noticing the old fellow at the plow, so clearly in view even at this distance.

"Oh, well, then," she said. "I'll just leave this with you for him." She gave him a basket from her arm.

Peter sniffed at it, and then smiled up at her. "An apple pie . . . by the Lord," he said.

Her eyes had widened a little under his smile. "I was going to town," she explained, very rosy of cheek. "I thought that I might as well leave a pie here on the way."

"There's no place where one will be more appreciated."

"Tell me," she said, abruptly getting on to another point, "are you helping Uncle Harry to put in that ground?" She turned and waved toward the river meadow.

"Do you know what he wants me to do?" he quavered.

"Well?"

"Stay with him permanently, and become his partner."

"Ah, ah!" cried the girl. "What a wonderful idea. Will you do it? Will you?"

XIII

It seemed a bit off to Peter that she should have said it in the manner of one making an appeal for herself rather than asking a mere question. In spite of himself he could not help remembering a certain thing that old Uncle Harry had said to him before.

"I don't know," Peter Blue said carefully. "I've thought of some such thing. But I don't know. You see, he has very sweeping ideas for fencing in the whole range to the crest of the hills, yonder, and putting all of the lowlands under cultivation . . . and ranging cattle through the hills themselves. Up yonder," he went on, watching her face cautiously, "he would have a house for me. A big house. For he says that, of course, I must marry at once."

Her face was crimson, and then white, and then rosy red once more. "It seems to me a beautiful idea," Mary said.

"If it could be done," Peter mused. "Do you think that a girl would be happy, living out here so far from town . . . such a very lonely place for a house?"

She answered hastily: "*I* think it would be a glorious place for a house. I can't imagine a better one."

"There would be a lake beside it, Uncle Harry says. He would dam the creek and make a little lake beside the house."

"The very thing, of course," said Mary Dunkirk.

"All that southern slope would be a lawn, perhaps, with spots of flowers."

"Why has no one ever thought of it before?" Mary asked.

"And the hollow behind would be the barns and

sheds and such things."

"To keep them from the northers, yes!"

"I suppose a yellow house with a red roof would look rather well."

"That's the finest color, of course."

"And it would be Spanish style, don't you think?"

"Anything else would be silly. Oh, of course, you'll stay and do it?"

"It's tempting, isn't it?"

"I've never heard of anything so perfect. I can see it all so clearly. I'll never be able to rub the picture out of my mind. That's a *happy* place for a home, Peter Blue."

All at once Peter, in turn, saw the picture that he had been describing—the yellow walls, and the glowing red of the roof above the oak trees, and the terraced lawn going down the hills, and the dim red roses growing there. It came breathlessly on him, and, looking from the hill to the girl, it seemed almost as though they had built the place together, out of their two minds, with thought and with love. He closed his eyes for an instant, and his face turned gray.

The girl was heedless of him, now, for her head was high, and she faced the proposed site of the house with eyes misted with delight. As she stared, she was singing softly: "Barnegat, Barnegat, take your stand. . . ."

"You know that old song?" he asked her abruptly.

"Uncle Harry is always singing it."

"Will you wait one moment while I write a note that I'd like to send to town?"

"Oh, of course."

It took him more than a moment. With painful care, sitting at the table in the kitchen, he scrawled the letters. It was amazing to see how his skill in the management of that left hand had grown. This is what he wrote:

Dear Livernash,

I promised to meet you, and now I'll give you the time and the place of the meeting. I didn't want to make too much of a disturbance out here; or else I should have finished you off the other day when you came. However, I'll come in tomorrow at noon and kill you in front of the hotel, where the rest of the town can see what's happening.

I want to give you a fair chance, Livernash. And since I've seen that you can't stand up against my right hand, I'll promise to use my gun in my left.

In case I don't have a chance to speak to you again except with a gun, I wish you a pleasant journey into the long night.

Faithfully yours,
Peter Blue

When he signed it, he smiled a little. He knew that bluff counts a great deal in this world. He had tried it many a time before, but he had not the slightest expectation that it would affect Livernash, except to make him thoroughly furious. But that was another way of gaining his point. For anger is almost as helpless as fear. He, Peter Blue, was always cold as steel when he went into a battle.

He went out and gave his missive to the girl.

"And," she said, taking it, "Mother wants to know if you can't come over to dinner . . . with Uncle Harry!"

He smiled faintly. "I don't think that your father would like that very well."

"Oh, don't you mind Dad. He's noisy and blustering. But he's a heart of gold. When he first came across you in the county . . . he . . . he didn't understand. But I'm sure that he does now."

"Do you think so?"

"Oh, yes. I told him that he was completely wrong."

"Ah?" said Peter Blue. "Thank you for that."

"But will you come?"

"Yes, of course. That is, I hope so."

"Then tell me when. Tonight?"

"Tomorrow night would be better."

"Tomorrow night, then. Mother . . . will be awfully pleased. So will Dad, I know. Good bye."

She whirled her horse away, and, as the mustang galloped furiously away, Peter heard the thin, sweet voice whistling down the wind.

Marty McVey, Marty McVey, Barnegat's gun will talk today!

As Mary Dunkirk rode into town, her head was high as the head of a flower, and her smile never died all the dusty way, until she drew up at the hotel verandah.

Half a dozen cowpunchers rushed to take the little envelope that she extended.

"It's for Stephen Livernash," she said. "Do you know him, any of you? Is he here?"

"He ain't a man not to know," said the brown youth who had got the envelope by sleight-of-hand. "Sure he's here. I'll see that he gets this, *pronto*. And . . . are you gonna be at the dance Saturday, Mary?"

"I don't know. I don't think so," Mary replied, and rode on down the street, singing as she went.

So up the stairs went the messenger and gave the letter to Stephen Livernash, who lolled in his room, industriously practicing with dice, rolling them on a blanket. He was averse to work, was Livernash, and he studied the easy ways of extracting coin from the pockets of absent-minded men. He took the letter and turned it twice over in his hand. He did not recognize the writing. It was big, sprawling, heavy, and the letters were formed with a curious clumsiness, a troubling clumsiness, like the handwriting of a child. Yet there was something about the character of the letters that was not the touch of a child. He opened it, and, with almost the first word that he read, he began to curse heavily. When he came to the conclusion, he balled the paper in his hand. Dashing it to the floor, he ground his heel into it. Then he picked up a gun and ran to the window, as though he half expected to see this hated enemy charging into view at that moment. But the street was empty, and then, with a second impulse, he went to the crushed letter, unfolded it carefully, and read it through a second time.

His face burned. It seemed impossible that any man would so dare to talk down to Stephen Livernash. As for the threat of fighting him with the left hand, that, of course, was the purest bluff. A bluff tried on Stephen Livernash! He had grown so furious with anger that he could not contain his wrath. With the letter in his hand, he went down the stairs into the lobby of the hotel.

"Hello, Steve," said the proprietor. "What's up, old man?"

"Hell's up!" said Livernash. "A damned fool is trying to drive us crazy. Look at this! Look at this!" He thrust the paper under the eyes of the hotelkeeper, then snatched it away and pinned it up on the bulletin board.

"Who brought that letter?" he called loudly. "Who fetched that letter in to me?"

"Why, young Mary Dunkirk done it."

"The sheriff's daughter? You don't mean her?"

"I do, though. There's only one Mary Dunkirk."

"Has the sheriff got a finger in this? Well, damn the sheriff and everybody else, and here's for Blue's letter!" He whipped out a pair of guns, and, firing from the hip, he blew a double succession of shots into the letter and the bulletin board behind it. Twelve liberal punctures tore through the paper. But when he had ended his shooting without a miss, the writing still could be made out by guessing a little at a missing word, here and there. A crowd came to stare and whisper. Livernash went out on the front verandah, gritting his teeth.

"Left-handed?" he heard somebody say behind him. "That'll be a fight. Blue is a cold-blooded devil, I guess."

"I'll left-hand him into hell," vowed Livernash, whirling on the speakers. As he turned back, he saw a pretty girl galloping briskly up the street.

"Who's that?" he asked.

"That's the sheriff's daughter. She must have some good news. Listen to her singing."

By she swept, and her song trailed behind her:

Barnegat, Barnegat, belt on your gun,
For Marty McVey is a-coming. . . .

Livernash, suffused with wonder and with rage, felt as though the girl had deliberately flung the threat at him as she swept past the hotel. She knew about the challenge and she was mocking him.

XIV

It was not very wonderful that Livernash was extremely excited, and after a moment he left the hotel and hurried across the first hill behind it. There, in the little hollow, he got his hand in practice by blowing fifty rounds of .45-caliber lead slugs at the stump of a tree. At thirty paces, he walked up and down, emptying his guns, and whirling about and trying snap shots, and, when he had finished, he walked up to the trunk and examined it. Some of the holes were blurred together, as many of the bullets had pierced the wood near the center, but, on the whole, the marksmanship had been excellent. He could count or guess at the marks that forty-five bullets had made. Only five had gone astray, and, when one remembers that the distance was nearly a hundred feet, the target five inches in diameter, and the shooting done when on the constant move, one can see that it was a startling bit of work. You who doubt, take a kicking, snorting, rearing, buck-ing Colt in either hand and try it out at a target of any size while you're walking up and down, to say nothing of whirling about and trying snap shots from the hip.

When Livernash had finished examining the state of his target, he grinned a little. In his heart of hearts, he felt that he was the greatest pistol shot in the world. There were others who could do better on a stage before an audience, but he felt that he stood on a stage by himself so far as man-to-man duels were concerned. There was only the one serious blot upon his record, and that was the day that he had failed to beat Peter Blue. But he swore that was an accident, and, with all the fervor in his heart, he had taken up the trail of Peter Blue as soon as his wound permitted him to do so.

Today, looking at his target work, he assured himself that there would be another story for the world to tell if he could make Peter Blue live up to his word the following day. His hatred of Peter was not based upon that single encounter. He had felt for many years that Blue had usurped a reputation to which he had no legitimate claim. He had always felt that his own record was more impressive. Certainly it was far more bloody. From Alaska to Argentina he had left his trail of dead men; what were the exploits of Peter Blue compared with this odyssey of crime? But men did not talk about his exploits so freely. They knew him as a hard fighter and a straight and quick shooter. But even the youngsters would take a chance against him, a thing that they would never dream of doing against Peter Blue, unless they were maddened with a hunger for fame or with a quantity of moonshine. Long and bitterly Livernash had brooded upon the thing. There was a real fame to be had in the working of an accurate Colt. Men got into books. Men were pointed out among their fellows. Men were hailed as immortals of the frontier because of their skill with weapons. Why, then, did they not write books about Stephen Livernash? Why did they not hail him as one of the immortals?

There was only one explanation, so far as he could see. It was not enough to do things. Performance was only a portion of the battle. It was apparent that two and two did not make four, humanly speaking. Otherwise, the great badmen would be rated according to the list of their killings, and that was not the case. No one said that Tucker, who had killed seven men, was as terrible a warrior as Chuck Moffit, who had killed only three. No one really compared Stephen Livernash, in spite of all his mighty deeds, with Peter Blue.

Why not? The burden of this injustice weighed terribly upon the brain of Livernash. It had kept him awake at night. It haunted him. Perhaps one will simply say that it was because Blue had met and beaten him. No, before he actually met Blue, the repute of Livernash was even lower than it was at present. After he had met, fought, and been dropped by Peter Blue, Livernash gained more fame through this defeat than he ever had possessed before. Was it a great wonder that the problem maddened him? For, indeed, the men who dared to stand before Peter Blue in a fair fight instantly became celebrities.

Why? cried Livernash to himself. He received no answer. It simply was the fact.

He wandered back to the hotel, warmed and comforted within by the knowledge that his skill never had had a finer edge than at present, but bruised and sullen as he reflected upon the injustice of the world and the capriciousness of fame. And there, in the street beside the hotel, he met the sheriff passing with his usual quick, nervous step. He stopped instantly and caught Livernash by the arm.

"What's all this nonsense, Steve?" said the sheriff. "What's all this tom-foolery? Blue to ride in here and fight a duel with you in front of the hotel at noon?"

"According to the word that he sent in," said Livernash, "that's about what's gonna happen."

"It can't happen at all!" cried the sheriff in great excitement. "I never heard of such confounded folderol. Am I the sheriff of this county or not?"

"I reckon that you are."

"Well, then, is the sheriff gonna let a pair of gents meet by appointment and try to murder one another?"

Livernash made a thoughtful pause, after hearing this, and stroked his mustaches. Then a glimmer of amusement came into his eyes and he said gently: "I see how it stands with you, Sheriff. But I would like to ask you a couple of little questions."

"Go on, then. Ask them. Fire away with them."

"What I want to know is . . . have I got the reputation of a gent that's too damn' good to associate with the rough ones? When I come into a town, does everybody breathe easy and feel safe and secure?"

"I dunno what you mean, Steve. You got a rough enough

name, if that's what you're driving at."

"I mean," said Livernash, "if I was to be bumped off in a fight, would there be a lot of wailing and carrying on and weeping and gnashing the teeth, and what not? Would there or wouldn't there?"

"Maybe there wouldn't," Dunkirk answered. "You've done a tolerable lot of harm to one man or another. You can't talk with a Colt, and talk straight, and still keep yourself loved by everybody. I dunno that you've ever put up the dough to run an asylum for the widows and orphans that you've made, Steve."

"Tell me straight, then. Would the county and the town, and the whole damn' state sort of breathe a sigh of relief if I was to be dropped dead right here in the street right in front of the hotel?"

The sheriff was silent, frowning, and the other continued: "Then take up the case of Peter Blue. Is he so damn' holy that the state is glad to spend money chasing him? Or has he killed enough folks to make the state hanker to drape a rope around his neck?"

"Blue is a sneaking scoundrel," said the sheriff, filled with his own grievance against the gunfighter.

"Aye!" cried Livernash, "that's a true thing that you've just said. He's a sneaking scoundrel. Then, I say, let him and me meet and shoot it out, and, if we both drop, it's a good thing for everybody. No matter how it turns out, nothing is lost to the state. Am I right or am I wrong?"

"Maybe folks would see it that way," the sheriff answered, musing.

"More than that," said Livernash, "if you was to try to stop this here fight, maybe you'd find it a tolerable dangerous job. Besides, who would thank you? This here town is set to see that fight, and they would call you partly a damn' fool for spoiling the fun, and partly a blockhead for not letting them die that need killing. You smoke a pipe on that and you'll see that I'm right. And when Blue comes prancing into the town, let us have our little party."

"With his left hand!" exclaimed the sheriff. "Confound him, I wonder if he really means to fight you with his left hand?"

"Pure bunk and blood!" bellowed Livernash. "He knows damn' well, down in his heart, that I'm a better man than he ever dreamed of bein'. I know it, and he knows it, and he's gonna use his right hand. You can lay to that."

"I don't know," Sheriff Dunkirk said, shaking his head. "I understand that he's been working to make himself ambidextrous. Working day and night to make his left hand as good as his right. And perhaps he's managed to do it."

"It can't be done," said Livernash. "One hand has got to lead. One hand has got to do the brain work. No, he'll fight with his right, and wish to God that he had two right hands instead of one, before I'm through with him. And now you tell me this, Sheriff. How come that Peter Blue has got such a name, anyway?"

"Why, man, he's fought for the name that he enjoys, I suppose that you'll admit."

"Fought? Fought? Well, who's he fought, then?"

"Why, Livernash, what are you talking about? Everyone knows how he killed Don King and young Lomax, for instance, when they went up Snyder Cañon to get him."

"Oh, hell, man, but I'm tired of that yarn! Is he the only man that ever faced two and killed 'em? Ain't I held my own ag'in' four and dropped two of 'em and made the other two ride like hell to get where they could tie up their wounds?"

"Ah." The sheriff smiled suddenly. "I understand what you mean, Livernash. You want to know why it is that he has such a great reputation, isn't that it? And here you are . . . as good a man as he . . . as you and I and some of the wise ones know . . . but without half as much fame. That's what you want to know?"

"Sheriff," said the tall gunfighter, "I sure do crave to know that from you. Can you explain?"

"I'll tell you how it is, old-timer," said the sheriff. "It ain't what a man does. It's the way of doing it that counts so much. When two gents is working hard, it's the one that don't seem to be trying that gets the applause. And that's the way with our friend Peter Blue. He handles himself so plumb graceful that folks worship the way that he does things."

Livernash gritted his teeth. "Let him handle himself plumb graceful tomorrow, then, because graceful dyin' is all that he's gonna have a chance to do!"

"Are you dead sure of yourself, Steve?"

"Am I? I'm gonna plaster that second-rate thug, and you can lay to that! Only, you tell me first how come that your girl works with Blue? Have you give him a chance to smile at her?"

"Works? For him? What in hell d'you mean?"

"She brung me his letter. And then she rode by singin' me a sassy song about beltin' on my gun, because somebody was comin'. . . ."

"I understand," said Dunkirk. "She's always singing 'Barnegat', you see. She couldn't have meant you any harm, and there isn't a chance that she knew anything about the challenge that was in that letter. But that Barnegat song she's always singing. Uncle Harry taught her."

"What Barnegat song is that?"

"The yarn about how Barnegat and McVey met, y'understand?"

"I've heard something about it. I forget what."

"McVey comes up to fight Barnegat, you see? Barnegat gets his guns and stands in the middle of the street, and McVey comes tearing in on him, riding a horse. And Barnegat fires a couple of times, then he gets scared, and turns and heels it to get away."

"Hold on! It ain't possible, Sheriff. No man would do a thing like that with a crowd standing by and looking on."

"No man? Barnegat was quite a man, as some will tell you. But he done just that. He got nervous. And nerves is hell, Steve. Nerves is hell!"

Livernash spat, and turned on his heel. "You get a good place to look on at this here fight yourself," he advised, "because there ain't going to be no holding of me."

So saying, he swaggered off down the street, and the sheriff watched him go with concern and yet with pleasure. He began to feel reasonably sure that Livernash would win, after all. For in all the sheriff's life, he could not recall a man who had approached a grave battle with such a boiling confidence in himself. And is not self-confidence half the fight?

XV

You may be sure that there was no self-confidence in the heart of Peter Blue the following morning. He knew that he had come to the last day of his life, unless a miracle saved him. As he looked across the hillsides, he told himself that he never again would see the glimmer of the early sun.

He did not go down to the shack of Uncle Harry. He had walked behind the ox-plow all of the preceding afternoon; he had wrung the hand of the old fellow when he said good night after supper the evening before. Although that might serve for a farewell, he decided that now he must leave some other note.

He sat down to write it, and scrawled out the letters with an odd swiftness and ease. Certainly that left hand was gaining a greater mastery every day, and he told himself that, if the battle with Livernash could only be postponed for another month, he might have a ghost of a chance to win. But as it was, he had to fight and die.

He wrote his letter, and then he waited until it was nearly eleven o'clock. It would take the greater part of an hour to ride into town. Dimly in the distance he could see Uncle Harry pursuing his way behind the plow, by the river, as he rode down the slope to the shack.

He entered, placed the sheet of scrawled-over paper on the table, and for a paperweight he laid his wallet upon it. Then he remounted and rode away, only pausing at the top of the rise to look back toward the shack where he had come to know the old man.

But when he rode on, the swarm of pictures remained clearly in his mind's eye. Uncle Harry, and the glowing stove, and the smell of comfortable cookery, and the lovely face of Mary Dunkirk smiling at him tenderly. . . .

Where was Mary herself on this morning? The sheriff himself had given her no word, not a syllable of the thing that was to happen on this day. But he had left the house late to ride in, and he had gone off carelessly, as if there were nothing of importance before him. Not even to his wife had he breathed a word.

But he was not well out of sight before a young cowpuncher galloped up to the house and sang out at the kitchen door: "Hello! Sheriff! Are you in?"

Mrs. Dunkirk thrust open the door.

"He ain't here. Hello, Tommy. What you wantin'? No more cattle rustlers, I hope?"

" 'Mornin', Missus Dunkirk. No more cattle rustlers. But I just wanted to know . . . is the sheriff gonna let the fight come today? Or is he gonna shut it off?"

"Shut it off?"

"I mean, is it gonna be worthwhile for us boys to ride in to see the fun, or is the sheriff gonna keep the game from coming off?"

"What game are you talkin' about, Tommy?"

Mary Dunkirk at her open window listened and waited, vaguely apprehensive.

"Why, I mean Blue and Livernash, of course. What else? I mean, are they gonna be allowed to fight it out, the same as Blue wants to do?"

"Fight it out?" echoed Mrs. Dunkirk. "The two of them wild men to meet?"

"Aye, at noon . . . if Blue can have his way. But if you don't know . . . maybe the sheriff is going to let them have their whirl . . . and if that's the way . . . I'm gonna be there."

He turned his horse in such excitement that he forgot to say good bye.

Before the rattle of hoofs died in the distance, Mary Dunkirk was down the stairs and rushing through the kitchen to the back door.

"Hey, Mary!" cried her mother. "Mary, darlin'. Mary, dear, where are you going? You can't do any good . . . it's the wild, wicked way of men . . . a woman can't stop them. Mary! Mar-y-y!"

But Mary was gone to the corrals, and a moment later, on her fleetest mare, she was dashing past the house, so that her mother had sight of only a set, pale face. And she knew that further protestation would do no good.

"Love and misery! Love and misery!" said the mother. "They always come together. Poor Mary. Poor dear."

But Mary was now far, far down the road. She did not check the gallop of her horse until she saw Uncle Harry toiling behind his plow close to the road. To him she went like a streak.

"Wait, girl, what's wrong? House on fire?"

"Where's Peter? Where's Peter Blue?"

"Pete? He's up at the Truman shack studyin', I suppose. No, hold on a minute. I seen him ride down to my shack a while back. Maybe he's still there."

She waited for not another word, but swept from the field and rushed for Uncle Harry's house. She swung from the saddle and rushed in. No Peter was there, but on the table she saw the time-stained pigskin of the wallet and the paper beneath. She snatched it up, and read:

Dear Uncle Harry,

Saying good bye to you is the hardest thing that I've ever done. But I couldn't say good bye and make a clean breast of everything face to face, so I'm doing it now in writing.

I'm about to ride into town and meet Livernash. He's hounded me into it, and I have to go. Besides, even if I dodge Livernash today, I'd soon have to meet some other gunfighter that's on my trail, and I'd go down. I've had my luck. Now I'm due for my bad time. It won't be long, because Livernash shoots straight.

You'll wonder why I've given up hope before even meeting him. I'll explain. You know that I've been playing a game about the left hand, Uncle Harry. Training it and working away with it. But as

271

a matter of fact, it hasn't been for fun. A bullet tore through my right hand and arm less than a year ago, and, when the wound healed, it left the right hand and arm good for nothing. I can't even write with it, let alone handle a gun. And that's why Livernash is sure to kill me.

Keep this a secret, though. I've written to him that I'll come and fight with him with my left hand. And when I go down, I want people to think that I went down trying to do a foolish thing, but taking a good chance. I don't want the world to know that my back is against the wall.

So much for that. Now for another thing.

Your boy will never come back to you. He lies in Eutaw Corners, buried in the churchyard. He walked into the saloon in that town, saw me in the gambling room, and drew a gun on me without warning. I shot him, and he died without speaking.

God knows that I wish that I could call that bullet back to me. But it's done, and can't be undone.

Go to Eutaw Corners and ask for the true story of what happened there that night. Your boy must have been nearly drunk. I know he was a clean lad, but the drink must have maddened him.

Try to remember me kindly in spite of that unlucky bullet I fired in Eutaw Corners.

I have no one to whom I care to leave whatever I have. I want you to have the bay horse. You'll find him sound and fit in every way. He cost me twelve hundred dollars, and after the education I've given him, he's worth something more than that today. He's a clean-bred one. Sell him and buy a plow team of horses. Besides, I have something in cash.

You'll find about eighteen hundred in this wallet. It's yours.

In exchange, I want you to keep Christopher if he lives through the fight. I almost hope that one of the bullets of Livernash knocks over Christopher. Because he and I have lived through so much together that we ought to die together, too. But if he lives, I know that you'll take good care of him. Let Mary ride him, if she pleases, but no other soul on earth. Let him have the run of a good pasture, and God bless you for any kindness you show him.

When Mary has married and her first child has come to her, I want you to tell her that I loved her. You can tell her then that I wanted to say good bye to her, but that I can't find the right words to put on the paper.

The best of fine luck to you.

Peter Blue

Twice and again she had to brush her eyes clear of moisture before she could go on with the reading. Now she crumpled the paper in her hand and rushed back to her horse. Her mind was whirling as she swung into the saddle. But there was no help for her except the speed of her horse. And how could she get to town before noon struck?

There was one possible way—the short cut across the unused trail over the hills.

That was the way that Mary Dunkirk galloped, leaning into the wind, her teeth set, and her face white, straining the good mare staunchly onward in that wild race against time, to tell Livernash and all the rest that a helpless man was coming that day to attempt a madman's battle. . . .

She dared not look at her watch. But with an upward

glance, now and again, she saw the sun nearing the zenith, and the heart swelled in her breast.

XVI

Outside the town, Peter Blue dismounted.

He took from the saddlebag a little whisk broom, and with this he went carefully over his clothes. He untied his bandanna from around his neck and shook the dust out of it. From another pouch he produced a small stiff brush and with that he groomed Christopher until the great horse shone like a glossy panther, and all the little leopard dappling showed dimly in the sun. The boots of Peter received an extra polish, now, and then he climbed into the saddle and viewed himself in a small hand mirror.

It is a pity that one must write down such unfortunate details of one who was riding in toward danger of death. But the fact is that Peter Blue wished to die handsome in act and in person, also. He was not above that smallness, and therefore it must be chronicled. In fact, he had never been the free-swinging, careless type of the range. There was something fastidious in his deviltry, from the very beginning.

Now, with all in place, neat, well-brushed, spotless as though from a bandbox, Peter Blue rode into the town. As he journeyed on, he saw that the houses on either side of him gaped forth at the street with open, empty door and windows. Everyone had deserted those houses, and he knew instantly what had happened. The news had been spread. Every soul in the countryside must have gathered there in front of the hotel to see the duel fought.

Well, that was as he would have had it. There was only one drawback—it was he who must fall in the encounter.

How, then, should he carry himself, so as to be ready for the critical moment, and how should he die with the utmost gallantry—in the eyes of the audience?

Vain Peter Blue! Even then he was thinking of his audience. Even then he was upon a stage! As he went slowly on, thinking, a song rose lightly in his throat. "Barnegat, Barnegat!"

Ah, what an apt song for this day! Except that McVey had not come softly in on a walking horse. He had come in thunder, with a flash and a rush.

Suddenly the thought took Peter by the throat. That was the way for him to die!

He touched Christopher, and a long, panther-like bound answered him. He spoke, and the stallion was instantly in full racing stride. It flared up the brim of Peter's hat. It whistled the wind into his face. And even as he rode in to meet death, he was filled with the joy of Christopher's matchless gallop. Did not Christopher himself know that a great moment was at hand? For what other reason would he have pricked his ears so joyously?

The street widened—he turned a corner, and saw the hotel not far away, and every window thronged with faces. And a wild cry went tingling up, and swept down the street and crashed against his ears!

"Peter Blue's coming!"

There were enough to make that death scene worthwhile! In front of the hotel he saw the tall form of Livernash, with the sun glistening on his long, saber-shaped mustaches. In either hand of Livernash glimmered a long, blue-barreled revolver. For answer, Peter caught out his own Colt, and poised it high in his left hand.

That left hand felt clumsy and thick in the wrist, and weak. He knew that he could never drive home a bullet true to the mark from the back of a galloping horse. But forward he rushed.

Then he saw those two long guns raised. A puff of smoke from the barrel of one, and a hornet singing at his ear. A miss.

A smoke puff from the other gun, and a heavy blow struck Peter over the chest. But he leaned resolutely forward. There was no pain. There was only a sense of numbness in his chest. He knew that he would be able to ride in to close quarters and there, perhaps, fire the finishing shot!

Calling to the stallion, he felt such a wave of joy rise in him that he could not help laughing, and as he laughed a cry of wonder and fear came from the throng of the hotel. For it seemed more than human that a man should ride down on a deadly marksman in this fashion with a laugh on his lips.

Then Peter saw a horse swerve into the street through an alley-mouth farther on, and, through the cloud of the dust, he saw that it was Mary Dunkirk.

Well, then, let Mary see how her lover could die! And with an unconquerable joy, he laughed still as he rode.

Again and again the guns spoke before him, but he did not hear so much as the sound of the bullets whirring past. He saw now that the legs of Livernash were braced far apart, as though to withstand a shock, and his mouth had sagged open, and there was in his face the horror of a man who sees a ghost walking at midnight.

Still the gun was poised stiffly in the left hand of Peter Blue. For suddenly he knew. It came upon him like a revealed prophecy. As with Barnegat in the song, so with Livernash this day. Yes, for suddenly the tall man in the street dropped his guns with a hoarse cry and bolted blindly toward the door of the hotel, flinging out his hands before him like a child running out of the terror of the dark toward a light. And Christopher flashed past like a meteor.

A mild uproar sounded in the ears of Peter Blue; Christopher was coming to a stop. He could not tell whether it was the roaring of a sea behind him, or the sound of many voices. And then, through a mist, a sweating mare flashed up to him, and he saw the face of Mary Dunkirk.

"Peter, has he killed you? Has he killed you?"

"Killed me, Mary? There aren't enough guns in the world to kill me today."

"Your whole coat is turning crimson . . . it's dripping with blood. Peter, Peter, come down to me, dear."

She was standing by the mighty shoulder of Christopher, and Peter leaned from the saddle, his foot slipped, he crashed headlong in the street.

But he did not die. Not all the guns in the world, he had said, could kill him. Not even that bullet, so terribly close the heart, could end his days.

In that hotel, in the best first-floor room, he came back to life, and to the white-faced smiling Mary Dunkirk, leaning above him.

"How could you dare to be so brave, Peter?" she asked him, another day.

"It was not I. It was a song that did the thing for me, Mary."

"Tell that to Uncle Harry. He's waiting to see you."

His face turned gray with sorrow.

"Hush!" said the girl. "He never read that letter. But *I* read it. And he shall never know. And who would dare to tell him . . . ever?" So she went for Uncle Harry.

"Hello, Peter," said the thin voice from the door.

"Hello, partner," said the sick man.

"You see, Mary?" Uncle Harry said, chuckling. "I told you that him and me was to start business together. And I dunno but that we'll have to take you in for a third member of the firm."

MAX BRAND®

JOKERS EXTRA WILD

Anyone making a living on the rough frontier took a bit of a gamble, but no Western writer knows how to up the ante like Max Brand. In "Speedy—Deputy," the title character racks up big winnings on the roulette wheel, but that won't help him when he's named deputy sheriff—a job where no one's lasted more than a week. "Satan's Gun Rider" continues the adventures of the infamous Sleeper, whose name belies his ability to bury a knife to the hilt with just a flick of his wrist. And in the title story, a professional gambler inherits a ring that lands him in a world of trouble.

MAX BRAND®

FLAMING FORTUNE

The three novellas collected here showcase Max Brand's outstanding ability to create living, breathing characters whose unforgettable exploits linger long after the last page is turned. In "The Cañon Coward," you'll meet Harry Clonnell, a tracker who refuses to carry a gun and shuns violence yet has somehow earned the reputation of one of the most notorious bandits around. Outlaw Lefty Richards is put in quite a bind when his dying friend asks him to turn over his guns to the local sheriff in "A Wolf Among Dogs." And Speedy, one of Brand's most enduring characters, takes on the job of sheriff in "Seven-Day Lawman"—a job where no man has ever lasted longer than a week.

MAX BRAND®
THE RUNAWAYS

Young Sammy wants nothing more than to get out from under the thumb of his overbearing spinster Aunt Claudia. When a tramp named Lefty wanders through town, Sammy is immediately taken in by his skill with a fiddle, his crafty charm and his trained bull terrier, Smiler. And when Lefty asks Sammy to join him on the road, the boy jumps at the chance. The two begin to con their way around the West—footloose and fancy-free. But Lefty isn't as free as he'd like to be. An incredibly dangerous hunchback named Jake has been chasing him across the country, looking to settle an old score. And when Jake catches up with them, there will be hell to pay, both for Lefty and for anyone traveling with him....

Dorchester Publishing Co., Inc.
P.O. Box 6640
Wayne, PA 19087-8640

_____5652-6
$5.99 US/$7.99 CAN

Please add $2.50 for shipping and handling for the first book and $.75 for each additional book. NY and PA residents, add appropriate sales tax. No cash, stamps, or CODs. Canadian orders require $2.00 for shipping and handling and must be paid in U.S. dollars. Prices and availability subject to change. **Payment must accompany all orders.**

Name: _____

Address: _____

City: _____ State: _____ Zip: _____

E-mail: _____

I have enclosed $_____ in payment for the checked book(s).

For more information on these books, check out our website at www.dorchesterpub.com.
_____ *Please send me a free catalog.*

PARTNERS

PAUL BAGDON

His name is L. B. Taylor, but everyone in Burnt Rock, Texas, calls him Pound. They also call him the town drunk. Pound used to be a schoolteacher, but he traded in his job—and his self-respect—for a bottle a long time ago. All that's changing today. Today Pound made a new friend, a stranger in town named Zeb Stone, and Zeb is about to take Pound under his wing, pull him out of the gutter, and teach him a new career. Zeb is a shootist, a hired gun, who's looking for a partner. Pound is going to learn to live without booze, to ride, and to shoot. But he'll also learn the hard way that riding with a shootist is more dangerous than drowning in a bottle ever was!

ZANE GREY

TONTO BASIN

This classic novel of the West was written in 1921, but only now is it making its paperback debut in the form Zane Grey intended. Finally readers can enjoy the full-length novel in all its glory.

Jean Isbel travels from Oregon to Arizona to join his family and force a final showdown with Lee Jorth and his notorious band of cattle rustlers. His savage hatred is tempered, though, when he meets and falls in love with Ellen, Jorth's beautiful daughter. Ellen, too, is torn between loyalty to her father and her feelings toward Jean. As the confrontation draws ever closer, emotions run high on both sides and passions flare, but can any good come from bad blood?

AL SARRANTONIO
WEST TEXAS

Lt. Thomas Mullin may be retired from the U.S. Cavalry, but he's still considered the best tracker around. So when a senator's son turns up missing, Mullin is the man called upon to find him. It doesn't take long for Mullin to figure out that quite a few travelers and cowboys have disappeared recently in the same area. And the desolate, inhospitable land is offering no clues—only shallow graves. As he investigates further, Mullin finds himself pitted against a killer stranger deadlier than any he's faced before.

LOREN ZANE GREY

A GRAVE FOR LASSITER

Even before his adventures in *Riders of the Purple Sage*, Lassiter was regarded as the mightiest gunslinger ever to sit a saddle. Therefore, it's no surprise he's the first man Josh Falconer calls to help save his business from the local tough trying to bankrupt his freight line. Though when Lassiter arrives in Bluegate, Josh is already dead and he finds his worst enemy, Kane Farrell, set to take over the line. With a price on his head, Lassiter doesn't get far before he's ambushed, shot and left for dead. But even death won't get in the way of his vengeance. He's determined the only man needing a grave will be Farrell.